RESISTING CHASE

SHARON WOODS

To all the beautiful women who are strong but need time to heal before committing, know that you are worth the wait. Find yourself a guy who will respect your journey and will be patient with you. He should be the kind of guy who will listen to your struggles and be there for you when you need him the most. He should be understanding and never pressure you to move faster than you're comfortable with. He should be someone who will love you for who you are and never try to change you. Find a guy who will be kind and supportive, and who will never let you doubt your worth.

CHAPTER 1

BENJAMIN

My ALARM BLARES THROUGH my silent house. Reaching for my phone on my wooden bedside table, I turn it off. Most people have the basic alarm that comes with the iPhone, a calming tone to ease themselves into a new day. Not me. Mine is "All I Do Is Win" by T-Pain, Ludacris, Snoop Dogg, and Rick Ross for the right kind of morning motivation.

Rolling myself out of bed, I flinch at my bruised and achy muscles. At least when I rub my eyes with my hands and stretch my arms above my head, there's zero fogginess. No hangover or nausea rolling in my gut from drinking the night before. The older I get, the less I can handle my liquor. After a couple of drinks, I'm sluggish the next day, constantly reminding myself never to drink so much again. I pick up my phone to check it, seeing there're no new messages or calls. Then I'm hitting the shower, hoping to wake up my muscles and ease some of the tightness before more training.

Being the second-string quarterback for the Chicago Eels has resulted in my body becoming a punching bag. But it's what I signed up for and I wouldn't change it for the world.

After a long, hot shower, I'm in the kitchen fixing up some breakfast, when my phone rings. Grabbing it from the white counter, I see it's Dad's name flashing on the screen.

"Mornin'." I continue to stir the eggs on the stove as I answer.

"I'm calling to see if you want a lift into training today?"

Peering down, I take in the white towel wrapped around my waist. "I just hopped out of the shower and I'm cooking breakfast now. But I can be ready in twenty. Will that work?"

I turn off the burner and grab a plate to transfer the eggs to.

"Yeah. I'll leave soon because I've got food your mom's made."

I shake my head, knowing he means I have a week's worth of lunches, dinners, and snacks. All prepared as per the nutrition plan the coach gives us.

"Does she realize I can cook?"

He laughs. "I keep telling her. But you know her."

I do. And this is her way of telling me how proud she is of me. After all the years she and my dad have sacrificed for me to do the sport I love, taking her meals isn't an issue. I wish I could repay her, but there isn't really anything I can do. Well, there is one thing. I shake my head—fuck no. Don't be ridiculous. An engagement is not happening any time soon. The only shiny, expensive item I want to see in my near future is a Vince Lombardi Trophy.

Thinking about winning it this year sends a wave of emotions through me. Nerves mixed with excitement. Most people would think I got here with only luck. Or a guaranteed spot because of my ex-NFL player dad, who now happens to be the offensive coordinator for the Eels. But instead, there was hard work and a lot of sacrifices that paved my way. And, if anything, having connections made me even more eager to prove myself and push myself harder each and every day.

When my dad turns up a little while later, I've eaten and dressed. I unpack the food he hands over before sending mom a quick text to thank her, letting her know I'll call her tonight.

Dad drops me off a short fifteen minutes later, then I'm walking the sidewalk, soaking in the peaceful Chicago sunlight toward training. Only, I almost trip over my damn feet, quite literally choking on my tongue a minute later from the sight in front of me.

A woman's bent over the front of her car, with the hood propped open as she looks inside. That's not what gets me walking closer, though. No, it's those navy-blue pants that hug her perky ass perfectly, and when she reaches farther, a sliver of skin becomes exposed from where her matching navy-blue top has ridden up. I'm certain this image is extra alluring because I'm not currently having sex. Otherwise, I don't think I'd be responding this way. The reasons are simple. Hard training sessions. Strict diet. Lack of sleep. Not from lack of attention, that's for sure. No, *that* I have an endless supply of. I just don't want the distraction. Keeping my focus on football is where my head needs to stay right now.

I run my hand through my hair and drink in her distracting frame one last time before I approach her.

"Hey there. You need a hand?" I ask, my voice a little deeper from the attraction seeping through.

As she turns, that interest only piques. She's gorgeous, especially with those sea-blue eyes. Eyes I could get lost in. Eyes that tell a story. I've never seen her around the headquarters before. And I would know, because I'd definitely remember her. When she turned to face me, I didn't notice the stick she was holding. And unfortunately for me, it flicked oil all over my fresh clothes. Specifically, my white top.

She gasps, a wince transforming her pretty features. "Oh my God. I'm so sorry." Her hand immediately covers her mouth as soon as the words leave her lips. Through her embarrassment, her eyes quickly travel over the expanse of my chest and arms, and I can't help but hope she enjoys the view. I know I am. Being taller than her is a plus, as I get a good eyeful of her full cleavage. Though, after a glance, I'm trying with all my might not to look again.

I'm just about to tell her it's okay. But I don't get a word in before she moves. Reaching out, she begins rubbing her hand over the splashes. I bite the inside of my cheek, not wanting to stop her. Instead, I watch on in utter fascination, lost for words. When she rubs harder, my stomach contracts under her palm, making her pouty lips part on an audible intake of breath. But she doesn't stop. The unexpected touch sends my body temperature rising by the second. As she moves a little lower, I swallow hard and coax down an impending erection.

Thinking she's done, she lifts her hands, and the color of her cheeks matches the scorching heat I'm feeling inside. She's not meeting my gaze, and it's as if she wants the ground to swallow her up. But, as if a switch flipped, laughter replaces her clear unease. A loud, hearty chuckle that causes the corner of my lips to twitch. I look down to where her eyes are trained, instantly finding the source of her amusement. The mess is definitely not ideal, but I'm about to change into training gear, so it's no big deal.

As her laughter subsides, her eyes meet mine again. They're wide as they look up at me, and shining brightly. "Remind me why I thought I was a mechanic."

I nod toward her hand with a grin. "Hey, don't sweat it. But maybe put the stick away?"

She closes her eyes briefly, mumbling under her breath, "Get your shit together."

And she doesn't wait, spinning to put it back. Only, she holds the stick in mid-air as she searches around the motor, clearly forgetting where it came from.

I step forward, biting back a laugh. She's adorable. "Here. Let me help." I take the stick out of her hand, putting it back in the oil. Tilting my head, I ask, "You finished here?"

She nods with a small smile. "Yeah. Thanks."

Twisting to face her, I lean my hip on the gray Chevrolet Blazer and stare down at her. Her sweet scent hits me hard at this proximity, and I suck in a deep, intoxicating lungful of it to hold on to. Her eyes stay locked on mine, still as large as saucers.

Neither of us speaks for a beat, but I'm the one to break the silence. "What happened?" I tilt my head toward the car.

It's a newer model, so I'm not sure how much help I can be. Cars aren't my specialty.

She folds her arms over her chest. "A light came on the dashboard, and it started making a funny noise."

I smirk at what "funny noise" could mean. "Did you need me to look at it? Or call a tow truck?"

She shakes her head. "No. I've got it, but thanks. You've helped enough. Sorry for keeping you."

"I don't mind."

She shakes her head. "I've gotta get to work soon. I'll deal with it later."

"Ben!" Levi calls out from behind me.

She seems relieved by the interruption, taking the opportunity to turn and rush off. Effectively ending our conversation. It's like she can't get away from me fast enough.

That's certainly not something that's happened to me before. And it has me standing here, momentarily stunned, like a fool.

I didn't even get her name.

CHAPTER 2

BENJAMIN

A FEW WEEKS LATER

"Hurry up, boys!" Levi calls out to the whole team.

It's loud with everyone chatting, and most of the players dragging their feet. We're all walking our way through the modern white corridor of the headquarters to a scheduled meeting. Today's agenda is to introduce new staff members.

"For fuck's sake. We will get our asses kicked if we're late," he grumbles as he glances down to check his watch, then meets my gaze with an annoyed look.

I offer him a nod, understanding his irritation. Showing respect is huge for the team. But that's not the worst of it. The punishment that our coach will hand out will be in the form of harder training. My body is too tired for that shit right now, so I'm happy to back Levi up and tell them to get a move on.

Turning around to look over my shoulder, I see them still not listening, and it irritates me. "You heard him. Move it," I grind out through clenched teeth.

After a few seconds, they shuffle a little quicker. Happy with them finally listening, I turn and approach the brightly lit conference room.

Entering behind Levi, I follow him to the head of the white marble table and take a seat next to him. I look around, checking the score of the game playing on the TV in the background, then quickly recognize a group of people standing at the front of the room. General Manager, Head Coach, all the coordinators, including my dad and our medical team. And then there are some who I don't know yet. I know how excited these new staff members will be, all recently signing a contract of their dreams. I've been there. Still, to this day, I can't quite believe it.

As I sit back in my chair, a loud clearing of a throat has the room quietening down. The last few staff take their seats, and my dad moves away, revealing a woman I wish I was more familiar with. I watch on in shock. My eyes can't believe what they're seeing. The car trouble beauty is in the same room as me. I know I'm staring, but I can't help it. I'm unable to tear my eyes away. She blinks rapidly as her gaze connects with mine. I smirk when recognition hits her. Even caught off guard, she's incredibly sexy. Long shiny blonde hair, bright blue eyes, and the poutiest, most kissable lips I've ever seen.

She crosses her arms over her chest as we stare at each other, before she caves and looks away, focusing on our General Manager, Dave, who's now speaking. I'm listening the best I can, but my eyes haven't left her once. Every now and then, her eyes flick to me, as if to check if I am still watching her. And every single time...I am.

I wonder who she's replacing. What's her role here? We've had a few staff recently change teams. And then others retire. I won't have to wait much longer; my question will be answered soon enough.

My mind goes back to that day a few weeks ago, her navy-blue outfit now making sense. At the time, I didn't see the logo because her flowy hair must've been covering it. However, I can't lie, the ample cleavage was a huge distraction too. She has great tits. What can I say? And speaking of her tits, the way her arms are crossed, it pushes them up higher for me to admire. I can't help but lick my lips. Thankfully, her profile is set on Coach and not on me being a total perv. She's hot, I can't help it. Her hourglass frame would be any guy's weakness. Curves in all the right places.

"Now you're all up to date on the news. Let's start the introductions. Starting with Jim." Dave carries on talking as my brow furrows, wishing it was her name being called.

I run a hand through my hair, frustrated, before focusing on the new recruits. My gaze bounces between looking at her and Jim.

Another couple of people are introduced before the next sentence has me sitting up straighter.

"Next up is the new physician working with John. Let's give a warm welcome to Doctor Natasha Blackwood."

I'm simply dumbstruck, watching as she bites her lip with nervousness before she rolls her shoulders back and waves at us. It's her. Natasha Blackwood.

A fucking doctor.

She's not just hot, but smart as well.

Shit. I wasn't expecting that. Hell, I wasn't expecting her to make my body feel like I've just played a whole game. I need a damn cold shower again. She does this. This woman, who I don't even know, has the ability to make me feel like I'm a horny teenager all over again.

Dave wraps up the meeting, and the room begins to rustle as people make their way out. Purposefully, I take my time getting out of the chair, choosing to wait until the room completely clears out, with hopes of catching Natasha for a chat.

"She's hot," Levi comments under his breath, so only my ears can hear it, plucking me right from my daydreams.

"Fuckin' oath," I say without removing my eyes from her. Only when Levi coughs into his hand to hide a laugh does my head twist to face him. A stupid smile forms on my lips at him, trying to cover it.

"You gonna try to hit that?" Levi asks curiously.

Am I?

"Yeah," I deadpan with a shrug.

Amusement flickers in his eyes, and he thrusts his chin out. "Let's go train."

Following his order, I stand and turn to leave. But not before I take one last look at her. Running my gaze over her body, I start from her eyes all the way down to her feet. Then I trail them back slower, finding her blue eyes holding mine unexpectedly. I wink at her, watching her cheeks pink, and she playfully rolls her eyes. Biting back a cheeky smile, I walk off.

CHAPTER 3

NATASHA

"MOM, IS THERE ANYTHING else you need before I go?" I ask, as I unpack last night's dishes from the dishwasher.

"No, love. Just go to work. I'm fine," she replies as she leaves the kitchen table, walking stick in hand as she goes to sit on her spot on the couch.

I read her profile to make sure she's speaking the truth. When I'm satisfied, I nod and turn to finish tidying the countertop before making her a cup of tea. My morning routine is still new to me because I've only been working for the Eels for a couple of months. I finally finished school and got the job. The hardest part is trying to juggle helping Mom and now working full time. I barely had a social life before, but now it's almost non-existent. I don't mind, since I've never been one for parties and nightlife, but I would love to see my girlfriends more often. Right now, though, I'm struggling to find any free time. It's hard enough to get in a workout or homemade dinner some days.

Taking the camomile tea to her, I don't hover to chat. With no spare minutes, I head to the bathroom to wash my face. The warm water is refreshing, but as I lean forward to pat my face dry with the towel, I can't help but notice the bags under my eyes.

Shit, when did my face become this puffy?

I would never have thought I'd be this exhausted. Isn't college supposed to be more draining than work-life? Except it's the opposite for me. I'm a real-life zombie.

After rubbing moisturizer onto my face, probably too roughly, I quickly add some bronzer, blush, and mascara to give myself some color. If I go to work without it, I'm sure people would think the doctor needs to see a doctor herself.

Tying up my hair into a neat high ponytail, I get my uniform on, before wandering back out to the kitchen and grabbing my lunch.

Mom smiles at me as I go to say goodbye for the day. "You ready, love?"

Leaning over, I kiss her cheek. "Yeah, I better go. I'll see you after work. Call me if you need me."

She picks up her tea and rolls her eyes, taking a sip. If you wondered where I got the eye roll habit, you can blame her.

I cross my arms over my top, staring down at her. She holds her tea in front of her mouth and peers up at me, amused. I try not to smile at her, instead reminding her she can always rely on me. "I'm serious, Mom. Call me."

"I will. But go to work. I'll be fine until you're home. Enjoy! See you later." She waves a hand to shoo me away before sipping more of her tea.

I squint as I check her over one last time, making sure she has her walking stick, blanket, remote, and frame close. Ever since her work accident ten years ago, I have been her around-the-clock caregiver, adding to my exhausting school and now work hours. Mom can use her stick or frame during the day, but by night-time, her muscles are fatigued, and the pain gets unbearable. Her movements become restricted, and she requires my help getting to bed. But I wouldn't change my life for the world. Mom's one of my best friends, and I'll always be there for her.

With nothing else to do for her, I say, "Okay, see you later."

I spin around, grab my purse from the counter, and leave the house. I don't want to be late and give John, aka, my asshole boss, any reason to be pissed off at me today. Ever since I started, he's been irritated by me, and I have no idea why. I follow his instructions to a T. Yet he huffs around and mumbles under his breath about missing the previous physician. A much older, *male* physician. Insert another eye roll from me at that. Since the other one retired, it's clear he's had no other choice but to tolerate me.

After my residency, I worked in a hospital for two years, receiving my sports medicine board certificate with high scores. Which I've mentioned to him on more than one occasion, hoping to win him over. But I only get a glum look or, if I'm lucky, a nod. No matter what I do or say, he won't warm to me. Not a hint of a smile, or one pleasant word. Just a flat expression that shows his disappointment. But I won't give up.

I've always wanted to work as a physician, and I love football, so studying and working as a sports physician for an NFL team was a no-brainer. When the job came up so close to home, I took it as a sign. It was meant to be mine. Hence why, I won't leave or back down without a fight.

Half an hour later, I stand on the sideline, clutching a board in front of me, watching the team train hard. And hard they are. Wide shoulders, thick waists, lean muscled thighs, and minimal body fat. Yeah, it's a sight I'm not used to. And I wonder if I will ever get used to it.

A player gets hit from the side, and I tighten my grip on my board. That's another thing to get used to: seeing injuries in action, not just after the fact. But they play on as if nothing happened, and my grip loosens, a breath whooshing from my lungs in relief. After starting this morning at nine, I can't help but yawn, but thankfully, the loud whistles are keeping me awake. The early rise to help mom get organized for the day and then the late nights caring for her are the cause of my chronic tiredness, not that I will complain. If she needs me, I'll be there for her.

It's just after halfway through the training session, and I'm scanning the oval, always on high alert, evaluating the players to make sure they are ready for the game. The team is playing so effortlessly today. It makes my job a little easier.

"What's going on?" Mia asks as she creeps up to stand beside me, causing me to jump.

And it just so happens that my new friend is also the head coach, Chris's daughter. Since I started here over a month ago, she has helped me settle in. There hasn't been a day we haven't chatted. We immediately clicked. It's nice to have her around, even if she is a bit out there.

"Not much," I say with a quick smile toward her, trying to keep my eyes on the game. "What are you doing?" I ask curiously.

"Taking it easy before I become flat-out."

Mia's a physiotherapist, but with her dad's position, she's able to get away with not following as many rules as the rest of us. Including wearing skinny blue jeans instead of the navy pants.

At least she wears the top...I guess?

I can't blame her, though. If I were her, I'd do it too. John is watching her, but she isn't worried, unlike me, who needs a job to support my mom.

So, I say under my breath, "I wish I could take it easy, but you know I can't."

She nods and then her lips twist into a wide smile. "How's Ben?" She peers around, clearly trying to find him, but of course, he's in his position—which is the second-string quarterback.

"The idiot doesn't want to listen to John." My bored tone is the complete opposite of how my stomach flips at the mention of his name. But I was dumb enough to tell her about my car incident with him. And now she keeps begging me to let her set us up on a date. Because, and I quote, *"He's single and you two would make the best couple."*

I watch him move around the field effortlessly with a fixed stare, his large frame bent forward in his start position, ready to go. I grind my teeth together as I remember how dismissive he was to John before the game.

"I'm fine," he had said simply, and then he gave us a charming grin, so John didn't press him further. He clearly thinks he knows how to smooth people over, but I didn't go to school for nine years for him to look at me as just some medic. I want to be taken seriously as one of the physicians here. Even as I stand here watching, he quickly rubs his knee as if no one will notice.

Yet I do.

I pull my pen out and make a note, hoping I can pressure him later to let me look at it. I still need to tell John. If he finds out I knew Ben isn't 100 percent and I didn't inform him, I'll risk losing this job.

As I watch Ben straighten, I can see his pinched brows that give his pain away. I know it's causing him grief, but he just refuses to listen.

Fucking stubborn.

I wish he would give up and let me do my job.

"I'm sure he'll be fine. Maybe he's been training too hard. You know they can't do anything, like partying, until the seasons over, so they over train," Mia mutters.

I don't believe any of these players follow the rules. I don't trust men as far as I could throw them.

They all lie, disappoint, and are completely selfish.

"Yes, I know, but this job is important to me, Mia. I have to get through and figure out a way to make him listen," I say, continuing to watch him run across the field. He shows no other displayed concern about the injury, so I move on reluctantly and scan the other players.

A minute later, my gaze hits a running player from my periphery—Ben. I frown. What's he doing? He's sprinting over toward us.

Oh, crap.

I straighten, expecting him to need me. Instead, he picks up the ball and tucks it under one arm. Lifting his top up with the other, he wipes the beads of sweat dripping from his face. With the fabric pulled up, it's hard to miss his tanned stomach, rippled with abs and a dusting of masculine hair. I blink rapidly and focus back up on his face, feeling the heat hit my cheeks. Unfortunately, when I lock eyes with him, he's sporting a smug grin and a cocked brow. I'm about to turn away, embarrassed for openly enjoying his body, but as he jogs off, he passes the ball and fails miserably. I gasp, and he turns to briefly look at me over his shoulder before he rubs the back of his neck and ducks his chin, sprinting off.

"He's so damn hot," Mia gushes, fanning herself.

I roll my eyes. "Ugh. In your eyes only."

Her head turns so quickly I'm surprised she didn't break her neck. "As if! You liar!"

I jerk back, my eyes widening in horror. "Shhh, Mia. You're so loud, someone will hear you. And I'm supposed to be working!" I giggle before adding, "John will have my balls if I step an inch out of line."

She elbows me.

"Ouch," I say with a wince, grabbing my side. "What did you do that for?"

"You don't have balls," she says and waves over my lower body. "Under all the dust is a vagina."

For fuck's sake.

I shake my head at her crassness, and suck in a deep breath to prevent another laugh that's bubbling. But it slips.

"Mia." I grip the board in my hands a little tighter, trying not to indulge her. Not wanting to discuss how long it's been since I last had sex.

A long time.

"What? It's okay to want it. They're the best in the bedroom. A little rough and the dirty talk..." she continues.

I don't know why I expected her to shut up. It wouldn't be her if she did. So, I let her go on and on as I continue studying the players.

"He would make you laugh too, and can you imagine the babies?"

She's already trying to marry me up, and I could not think of anything worse right now. I worked too damn hard to get where I am now. To get further ahead, to let a man impede where I want to go with my future...love isn't on my agenda.

I'm not about to depend on someone again, hence why I want this career. No, I need it.

"Well, you're dating Levi, so shouldn't you keep your eyes on him?" I ask with a raised brow.

She and Levi aren't in a relationship when her dad is around. He would not approve of his daughter dating a player from his own team. It's a secret we all keep, but I continue reminding her that secrets have a way of coming out, so she's better off being open and telling him than him finding out from someone else.

I move my gaze onto the subject at hand, sitting on the side-lines, more solid than Ben, but at the same height of six-three. As I flick my gaze between the two, Ben takes a three-step before throwing the ball. Every day, there's a moment when the sheer excitement of doing my dream job causes me to smile. And this is it. I almost don't realize Mia is talking again.

"I am, and Levi is sexy, but that doesn't mean I'm blind. Ben's just charming, like, look at that cheeky boy grin." Mia's words pull me back to glance at Ben. That part I can agree with. The small snippets of charm he's directed at me are hard to ignore.

"Mia, you're not helping the situation," I say with a groan. "This is not how you speak when you're with someone. The only person who should matter or who you find attractive is the one right in front of you. The one you can't stop thinking about, breathing about, and dreaming about. Your whole life revolves around that one person's air." I tsk and turn toward her.

She flicks her long black hair over her shoulders, and I'm reminded she doesn't wear a nametag. I have argued with John, but he insists on making me wear one all year round.

How embarrassing, as if the guys won't remember my name on their own.

"See, that's where you're wrong," Mia argues, and it makes me smile, waiting to hear her take on it.

"You overthink everything, Tash. The way you talk about love, it's just so beautiful. You really want to be with someone. It's just we've got to find you the right guy. Not every guy will let you down, and I know one in particular who's totally into you." She pauses, her gaze moving back to the field, and then she continues. "And there is nothing better than a tall, delicious, sandy-blond man with blue eyes to have you falling head over heels for."

I snort. "There is no need to find love. I don't need it or want it. I'm trying to juggle a new job, John, Mom, bills, and maybe just a minute of time for myself. I can't possibly put a guy into the mix."

"Bullshit," she coughs into her fist.

I purse my lips to stop the smile that's trying to split open on my face. "John told me his rules and expectations. And one specifically includes not dating a player."

"No!" she gasps, grabbing my upper arm and facing me with a surprised expression.

I nod. "Yep. He even made me repeat what he said, so he knew I was listening."

"What an asshole!" she sneers, her eyes narrowed.

I snicker. That I can't disagree with.

We stay silent after that. And I'm kind of grateful. With only ten minutes left, my eyes keep drifting to Ben. I'm unable to deny that I would be interested in somebody like him. But as I rake my gaze over his gloriously fit body that's glistening in sweat, I internally kick myself for thinking about him like that. John made it loud and clear, and I need to focus on my new job. I don't want to risk losing this incredible opportunity for a fling. It makes me physically sick thinking about it.

Ugh.

"I think they have a very good appetite," Mia says with a chuckle, still looking at the guys, breaking up our peaceful silence.

"Talking about them eating like pigs isn't appealing," I mutter with a shake of my head, and wonder what she's on about.

She tips her head back, laughing. When she straightens, she says in a whisper, "Oh, you idiot. Not that kind of hunger."

She wiggles her eyebrows at me with a funny expression written across her face.

The penny drops.

Her mind is back in the gutter.

Oh.

"Oh my God." I laugh, but it's strangled with shock.

Ben moves close to us again, and I drop my gaze to the board, avoiding eye contact with him. When I feel him jog away, I peer back up and finish the conversation with Mia, ignoring the tension coiling in my back.

"I really need to concentrate, Mia. John will be up my ass, as per usual, if I don't keep my mind on the job. He *hates* me. I heard him mutter today about this being a man's world," I say, trying to not let the comment get to me. Even if it has already stung the way it was intended to.

After a few deep breaths, I'm feeling my body slacken, and I'm able to focus back on the task at hand.

"John is an asshole. Women can do just as good of a job as any man. I'm proud of you. Don't let him get the better of you."

I smile at her comment. "No chance. This is my dream job. I'm not going anywhere."

"Good for you, babe. Well, I better get back and leave you to it. Come find me after the game, or should I say, *training*." She air quotes the last bit before kissing both my cheeks and pulling back.

I smile as I watch her walk away.

Returning my gaze to the game, I spot that sexy blond and mentally run through different ways to convince him to let me assess his knee. If he does, I'll need to not get lost in how dreamy he is...or worse, get swept up in his boyish charm.

CHAPTER 4

BENJAMIN

"Let's hit the showers," Levi yells across the field to all of us guys.

I want to argue, and practice longer, but I can't. It's not as if I can tell the quarterback no. Friends or not. Rules are rules. With my head hung low, I walk toward the locker rooms. My hands on my hips, I suck in deep breaths, refilling my lungs that have been deprived of oxygen.

"You coming to my house tonight?"

I lift my head to meet Levi's questioning face. Dropping my hands, I swipe a bottle of Gatorade and down the cold, refreshing liquid before I give him an answer.

"As in, you're hosting a party or playin' PlayStation?" I ask, with a raised brow, knowing he likes to push the rules.

"Are you actually going to attend a party?"

His tone is laced with a mix of humor and accusation, but I laugh it off.

"Not unless it's for work. And Coach will kick our asses if we aren't following our regime," I say, reminding him of our rules.

"I know," he mutters, before taking a decent guzzle of his own orange drink.

"So, it's not a party?" I press, not wanting to get caught off guard and end up attending a non-team organized event. Training twice a day is wiping me out. I'm not gonna lie. My body is tired, sore, and achy. I don't want to jeopardize my position for a stupid party. Even if hot girls are offered on a silver platter. That means very little to me and always has.

My relationships with women have always been casual. Life as a pro football player has me traveling too much for commitment. If I need stress relief, I find a no strings attached hook-up.

He bumps my shoulder, and I stumble for a second as I steady myself. "Nah, no party. Let's just have a beer and play COD."

I shove his shoulder back with a sly grin, watching him now fumble and the orange liquid spilling out. I chuckle as I watch him recover. Beating his ass in Call of Duty again sounds good. "No beer for me, but yeah, I'll come for a bit. I can't stay too long, though. These two-a-days are wiping me out."

"Yeah, they are lethal, but fuck, man, you're killing it. I've never seen you work harder."

A slow, stupid grin forms on my face from his words. I know they ring true. I've been working hard with my trainer. I love the feeling of pushing myself to my limits, even in practice. Nothing satisfies me more than my job.

Walking into the shower, I welcome the water on my tired, achy muscles. I make it a quick one, because I'll need another after strength training later. Knowing a few players will skip the second training session, but I can't. This is my life. My eye is on the prize—win the Super Bowl. Keep outside distractions to the minimum and follow all of our coach's rules.

Nothing and no one will stop me.

Well...fuck, except maybe Natasha. It's as if fate drew us together after meeting that first time, and ever since, I've found my mind wandering more than I'm used to.

As I walk out of the shower, I look over at her now. She's holding a clipboard in her hands, sporting the biggest shit-eating grin I've ever seen at practice. She's so damn hot. But, as John steps toward her and speaks, her stunning mouth closes, and the lightness on her face quickly fades. I frown, wondering why the change. As I come closer, I run my gaze over her. As usual, she's wearing the boring ass uniform, but on her, it's eye-catching. That fabric can do nothing to hide her tight figure when she moves.

The closer I am, the more a thrill catapults inside me. My heart beating a little faster and my body temperature rising. I don't know why my body keeps having this reaction to her. I'm not mad about it, just...more confused. She's much better to look at than John, that's for damn fucking sure. I've only seen glimpses of her in the corridor or around the field, and every single time I catch her eyes, there's a spark between us. She's quick to look away, but not before I take a moment to let my gaze explore her high cheekbones and luscious lips that her silky blonde hair can't hide. Her full lips were made to be kissed.

That single thought makes me hard.

A smack on my back pulls me away from Natasha. I grind my teeth. Goddamnit. I just wanted to soak her in a little longer.

"You killed it out there." Andrew slaps my shoulder, and I tilt to look up at our offensive lineman. He's a big bastard. About 6'5" and weighs fifty pounds more than me.

I chuckle. "I could say the same about you." And I slap his shoulder back, but he barely moves an inch.

"We're in the best shape of our careers. Nothing can stop us. Now, I need a shower. I fuckin' stink," he says, still out of breath.

I nod. But as we hit the locker rooms, a gush of air leaves my lungs at the sight of the stunning blonde squatting. She's picking up a large number of scattered papers. Without thinking about my lack of clothes. I step toward her and squat down. As I help, I can't help but take in her pretty face from being this close to her. Her cheeks are dusty pink and when she looks up, I swallow a growl. Her eyes are wide and so vibrant, the blues brighter than I've ever seen before. They are so damn hypnotizing that until she moves, I've forgotten what I was doing for a moment.

The air has shifted, and the already steamy room is now combustible. She stands and I follow. My over six feet frame means she has to tilt her head back to look at me. I don't miss the way her eyes trail up slowly over my almost naked body. It sends a warm thrill through my chest and a knowing smirk splits on my face.

When she finishes her assessment, I cock a brow and hold out the papers. "Here you go."

I pass them over and, with purpose, I touch her hand with mine. Static scatters over my skin and up my arm.

She stares and licks her lips before muttering, "Thanks for your help—again."

Taking the papers from me, she loses her footing and falls. She curses under her breath, and I can't help but break out into a wide smile.

I'm quick to bend and give her a hand up. "I seem to have that effect on women."

I wink when she meets my gaze.

She rolls her eyes and the words, "Lucky women," leave her lips in a dry tone.

I frown, not understanding what I said to get that reaction.

She turns to leave, and a piece of white paper catches the corner of my eye.

"Wait up. You missed a piece." I pick it up and step over to her. I hand it out and she's quick to rip it out of my hands. She's avoiding touching me. The knowledge causes me to grin. Glad to not be the only one affected.

I don't want her to leave just yet. Before she turns, I blurt, "Congratulations on your new role." Not the best conversation starter, but she seems a little weary of me and I couldn't think of anything else on the spot. It's like her beauty stole my brain.

She stares at me before giving me a small smile. "Thanks."

"Nice to meet you." I grin and thrust my hand out.

I want to kick my own ass right now. Where the fuck is my game? Why am I wanting to shake her hand? It's not as if I can take it back now.

She looks at my hand briefly before awkwardly putting her hand in mine and shaking it. Adding to my already embarrassed ego. She's quick to yank her hand away. "Same. I've gotta go. John needs me."

Before I have a chance to argue and say he's busy talking to Andrew, she's gone. Leaving me standing there in the middle of the locker room. With my mouth hanging open and my hand tingling from the way her dainty hand fit perfectly in mine.

CHAPTER 5

BENJAMIN

THE NEXT AFTERNOON, I'M leaving the gym after stretching and conditioning, when I see Natasha walking ahead. She's holding a book and there's a pen tucked behind her ear, clearly on display thanks to the way she's tied her hair up into a slick bun. Her exposed neck is sexy, but the pen gives her the irresistible-nerdy-girl vibe. I can't deny she's tempting. My feet seem to move on their own accord as I pick up my pace, heading behind her toward her office.

Once I approach, I notice she's removed the pen, and she's now sitting behind a large wooden desk. She opens a book, nibbling on the end of the pen as she flips through the pages, looking for something. She's too perfect, and now is my chance to have a conversation with her that doesn't have her running away from me.

Knocking on the wooden doorway, her head lifts as she jumps slightly in her seat, surprise written on her face. She lowers the pen away from her mouth and down to the desk but doesn't say anything.

"Hey. Can I come in?" I was going to ask if she's too busy, but then she might say yes, and I didn't want to give her the option.

"Is everything okay? Are you hurt?" Her eyes scan my body quickly.

I like her attention on me, but not when she thinks I'm injured.

I let out a sigh. "No."

Curiosity flashes across her face before her eyes narrow a bit. I step to the vacant seat in front of her desk, figuring if she isn't telling me to leave, I have five minutes to get to know her better.

"What is it, Ben? Is there something I can help you with?"

Pursing my lips, I contain any smartass comment from leaving my mouth. I don't want to fuck this up. "Just checking in on you."

Her face is perplexed, and I chuckle, a soft smile sitting on my lips. "No one checks on you, Doc?"

"To be honest, no." Her eyes flash with sadness before I sense a wall going back up. I already had a feeling she would be hard to crack, but this proves it could be harder than I thought.

I draw my mouth into a thin line, staying quiet for a beat to think before I speak. "That's sad. You deserve to be asked if you're okay, just as much as you ask any of us."

She leans forward, putting her hands under her chin. "Is that what you think?" Her eyes bore into mine, not giving anything away. I think that's what has me so interested. There's something about her that's alluring without trying to be.

"That's what I know," I say, and lean to one side of the chair.

She laughs at that. And there's a little softness to her eyes now as she drops her hands to the desk. "That's kind of you. But I'm a big girl, and I don't need anyone checking on me."

"But what if I wanna check on you?"

She blinks, looking a bit nervous as her fingers move to tug on her earring. Simple white gold studs. They suit her. She doesn't seem to be a woman who needs large diamonds, unlike most women I've met. "You'd be wasting your breath, Mr. Chase."

My dick twitches at the way she says my name.

"Mr. Chase...mmm." My thumb grazes my lip, and my eyes never leave hers. I don't miss the way she watches the movement. "I like that. But just so we're clear, you wouldn't be a waste of my time."

She looks conflicted, but then she shakes her head. As if to snap herself out of it. Then she's putting on her smooth, controlled, professional voice, which I've come to look forward to hearing. Peering around her office, I take in a frame on her desk, and without hesitation, I grab it. Reading the contents of her certificate.

"Is there anything else I can help you with, Ben?"

Lowering it back down, I shake my head. "I liked Mr. Chase better," I tease, as a smirk forms on my lips.

She rolls her eyes again, and it stirs something in me. She hasn't left my mind since the moment I met her. Every one of her mannerisms, and the way she speaks, how she looks at me, it's all impossible to ignore. The only problem is, she's the one woman who won't give me a chance. No matter how I look, my celebrity status, or what flirty advances I attempt.

"Well, *Mr. Chase*, if you want to help me, you can let me assess your knee."

The way her face lights up with amusement...I want to see more of that.

I know she's challenging me, and fuck, I'm competitive by nature.

Staring back at me, wearing a smug smile, she knows it.

She knows she's won.

CHAPTER 6

Natasha

"Fine. Let's do it. Even though I think you're wasting your time," he says, sarcasm dripping from his voice.

I swallow the lump that's formed in my throat from the nerves. I'm about to touch his knee, while being in close proximity, alone in this office. His large frame already fills up too much space, making it hard for me to breathe without sucking in his dizzying, masculine scent. Pushing out of my office chair, I stand, grateful for my wooden desk to lean on. Because the second I stood, he followed suit, immediately ripping off his black training top.

My stomach flips with butterflies, and I want to scold myself. It's not like I haven't walked through the locker room, having seen many players half-dressed, with their dicks out, or asses on display, and hell, it's not like I haven't seen a naked man, but I'm not gonna lie...it's been a while. And by a while, I mean a couple of years.

Ignoring the way my body is responding to all his testosterone in the room, I look down to gather my thoughts. I need to avoid staring at his hot, toned body that's currently making me flustered.

After a moment of gathering my wayward thoughts while pretending to look over a paper on my desk, I straighten my spine.

"Ready?" he asks, popping a brow as I meet his curious gaze head on.

I gesture to the exam table. "Let's. Please take a seat."

Happy I sound in control.

He winks at me, and I roll my lips to prevent a smile from forming. I watch his magnificent frame follow my instruction as he turns, giving myself another internal pep talk to not fumble and fall on my ass this time.

I move to stand in front of him, peering down at his enormous frame. He's even more handsome this close, with his chiselled jaw, blue eyes, and athletic frame. My throat itches from the heat. I reach up and scratch the base of my neck, clearing my throat to speak. "So, do you have any aches or pains in this knee?" I point to the left, knowing it's not the troublesome one.

His blue eyes glow under the room lights, making me burn up again. Then his lopsided grin is back, and I melt into a puddle. "Nah."

"What about the right knee?"

"Nah, I'm all good." He shrugs it off, but there is a twitch in his smile and the hardness of his expression that makes me think he is bluffing, telling me what he thinks I want to hear.

"Hmm, but I saw you rubbing your right knee. Did it pull or feel tight?" I ask.

A flicker of surprise hits his face before his eyes narrow on mine.

I'm glad to be standing above him at this moment, so he doesn't make me feel so small. But just as quickly as that scowl's there, he's smiling again.

A totally fake one this time.

"No, there is nothing wrong with it. But I do like that you're checking me out." Once again, he's dismissing me with a panty-melting smirk and a playful wiggle of his eyebrows. He extends his knee and lowers it again, as if trying to prove a point. After a few in a row, he raises his brow at me, thinking he's in the clear.

"Doing my job, you mean. Let me have a quick feel, then." I lift my own brow in a challenge.

He waves his hand. "No need."

His tone makes me grind my molars.

Why is he being a jerk?

This is the first time I have seen this side of him. Doesn't he realize I'm just here to help?

I take a deep, steady breath. John will be on my back if I don't sort this out now.

"You know, if you get it checked out, it might be nothing, but if you let it go and it becomes something, it causes more damage in the end. I promise, I'll only be a few minutes."

As I stand waiting, I think he is going to shrug me off. But then he sighs and dips his head before looking at me again. A fixed stare has me under his scrutiny, and I hold my breath.

Please. Please. Please. Let me just assess you. Don't make this harder than it needs to.

"I don't want to, but fine. You've got two minutes."

I drop to my knees in front of him, hearing a hiss escape from his mouth. Panic rises in my veins from the noise, and I peek up at him with worry. "Are you okay? Did I hurt you?" I reach up and touch his leg. His eyes are staring back at me with an unreadable expression, and I notice they've grown darker. My gaze drifts down to notice his hands gripping the seat on either side of his thighs with white knuckle force.

"No, it's fine," he grunts, but he's still sitting upright, stiff as a board, and I have no idea why.

He said it wasn't pain, so what is it, then?

I have to shrug it off and begin the assessment.

He grunts again. "There's nothing wrong with it. You're wasting your time."

Keeping my focus on my job and away from whatever weirdness is going on with him, I continue. Why is he so angry all of the sudden?

"I hope you're right. I hope I'm wasting my time. But I need to check your knee, otherwise, John will be on me if something happens." I slam my lips shut, unable to believe I let those words fly out of my mouth. It's not professional of me to speak about John to a player.

He chuckles darkly above me, causing my eyes to flick up to his. The softness I've become familiar with from him is back in his features. "Yeah, John can be a royal pain in the ass."

As I shuffle my knees closer and my fingertips touch his warm skin, my body flushes. Thankfully, my chin is down to my chest, so he can't see my body's reaction to him. His toned thigh above shows his strength, and luckily, I don't need to venture up higher. Keeping my assessment on his knee only. *A safe zone.*

I do my usual tests, and he doesn't flinch.

Passing.

But I still know in my gut something isn't right. And it's time to tell him what I think and how to treat it.

Without lingering a moment longer, I stand, feeling better when I'm up and getting out of his space.

I meet his gaze. "I think you have a strain in your knee. You need to rest for the next two days, with your right leg elevated. Ice it for twenty minutes every two hours, and then I can get one of the trainers to bandage it."

"I don't need ice or a bandage from one of the trainers. I need you." His mouth forms a crooked smile, and I can tell he's feeling all smug with himself.

I'm caught off guard by his forward advance. It's not the first time, but I brush it off and refocus on him. Why on earth is he trying to ignore his injury? It isn't fooling me. And if he doesn't listen, the strain will become a more permanent problem, therefore ending his season before it's even began. Maybe even his career. "If you don't, you might not be ready to play in a couple of weeks."

His shoulders slump, and I don't miss the way his jaw ticks at my warning. "I'm aware of that. Obviously."

The snide tone annoys me, but I keep my cool and watch him stand. With the assessment over, he puts his top back on. I refuse to look at his perfect naked torso. It gets me thinking...why did he remove his top in the first place?

Probably to distract me.

Ignoring where my mind wants to go, I say, "If that's all, I'll see you in two days. You know where to find me if you need me before then. Please don't hesitate," I say, then promptly step back from his personal space.

"Trust me, I won't," he replies with another wink and jumps off the bed, towering over me again.

I quickly turn to find a gorgeous woman standing at the door. Who is she? I've never seen her before. "Can I help you?" I ask, wandering back over to my desk again.

Not missing Ben's loud curse, I ignore him, watching as she eyes Ben longingly.

"I was looking for Ben."

My stomach drops, but this gives me a reason not to drool over him anymore.

"I'm busy." He tries to dismiss her.

She visibly winces, and I feel bad for her. But she's quick to recover. "I'll just wait in the—"

"Later," he warns.

But knowing I'm finished assessing him, I speak up.

"No, it's fine. We're done here." I swallow the mix of hurt, and I'm unable to hold back the displeasure that drips from my voice. Why I even feel that way, I'm not sure.

"Okay, great. I'll just wait out here." She smiles and turns around, her heels clicking away.

I sit and return to my paperwork, avoiding his eye contact. I can feel his gaze on me, but I'm relieved when he doesn't argue. Instead, I hear a heavy, exasperated breath leave his mouth.

My control is firmly back in place, and I still don't look up to watch him leave.

CHAPTER 7

BENJAMIN

THE NEXT DAY, I'M talking to the coach Chris. Well...I was until Natasha caught my eye. She's talking to John. The way we left things yesterday felt awkward, and fuck, totally uncomfortable.

After finishing up with Coach, I see John move on to speak with Levi. Perfect opportunity for me to talk to her alone again. I head to her office, moving quickly and making sure no one else is around. This time, before I can knock, her eyes look up from the paper in front of her. My lips twitch as her eyes widen in shock. But then they return to normal, hiding her true feelings once again. Approaching her desk, I forget my manners, not even asking if I can have a moment. Because the slight annoyance mixed with mysterious hurt staring back at me has me guessing she'd say she was busy. Therefore, I'm not giving her an option. I don't plan to take too much of her time, just enough to apologize for the debacle yesterday.

"I'm busy, Ben. Can you come back later?" She looks at me directly, with a pinched expression.

Her bossy voice sends my dick twitching. It's hot, and the way she's focused on work is a major turn on. I'm too excited right now to put forth a better conversation.

"I'll be five minutes, tops." Taking a seat in the chair across from her, I know I won't want to leave that soon.

Yeah, I'm definitely not thinking straight.

She narrows her eyes at me. "Well, spit it out, Mr. Chase."

I swallow the growl that's threatening to leave my chest. Instead, I smirk. "Well, Miss Blackwood..." I purposefully purr out her name, but of course, her façade is unwavering. "I wanted to apologize to you for the interruption yesterday."

"Are you here just to say that? Because, thanks for the apology, but I really don't need a rundown of your sexcapades, Ben," she deadpans.

I almost choke on a laugh.

"I know, and I'm not. This is me wanting to find out more about you. That was why I came in yesterday."

She shifts in her seat, as if she needs to get comfortable with this conversation. "Ben, I can't get to know you like that."

My jaw ticks, irritated. "Why?" Surely not because of yesterday.

She runs her hand over her neatly pulled back blonde hair. Blowing out a long, strained breath, she answers, "Because it's highly inappropriate."

I sit, waiting, expecting her to elaborate, but she doesn't. She just sits back, staring at me.

"We're just talking," I say, like the smartass I am.

Easing back into the chair, I watch her tap her pen on the papers.

"And that's all it will be. I'm still new and finding my feet." She says, shaking her head.

I'm hoping for a little more personal information, but it's like she reins herself back in. She's the total opposite of me.

"I can help you settle in," I genuinely offer. I want to earn her trust and spend more time with her, whatever that entails.

Her eyes narrow further as she scrutinizes me. "How?"

"First, help you go through the paperwork. Then maybe set up your office." I scan the boxes scattered around the room. Unpacking alone will take her a big chunk of time. "And then end it with some dinner?"

Her jaw drops at my last offer. I couldn't help myself.

"Ben, what are you really doing here?" she asks, sounding tired and a bit frustrated. Ignoring all the offerings and just focusing on me inviting her to dinner.

"Getting to know you and offering you help," I reply with a shrug.

Clasping her hands together, she's about to speak, when John's booming voice cuts in. "Were you looking for me, Ben?"

"No," I reply at the same time Natasha says, "Yes."

My earlier smile fades.

"Yes, he was," Natasha repeats, looking right at me with a little smug smile.

I smirk back at her, at a total loss. Why is she the one woman who won't give me a chance?

Needing to answer John, I twist to face him and tell him, "Seems I was." I flick my gaze back to her and see her beaming like the Cheshire Cat.

"Right. Well then, let's go to my office," John says, walking out.

Standing out of my chair, I lean over her desk, my hands flat on the cold wood. She swallows roughly as her head tilts back to look up at me. Her eyes hold mine, and we don't move for a beat. Just our heavy breathing is exchanged. Then, without warning, I push off the desk and step back. I don't miss the exhale that leaves her lips and the involuntary body shiver that takes over her as soon as she thinks I'm not paying attention.

"We are not done here," I say, then leave her in her office with a smile plastered on my face at knowing I have an effect on her.

CHAPTER 8

NATASHA

IT'S SUNDAY MORNING, AND I'm doing my weekly chores at home. I wish I'd been able to sleep in, but I have errands to run before work tomorrow.

I'm stirring my oatmeal when Mom's footsteps sound from her room. She's always less uncomfortable in the mornings, so she only uses her walking stick for some support. But by the evenings, her back is in too much pain, and the frame is more stable. After she had a few accidents, I encouraged her, using my doctor's voice to really drive home how important it was.

"Morning. How are you feeling?" I pause to look at her.

She takes a seat at the dining table, awaiting her breakfast, albeit stubbornly. The number of arguments we've had because she doesn't want me to help her is ridiculous. But it's my job as the daughter.

It's just us two. So, I'll always be there for her. She's part of the drive I had to study sports medicine. Her injury enhanced the desire for me to help other people in any way I could.

I move to prepare her cereal, tea, and pills. And a few minutes later, we're eating side by side. Weekends go by at a much slower pace. A tiny bit of extra sleep is nice, but it's not enough to cure the sleep deprivation. There's still so much to squeeze into two days.

"I'm fine. Stop worrying about me. Are you going out to-day?"

I frown, not understanding what she's asking. She knows the Sunday routine. I'm all about sticking to a strict routine. It keeps me from spiraling. I like knowing what I'm doing and at what time. The control of organization keeps me calm. I definitely am not a go-with-the-flow type of person.

"Please tell me you have something for yourself to do today?" she asks as she dips her spoon into her cereal, taking a bite and chewing as she waits for my response.

I look down at my milky tea, and then back up, shaking my head. Did I forget something today? It's no one's birthday. I don't get it. "No, I thought we could go to the market."

She leans forward, her hands resting on the table. "You haven't seen your friends much lately."

It's like she's read my thoughts. I take a bite of my oatmeal. "I saw—"

I stop talking when my stomach drops because I haven't seen Mia outside of work. And with my other friends, well, I haven't seen them for a month...or is it months now?

I shake my head and smile, shrugging it off. "It's fine. I saw them recently enough."

She sighs heavily. Her face is tight, and her blue eyes sad. "You need to go out on your weekends off. I'm a big girl who can stay out of trouble for a couple of hours. I do it when you're at work."

I raise my brow at her. Hating the fact she thinks she's a burden. Or that I don't want to be doing this and that she's holding me back from living my life. Which isn't at all true. I'm a homebody at heart, and I love that. There isn't anything wrong with enjoying your own company.

"Your caregiver comes during the day while I'm at work," I remind her.

"She isn't here all day." She lets out a frustrated breath and continues. "Please, just go out for a couple of hours with your friends. Maybe they would like to go to the market with you? Just bring me a cinnamon donut back." She winks before sitting back up and returning to her breakfast.

I could go out for a little while...I would like to get some flowers, and if she wants a donut, I'll bring one back. My stomach rumbles, loving the sound of a delicious, melt-in-your-mouth cinnamon, or even a glazed donut.

My shoulders drop, and I give in. With Mom, she knows she can always convince me somehow. I'm a tough cookie, but I'm all gooey and soft for her. "Okay. I'll call and see if one of them is free."

Once I've finished my tea, Mom moves to the couch, and I call my friend Sara.

"Oh my god, you're alive! I have been texting you for weeks. Where have you been?" she rambles off, like I've been gone a year.

I laugh, taking a seat on my bed. "I answered them."

"Yes, but I haven't seen you. Are you avoiding me?" she asks directly.

I run my hand along the white cotton bedding under me, feeling a wash of guilt. Maybe Mom was right, and I need to make more of an effort. "No way. I've been busy with work and Mom."

"Fair enough. But I miss you."

My stomach knots further because of my simple explanation. They react with no bullshit or rude comments; they accept me for me. And they're there whenever I need them. I just wish I was a better friend in return. Time is a wondrous thing, and I just can't seem to find enough of it...for everyone and everything going on in my life.

"I was actually calling to see if you're free today?" I say, hoping she is, because I need this. I didn't realize how much I needed my friend until hearing her voice.

"Yeah! What do you have in mind?" she rushes out excitedly.

"The market." I check my watch and add, "In half an hour? I want to be back by lunch. I'll pick you up."

I know it's not a lot of time, but Sara doesn't push. "I can't wait."

I hang up and practically jump off the bed to shower and get dressed.

When I pick her up for the market, I can't help but feel lighter from just being in her presence. She hasn't shut up since the moment I picked her up, but it's made me smile from ear to ear the whole time. To add to this perfect Sunday, the sun is out, and the buzz of people at the market is making me happier with every passing minute. For the first time in a while, I feel relaxed.

"Where should we start first?" Sara asks as we look ahead at all the stalls.

I point to the other side, noticing the stands I want to stop at last. "How about there, because I want to grab donuts and flowers before we leave."

"Good thinking." She links arms with me, and we wear silly smiles as we mosey up and down each aisle for the next hour while catching up about what's been happening in our lives. Sara is in fashion design, so she always has extravagant stories. Listening to her has me forgetting about my life for a moment. I wonder what it would be like to step into someone else's shoes, someone without responsibilities and totally carefree.

We're finishing our walk around the entire market when we stop at the flower stall. I grab a bouquet of white tulips and we make our way to grab a box of fresh donuts. The aroma in the air is full of delicious sugar. Instantly, my mouth waters, and even a small moan slips from my lips. We both order and then wait to the side for them to be made fresh.

"I changed my mind. I'm going to grab the candle I saw back there." Sara points toward the direction of a stall we stopped at earlier.

I smile, knowing the exact one she wants. It has the coolest purple crystal pieces set in the top of the white wax. I was surprised when she didn't grab it. "I think that's a great idea. They were so pretty."

"And smelled amazing. I won't be long." She hurries off, and I stay waiting, my eyes searching the stalls nearby for anything fun I may have missed.

"You know that's not good for you, Doc."

My head whips around at the sound of *his* voice.

What's he doing here?

I face him slowly to see his athletic frame in a tight white shirt showing off his broad shoulders and wide chest. His fitted light-gray jeans hug those thick thighs I've had my hands on, and his white sneakers top off his casual look. Yet, for some reason, he looks anything but casual. I can't deny how hot he is.

However, it seems like he's trying to stay under the radar, because he also has a baseball cap on, hiding most of his unruly blond hair. Players can't go out without being stopped for pictures or signatures. It must suck to have no privacy.

As much as I prefer him without a hat, I think it's saving me right now. Between that and the sun in my eyes, it makes it harder to get lost in his piercing blue gaze.

I stuff my hands into my skinny jean pockets, not holding back my eye roll. "I'm not eating all those myself."

His mouth clamps shut, and his body stiffens, the small tick in his jaw telling me he's jealous.

"Who are you sharing them with?" he asks through clenched teeth.

I pinch my lips together to prevent a smile from spreading across my face. I ponder making him sweat it or putting him out of his misery, but I don't have long to wait because Sara interrupts, saying, "Her mom."

I don't know if I'm sad she told the truth. I felt good when he was all green-eyed, thinking I was buying it to share with a guy...

My order is called, so I grab my box and Sara's. Handing her box over to her and opening mine, I decide I can't wait.

"What are you doing here?" I ask as I take a quick bite while it's still hot. I figure if he's being nosy, so can I.

The sugar melts on my tongue and the fresh dough causes me to close my eyes for a second and moan before I can stop myself. "So good." I lick my lips, getting the residue of sugar off.

"Meeting friends, but you're tempting me to grab a donut." His voice is deeper and more seductive than when he greeted me, and I catch my breath when I watch his Adam's apple bob from a strong swallow.

My mouth hangs open, and I freeze when he reaches out to dust sugar crumbs from my bottom lip. The feeling of his calloused thumb causes me to tremble. He's never touched me before, and I'm surprised I don't hate it. In fact, the warmth that flows through me has me thankful I can't see his eyes right now. I'm beginning to overheat from our close proximity.

His other hand tips his hat up, and I gulp for air. The way his blue eyes are staring through me, making me feel naked, he's suffocating all my senses. When his mouth splits into a sexy smirk, it's like he can read my mind. He knows how tempted I am right now.

Tempted to do what...I'm not sure. But whatever it is, it wouldn't be good.

As he holds me in an intense eye fuck, we're silent, his hand still on my face. Then, before I can react, he grabs a donut out of my box and takes a huge bite. My gaze can't tear away from his mouth; I'm totally fixated on it. Watching him lick his lips, cleaning the sugar residue, sends my achy core into a burning inferno.

I don't know whether to be mad he stole one of my donuts or be disgusted with myself because I want to kiss him so badly right now. This is the boldest attempt he's made so far, and I hate that it's working on me. My mind drifts effortlessly into the dangerous territory of imagining what his mouth would feel and taste like pressed against mine. I bet it would be lethal. A strong mix of cinnamon, sugar, and *him*.

I watch him finish the donut and lick his fingers clean, and of course, my body shudders. Could I be any more obvious? Those fingers, that mouth, it's all too much. I shake my head, needing to snap myself out of whatever is happening right now. It has to stop. We're in public.

I hear Sara clear her throat beside me. I totally forgot she was standing there.

"I'm sure you could have afforded to buy your own," I say in a voice that doesn't sound like mine, although I'm trying with all my strength to be sassy.

He smirks. "But I know yours tastes better."

I blink rapidly. He is too fucking much. "You owe my mother a donut now."

"I'd be happy to visit her with some."

My mouth opens and closes.

No.

Then he would know and feel pity for our life. I don't want that; Mom and I are happy and, frankly, I don't want to answer any questions or bring up the past.

I'm about to respond—with what, I'm not sure—just as a male approaches.

"There you are," he says, holding hands with a blonde woman.

"James. Abigail—" Benjamin says, about to introduce them to me.

"We have to get going," I interrupt him, pulling Sara along. I don't want to meet his friends or get personal with him. That would be too much right now. My heart is beating frantically in my chest with the need to get out of here. I'm high on sugar and, well, him.

A flash of something unreadable hits his face, and he drops his chin. "I'll see you tomorrow."

"Yup!"

I wave and turn without another glance at him. I hear Sara say goodbye and follow me.

She hooks her arm through mine, as I concentrate on taking one step at a time on my shaky legs.

When we are almost at the car, she whispers, "Who was that?"

I shrug and whisper back, "It's just Ben from the team."

Sara wouldn't know who he is, because she doesn't have a clue about football. But I hope I come across as unbothered by him. Or that she didn't pick up on our weird exchange, but as soon as I think it...

She spins to face me with an amused expression. "Just Ben? I don't think so. You two are hot for each other."

I scoff, waving it off, even though my heart feels like it's about to beat out of my chest. I'm scared he's following us, and I don't know what I would do if he touched me again. "No. I'm not interested in dating."

We arrive at the car, opening our doors. "I'm sure if you explained—"

"No," I answer firmly, cutting off her thoughts and sitting in the driver's seat.

That's not my life. My life is work and Mom, bottom line. There's no room in my heart or life for a man. And definitely not for one who could break it.

"It's up to you. But it's a damn shame if you don't go for it. I wish someone that attractive looked at me like that." She buckles up and sits back.

As I drive off, I replay her words in my mind: *looked at me like that.* I remain silent, not letting myself indulge in fantasies because, really, they are just that—*fantasies*.

CHAPTER 9

NATASHA

IT'S BEEN A BUSY week. I stand watching the last ten minutes from the sideline, engrossed in every bit of the game. It's intense, and I have a huge smile on my face the whole time. Loving every second of this nail-biter.

In the last few minutes, the ball gets tossed into Levi's hands, and he takes off in a sprint. He clashes into a teammate, and when he bounces backward, I think nothing of it. That is, until he clutches his right hand to grab his left shoulder and the wince on his face makes my stomach drop.

He's injured.

Shit.

The quarterback's down.

I try to signal the head referee. He blows the whistle when the coach calls time out. After what feels like forever, but has only been a minute, the head referee turns and waves me on. Adrenaline rises in me as we get closer. I drop the board I'm holding and run out across the field as fast as my legs can take me, catching my breath when I approach. As I squat down in front of him, I feel the presence of the team watching.

"Levi, are you okay? What happened?" I ask, keeping my tone as even as possible. I'm trying to keep him from panicking, but when he looks up at me, the fear in his eyes freezes me on the spot.

His gaze moves to the area on the field where it happened. He blinks and keeps his eyes on the spot as he speaks in a quavering voice. "My shoulder...I don't know what I was doing. I just ran like I always do, but the impact was harder. The noise wasn't right and the pain in my shoulder straight after..." He pauses to shake his head, and his eyes meet mine again. "I have never felt anything like it."

Suddenly, my stomach rolls with nausea. His face and that description are giving me one idea, and I just hope I'm wrong.

I take a long breath and keep my face neutral, and with a calm voice, I say, "Okay. I want to get you back into the locker room, and I'll look at you properly there."

He nods, and I stand.

Just as I'm about to help Levi up, I hear a barking order directed at me. "Wait a minute."

John. Aka, the boss from hell.

My shoulders stiffen at his tone, and I know I'm about to be pushed aside. It makes my blood boil. The fact that he doesn't take me seriously and doesn't let me do my job pisses me off. I can do this. I can assess Levi on my own, for fuck's sake. My hands curl into fists by my sides to hold in my temper, threatening to spill.

I want to ask him why he won't just let me make a decision? I passed all my schooling, and I was hired for this job. What's his problem? But instead, I swallow it down and grind my teeth together, waiting for his direction. Levi is the priority right now.

"Levi, let me look at it," John insists. And I watch him walk straight up into Levi and help him stand. He stares into his face and even I can see Levi looking a bit uncomfortable, not meeting my eyes, keeping his head hung low. I think he feels sorry for me and that makes me feel worse.

Fucking John.

I don't want anyone to feel sorry for me. But when John barks orders instead of talking to me nicely, or with even an ounce of respect, not even trying to listen to me, it makes people not take me seriously. I'm just the dumb woman who shouldn't be a part of the man's world.

As I watch on, I don't say anything. John asks a bunch of questions as he touches Levi's shoulder, doing all the things I could have done in the locker room—in silence, with none of the other players watching.

I can see the worry in Levi's eyes as John examines him. When John grazes a sore spot, Levi winces again. Football players take a beating on the regular, so this is obviously painful for him to be visibly reacting.

It's not a good sign.

John orders him to get to the locker room.

Which is what I said five minutes ago, but, of course, John wouldn't listen.

John and Levi walk past me. John with his chest up like a king dick, and Levi clutching his shoulder, head down. All the other players watch in silence, not knowing what to do. I step forward but hear one voice that prevents me from moving...an all too familiar one.

It makes me tingly all over, and the hairs on the back of my neck stand on end. He always has my attention, like it knows him intimately for some stupid reason. I'm sure my body is just responding to what happened at the market. Yeah, I'm sure that's it.

"Let's finish the game, guys," he orders the team in an authoritative tone.

As they follow his instruction, he continues. "Don't worry about Levi; he'll be fine."

Will he?

I want to believe him, even though I know the likelihood of that not being the case at all.

I force myself to move, walking back to the sideline to finish watching the game.

Afterward, I head into the locker room at a slow pace, rolling my shoulders back and putting on my fake smile to check in with the players. Doing my job on autopilot, because I don't need John telling me I can't do this too.

I take my time to speak with each player, purposely leaving Ben second to last, and Levi for the very end, not wanting to intrude when he's with John.

Moving toward Ben, I feel my heart beating inside my ears. His head reclines when he hears me approach, and his face breaks into a smile. But let's see how long it lasts after I ask him how he's feeling. That seems to be an instant mood changer. Or is that his normal behind-the-smile personality that no one else sees?

His face is flushed and sweat beads drip down his neck from his face, the sign of a hard game. I move my gaze to the board, and biting the inside of my cheek, I look back at him. Watching as he runs his hand through his wet hair, he pushes it off his face, letting his eyes hold mine. He sits in his training gear, not bothering to change, and I pray he doesn't take it off in front of me again. That would be way too distracting.

I stand tall on the spot, trying to seem unaffected by his presence, even though the tension between us causes a shiver to run down my spine.

Focus on your job.

"How are you feeling after the game? Do you have any areas of concern?"

There is a gleam in his eye. "Well, I do have this one spot." I move closer, and he says with a chuckle, "Had you, didn't I?"

I roll my eyes, but I can't help but laugh at his light, cheeky tone. "I'm serious, Ben."

He nods, but his playfulness stays stretched across his handsome face. "I know. I'm just having fun. I wanted to see you smile. You're so beautiful when you smile."

He's rendered me speechless, but in a good way.

"But to answer your question, no, I'm good." He gives me a soft sigh.

With nothing else to say, and not wanting to hang around to see him undress, I give him a small smile and turn to walk away.

"Hold up. What about you?" he questions to my back, making me pause.

I turn back around to face him, my brows pinching together. What's he talking about?

The way this man looks at me makes my stomach harden. And I don't know which part he's referring to. I wonder for a second, but then shake my head, reminding myself he doesn't know about my mom.

I clear my throat to ask, "What about me?"

He smiles, head tilting as he repeats, "How are *you*?"

Oh.

I lift my eyes, darting them around, trying to avert his intense gaze. No one asks about me.

Only him.

Knowing I need to answer, I bite my tongue and fake how I feel. I'm not willing to talk badly about John, even though that's at the forefront of my mind.

"Oh, I'm fine." I wave my hand out. "I'm sure everything's going to be okay. Levi will be fine. All is fine."

His head tips back, showing me his thick, tanned neck, and a deep chuckle leaves his chest. The sound does something to my body I'm not willing to address. I stare at the vein along his throat, where the perspiration still clings to his body, licking my lips and wishing I could run my tongue along it. I want to taste his sweaty, masculine skin. My mouth is now dry, and my sex throbbing.

Stupid traitorous body.

He straightens his head back up, and his eyes darken. I fear he caught me with my dirty fucking mind.

"With the number of times you said *fine*, I'm pretty sure that means you're anything but."

Shit.

Totally busted.

I shake it off and snort.

Can the ground swallow me up, please?

He laughs again, shaking his head at me with a sexy smile.

But this time, I can't help but smile back before biting down on my bottom lip and rolling my eyes. "I *am* fine."

And I'm leaving before I say anything else. I spin on my heel, hearing his throaty chuckle again, but I don't turn back. Instead, I proceed slowly, step by step, toward John, who's still speaking with Levi. I take a deep breath, pausing a moment to calm my rattled body down. As I move in closer, it's as if they can sense me.

Levi's eyes look glassy. That's no good. It's heartbreaking to see him in so pain. Both emotional and physical.

And then John's icy glare, which instantly annoys me. I know he doesn't want me here, but I'm not about to let him push me around.

My emotions are all over the place from being dismissed. I want to help; this was why I became a doctor.

I wait for my shaking body to ease before I ask nicely, "Can I help you with anything?"

"No, I've got it," John sneers. "Go see if anyone else needs a hand. It's a big game next week."

As if I don't know that.

Then with pride, I say, "I have. They're all set for next week."

He has already spun around to face Levi again, his back to me. "Well then, go home."

Staring at his back in disbelief, I grind my teeth together.

I can't argue to stay, so with no other choice, I walk out, not giving the asshole another breath. It would be a waste of my time anyway.

I grab my bag, and as I turn around, I see Ben, his attention still on me. He clearly heard the exchange. The whole fucking room probably did. The backs of my eyes tingle, and I'm more than pissed off. I'm on the borderline of breaking down from embarrassment. I don't want to talk to anyone right now, don't want to lose it.

As I rush out of the locker room, I hear my name leave Ben's lips. "Natasha, wait."

But I don't stop until I'm in my car, crying all the way home.

CHAPTER 10

BENJAMIN

NEXT WEEK, AFTER PRACTICING for three hours straight, I hit the rooms and toss my helmet in my locker. Coach Chris walks in yelling, "Listen up."

Closing the door, I turn to stand with my hands on my hips, sucking in deep breaths. The chatter in the room quietens.

"With Levi being out for the season, I'd like to announce Ben as quarterback for this week."

The room breaks out in a chant, and we're all jumping up and down. This shit can't be real.

Chris interrupts the celebrations to add, "This calls for a team bonding session."

The room is buzzing with new energy. Music is turned on a moment later, causing us to become even louder.

After the chant finishes, the guys all come slap me on the back, bumping shoulders or yelling, "*Fuck yeah*" and "*well deserved*."

I duck my head and punch the air. I fucking did it. Everything is lining up as it should. Age is just a fucking number. I just crushed one of my goals.

When the room calms down and the guys take their seats or begin packing up, I clear my throat. "Guys. Not only do I want to thank Coach for giving me this opportunity, but I'd like to request a bonding dinner at my house tomorrow night."

They nod or give me a yes back.

"Now we're going to win this week for Levi. So, let's fucking go!" I yell.

They cheer loudly again and my gaze flicks to Natasha watching on from the side of the room. Her face is slack and totally bewildered. My legs move on their own accord, and when she sees me approaching, she moves forward to meet me.

When we are toe to toe, she stops nibbling on her lip. "Congratulations."

"Thanks. Wanna come and celebrate it with me tonight?" I tease, but I'm actually serious.

She rolls her lips, and I'm fucking fixated on it. High from the announcement, but it's more than that. She's so fucking sexy, especially when she does these little things that show her shyness.

"I can't," she says, looking away from my staring eyes.

"You can." My voice sounds almost desperate.

My hand lands on her hip, holding her gently.

"No. That's not happening. Celebrate with your team-mates," she argues, turning to meet my gaze head on.

I sigh in response, running my free hand through my hair. "Well, I guess you're celebrating with me anyway."

"What do you mean?" she asks, rapidly blinking.

I lick my lips and rub them together, not missing the way she watches me. "The dinner involves the whole team—including you."

I watch her swallow the words. And there is fear mixed with something else in her eyes. Something that resembles desire, or is it irritation?

"So, either way, you're celebrating with me, Natasha."

A few hours later, all the guys have left. I'm standing on the open field with the stadium lights shining down on me, still wearing my gear. I toss the ball into the air; it sails through, to land perfectly in my dad's outstretched hands. He clutches it to his chest with a wide smile. Jogging in a circle, he tosses it straight back to me, and I catch it easily.

We continue the back-and-forth, neither of us speaking. I'm still shocked that part of my dream is being fulfilled and it's bringing me one step closer to get the other goal of winning the trophy.

I need to train harder. Put in more hours. Practice more. I need to be perfect during the season to keep my position secure.

I keep tossing the ball, pushing past the tiredness and pain in my shoulder. I do not know how much time has passed, but the fatigue of the day is well and truly catching up to me. But standing on the grass in my boots and gear gives me the drive and determination like no other.

"How did you feel during the game?" Dad shouts across the field.

I throw it back and answer honestly. "Great. We have a real chance at winning this year."

The last ten years of not winning the final have been hard. But in the last few years, our team has stayed consistent and strong, working well together. And this year, it's our team's time. I don't have many years left before I'll be retiring; being thirty-four, I'm not getting any younger. So, I need to make every second count to get that win.

He tosses the ball back to me. "You've got this. Now you're the quarterback, with a strong team behind you. You should see yourselves. I'm proud of you, son."

I nod and catch it, tapping the ball with my hand. My chest is tight from his words, and I blow out a breath. My dad and I love to spend time after practice just tossing the ball back and forth and talking about how I felt during practice and how I can improve before the next game. The bond we share is unlike what I have with any of my friends. I'm lucky to have him to push me to be better, but also to support me when I need a break. He's one of a kind. My best friend. And since he was an NFL player too, he understands the sport better than anyone, so I always listen to his advice.

"I have a good feeling about winning this year," he calls out.

I hope he's right. I really fucking want it.

"Yeah, I hope so. I just have to keep up the practice. Eyes on the prize."

"But, son?" he asks, walking closer to me across the field and closing the space between us.

"Yeah?" I ask, squinting at him as he approaches until he stands face to face with me. I stare into the same blue eyes as mine and see his face etched with a hard expression. "Your form and body are looking better than ever, so give yourself some proper recovery time."

I swallow the worry that's been in the back of my mind since Little Miss Blackwood poked me. My knee isn't a hundred percent, and I worry I won't get my chance to play in the playoffs. It's always been my goal, and I'm close, but...no, I shake my head. I can't think about not getting there. My knee will hold out.

I need it to.

"Otherwise, that old body of yours will give in like mine." He rolls his left shoulder slowly, showing his restricted movement on that side.

My dad had a bad shoulder that took him out of the game. He never made quarterback or won a Super Bowl. He never fulfilled his ultimate dream. So, he wants to live his dream through me. He wouldn't mind if I didn't, but I'm hungry for it. I want to see his face when I play in a Super Bowl game, and even more so if we won. Yeah, that would be priceless.

I want to do it for us. Put our family in the history books.

I run backward and toss the ball back harder, faster this time. When he catches it, I grin wide, really loving this time we share when no one else is around.

I laugh at the ease with which he catches the ball. He's still got it. No matter how old or injured he is.

This is perfect, being here with my biggest supporter, and making him proud.

Until his ringtone breaks my thoughts.

My dad tosses the ball back to me, and I catch it, holding it under my arm as I wait to see who's on the line.

"Yeah?" he answers. A wide smile breaks out on his face, his eyes shining brightly at hearing her voice.

It's Mom.

The way he talks to her and looks at her, it's true, earthmoving love. If I ever felt that, I would hold on tight and never let it go. I've never had a relationship give me an all-consuming feeling. I want a relationship where we challenge each other and push one another to be the best versions of ourselves. But I also want that lasting comfort and longing that comes with finding your match. Witnessing my parents' love has me chasing what they share.

I can't help but smile too and move closer to him. I'm tired now that I've stopped moving.

I try to listen, but I can't hear what she's saying.

He's got a goofy smile on his face when I look up at him again. "Okay, okay. We'll be home soon." He takes a breath, then says, "All right. All right. Love you too."

Stuffing his phone in his pocket, he meets my gaze. "She wants us home, son. Let's go. She's got your favorite dinner on the table to celebrate."

I nod, and he wraps his arm around my shoulder. We walk in silence to the car, but only because thinking of relationships also has my mind drifting to a certain blonde. And she stays in my thoughts that whole night, even in my sleep.

CHAPTER 11

NATASHA

"I DON'T HAVE TO go," I say as I stare at my clothes hanging in the wardrobe. Moving one hanger at a time to inspect each piece, I sigh when nothing stands out. Glancing down at my watch, I'm running out of time; I need to find something to wear to Ben's hosting dinner.

"Yes, you do. This is an exciting opportunity to bond with the team," Mom says as she sits on my bed.

"Exactly. It's a bonding session. It seems silly that I got an invite."

But the real reason I don't want to go is the nerves taking over my stomach at the thought of being around Ben. Our interactions have been getting increasingly dangerous; he can get to me now, and I hope he doesn't know it. I don't want him to have that power over me. I like having power over my thoughts and inner desires. The sexual tension between us is palpable, but maybe that's all we have. Risking my job or taking focus away from my mom for just sexual relief isn't happening to me.

"If your boss is expecting you, then this must be important to the team," she encourages with a gentle smile.

"Hmm. I guess you're right." I look over my shoulder briefly at her, and then back at the clothes.

I can't say no, can I?

"Now choose something to wear." I think she's more excited than me. Sometimes I wonder if she just wants me out of her house because she feels guilty for holding me back, but I don't see it that way. I enjoy being home with her in my bubble.

I sigh, staring at all my basic clothes. All jeans and sweaters, but nothing nice enough for a dinner party. "That's the problem. I don't have anything," I moan. "This is why I can't go."

"Call Mia. Ask her what's she's wearing?" She ignores my attempt at bailing again.

"Hm. That's actually a good idea."

Without hesitation, I grab my phone and call Mia.

"Hey," she answers on the second ring.

"Mia, I need help. What are you wearing tonight?" I rub my eyes, wanting nothing more than to cancel. The words are on the tip of my tongue.

Dropping myself down to the bed beside Mom, its softness has me lying down. I lower my back and sink in deeper, closing my eyes when my head hits my cozy blankets. I feel relaxed and wonder if I have time for a nap. But I push the thought aside when she replies.

"A dress. Think of it like a cocktail party."

I grumble down the line. Even worse. I don't attend fancy parties, so I don't buy nice evening wear.

"I have nothing fancy like that to wear to this dinner."

"Let's go to the shop. I'm sure we can find something," she offers.

I tilt my head and look at my bedside clock and mutter. "No, we don't have time."

"Call Sara. I'm sure she has something she can lend you," Mom whispers.

My eyes flick to hers, a small smile lifting my lips as I nod.

I get up with a new spring in my step at the idea.

"It's okay, I've got an idea," I tell Mia with more enthusiasm than I have all night.

She chuckles. "Okay, well, I'll see you soon."

I hang up and call Sara, who says she will drop off the perfect dress.

An hour later, I rush in for a shower and style my hair in soft curls. Then I work on applying some natural makeup. As soon as I slip into my new figure-hugging black dress and strappy black heels, I feel sexy. Happy with my reflection, an odd sense of giddiness washes over me. I flick my hair with my hand over my shoulders and wait for Mia and Levi to arrive.

The doorbell chimes to the house, and I kiss Mom on the cheek. I organized a caretaker to help her get to bed tonight, and that has me swallowing a lump of guilt.

"Have fun!" Mom calls out as I'm heading for the door.

I pinch my freshly coated glossy lips together as I open the door and Mia stands with an enormous smile on her face. She looks over at me slowly, her brows lifting.

"Holy shit, girl. You scrub up hot."

I giggle and shake my head, taking in her tight red silk dress. "And you can talk?"

She spins around, clearly loving the compliment.

The car horn scares the shit out of me a moment later, and we both jolt. Levi's unable to drive because, as I predicted, his shoulder injury was a dislocation, and he's got a long recovery ahead of him. Months, to be more accurate. The season is over for him before it really began.

"For fuck's sake," she mumbles to me, and then spins to yell toward the car, "We're coming!" She returns her gaze to me with an eye roll. "Men."

"And you see why I'm single." I chuckle.

"No, I don't, but I don't have time to argue with you because he'll be out of the car if we don't get moving."

I giggle again. Knowing the night will be fun since I'll be with these two friends.

She pivots and walks down toward the black car, and I follow behind. I haven't been in heels in a while and now isn't the time to roll an ankle.

Before I know it, we're parked at Ben's, and my stomach churns with nervous energy at seeing him outside of work again.

Levi and Mia exit the car and their doors slamming shut get me moving too. I push open the door and straighten my spine, walking on shaky feet with Mia behind Levi. Our heels click with each step across the concrete, and the closer we get, my heart picks up speed. His house looks incredible. A double-story red-brick beauty, with a small garden in front. As we take the few stairs up to his front door, I feel lightheaded. But I don't get long to think about my increasing nerves, because Mia and Levi are stepping into his house a moment later.

"This is amazing," I whisper in Mia's ear as I follow them inside.

"Isn't it?" She flashes me an enormous grin.

The first thing I see is Ben as we pass through the entryway. His face lights up when our eyes lock, causing warmth to spread across my chest.

He inclines his head. "Welcome, come on in."

"Thank you." I give him a small smile.

He gives me one of his panty-melting smirks, and it hits me right in the chest. As I move to step past him, his hand reaches out and touches my hip. I pause from the contact and try to control the flutters in my stomach from taking over my every thought.

He edges even closer to whisper in my ear, "You look incredible." I can feel the heat from his body against me, our bodies only inches apart.

I gulp some air and try to find my voice. "Thanks."

"Am I making you shy?" he purrs, and I know he's teasing me about how breathy I sound.

I blow out a slow, shaky breath. "You wish."

A deep chuckle leaves his throat. He keeps upping the ante every opportunity he gets. I pull my head back to stare at him with a challenging look, keeping my desire buried deep, even though he makes it difficult. I'm scorching from our close proximity and his hungry eyes. We need space. With every ounce of strength I have, I peel his hand from my body, ignoring the buzz from our skin touching, and remember someone from work could see us. He reluctantly drops his hand, and I brush past him.

He closes the door behind us and walks us farther into the house that's styled like a magazine. Everywhere I look, it just gets more gorgeous. I take everything in, unsure where Mia's gone. I find myself standing inside his living room, where there are a few people standing around talking.

"Did you want a drink?" Levi asks, breaking my trance.

Looking at him, I see the bar straight ahead, and that's where I find Mia. The thought of alcohol sounds perfect. I need to take away some of the nerves swirling around my gut. I feel different in this tight dress and being here is so different from anything I've ever attended in the past.

"Please," I say with a smile.

Walking over, I pass a dining area where no one is sitting yet. All the players and staff surround the large bar instead.

Illuminated by softly lit lights, it makes me take notice of the rows of alcohol.

Levi and I amble over to a waiting Mia. Needing a strong hit, I say, "Tequila?"

I know Mia won't turn me down. I see the wicked grin split her face. "Yes. That's my girl."

She moves her gaze toward Levi and the look they share is intimate. It's so loving and heartfelt that I have to glance away for a moment. Who doesn't want to be looked at like you're the only person in the room? That no one else matters.

After I do another scan of the house, I find the bartender pouring the tequila into shot glasses. We each pick up our glasses and face each other, clinking, before tossing them back. The burn down my throat causes a warm shiver to roll through my body.

"Another?" Mia asks.

"Yeah, why not?" I answer with a shrug.

The second shot gives me the buzz I was hoping for, calming my nerves and putting me a bit more at ease.

"Where are we sitting?" I ask Mia as I stare at the table.

She turns around to look. "Over there." I follow to where she is pointing to a table lit from a chandelier.

"Should we go grab our seats?" I want to sit down to relieve the pain in my feet. My heels are already becoming unbearable. I'm definitely out of practice.

Mia scrunches up her face at me like she is sucking on a lemon wedge. "Not yet. Calm down, eager beaver."

I giggle. Not wanting to complain about my feet, I use a different excuse. "I'm not eager. I'm hungry."

Her eyes narrow, looking at me curiously.

"What?" I mutter under my breath, so only she can hear my annoyed tone. I'm definitely getting hangry.

"Who are you really trying to impress at the dinner?" She crosses her arms over her chest and leans her back on the bar as if getting comfortable for a long conversation.

Hell no.

She is reading way too much into this. It didn't even cross my mind that I want to sit down at the table for Ben.

"No one. Don't be ridiculous. I'm starving. I'm about to eat my arm off."

She raises a brow, disbelief displayed across her beautiful face as she says, "I'm pretty sure there's a single, tall, sandy blond, blue-eyed guy who can't take his eyes off you. So, I bet it's him."

My body tingles from her letting me know he's watching me. Shaking my head vehemently, I argue, "You're seeing things. Him and I are a no go. Never. Going. To. Happen!"

"Why?" she asks with a frown.

I swear this woman gives me a headache. I love her so much, but her poking into my business makes me crazy. I have told her why before, so I hate having to repeat myself.

Crossing my arms over my chest, I explain. "I don't date and definitely not football players. I don't know how you do it. Men cheat, then leave, and you simply can't trust them. But also, Mia, you have your path laid out for you because you're the coach's daughter, whereas I have to focus on my goals and prove myself."

She straightens, and I can sense I have hit a nerve because of Levi. I'm sure she doesn't think Levi will cheat or leave, but no one enters a relationship expecting that to be the case. It evens happens to the best couples.

"That's unfair. You're putting all men into the same box. Aren't you trying to get John to see you differently from other women and give you a chance?"

I swallow.

Well, fuck.

She has me there.

"Yes, but they can't be trusted. Women hit on Levi when you're around. Remember, a few weeks ago, you told me at the bar you stood right next to him, and a chick came up and sat on his lap, lifting her top, to show him her tits."

I shiver at the memory. It sounded disgusting. Mia said the chick was stone-cold sober when she did that, deluded to think that would attract him. Well, I'm sure some men would fall for it, just not in front of their Mrs. Or, at least, you'd hope.

She holds up a hand. "Okay, hold up. One thing first. He kicked her off straight away."

"Because you were there," I argue with a raised brow.

"Levi has done nothing but shower me with love. Just because he's an attractive, successful football player doesn't mean he will leave or cheat on me."

"Never, baby. You're more than enough for me," Levi says, slipping in behind her and wrapping an arm around her waist to tug her back against him.

"See. Come here, sexy." Mia spins to face him. Levi smiles and kisses Mia passionately on the lips. But it's the hard glare from the handsome statue next to him that has my stomach somersaulting.

Shit.

How much did he hear?

CHAPTER 12

BENJAMIN

I'M TREMBLING WITH A mix of anger and desire. Listening to her say that all men do is leave and cheat pisses me right off.

I'd do no such thing.

It's hurtful to even listen to that shit.

And has she even dated a football player to even know that?

I fucking doubt it.

Yes, some players cheat, but most of us are loyal.

Isn't that the risk with any person you date, though? Not just football players.

When I first noticed her across the room in her stunning little black dress, I just wanted to touch her again. Feel her delicate curves under my palms, to wrap my hands around her waist and squeeze. Now, I look at her and I want to make her sorry that she ever thought that about me. Even though she didn't specifically say my name, I fall under the umbrella.

Little does she know, I idolize my parents' relationship and want that very feeling for myself. I didn't think I wanted it right now, but when she entered, or should I say *barrelled*, into my life months ago, it sent my heart into overdrive. She's going to be mine. I just don't know how yet. And I know it sounds ridiculous because, fuck, even to my own ears, it is, but for some reason, I need her. I also need to get her on the same page as me.

As I stare into the eyes of Natasha, I want to tell her how much of a one-woman man I really am. Or show her.

I see her wide eyes staring back at me. Dropping my gaze to her feet, I admire her long legs in high heels, slowly appreciating every square inch of her as my eyes travel up. Reaching her face, my lips curl at her seeing her magnificent blue eyes, only standing out more with the natural makeup she's wearing. I could totally get lost in them.

There's something about her that has me fixated. I'm going to prove to her how wrong she is about men...or more specifically, about me.

I may be angry, but I can't deny what my body wants. I love her beauty, but it's not what draws me in. It's our chemistry and her brain. Her attitude differs from any other woman I have met. It's challenging and exciting all at the same time.

I can't help but want to play with her more. Make her feel sorry that she let me hear that. My heartbeat picks up, knowing I'm going to annoy the fuck out of her.

"Are you ready to take your seat next to the players?" I ask with a smug grin.

Her eyes narrow, and she tilts her head, as if not understanding.

"You know, we all cheat, so we are the players." I wink, and she screws up her face in disdain. "You said it, not me, so come on. Let's go have some dinner with all your favorite people."

I hold back a chuckle as her lips purse. Her face staring at me right now is priceless; it's like she's holding back a lashing. It's so fucking cute.

She really isn't happy with me right now, and inside, I'm laughing. I can't wait for her to argue. I know it's coming soon.

She looks around us, and when she's happy no one is watching, she answers quietly. "Yes, I'm hungry, if that's what you're saying. But I didn't say you're all cheaters. It's just—"

And she pauses, not knowing what to say.

I chuckle at her speechlessness. "It's just what?" I ask, genuinely wanting to hear the rest.

She glances at the floor and then huffs out a breath. "Everybody knows football players do a lot of off-field playing." Her tone is clipped and laced with annoyance as she continues. "Have you seen *TMZ* or the news? Do you not notice they feature you guys a lot?" I know she's poking me, but I'm not catching on.

"Yeah, obviously, but that's because we're in the limelight." I shrug, not understanding where she's going with all this. "You should know. You've got a big brain, don't you, Doc?"

As soon as the words leave my mouth, I instantly regret it. The wince on her face doesn't help matters. Realizing how badly that came off, I suddenly swallow the lump of guilt and reword it. I reach out to touch her shoulder without thinking of who's around. Her eyes widen at the contact, and I rub my brow at the mess I've made again, feeling stifling hot.

"I didn't mean it like that. I'm so sorry. I'm just—you should know that we have a microscope looking at us, which is totally unfair. Average people don't live like this. We should be treated just the same. Anyone can cheat if they choose to. But you don't go into relationships not trusting your partner, right?"

I stuff my hands firmly into my suit pockets, watching her body soften and shoulders sag a little as she thinks about it. Still, I'm expecting a smartass response.

"No, you shouldn't go into relationships not trusting. Maybe I'm being too judgmental."

I nearly fall backward. I wasn't expecting that to come out of her mouth.

Maybe there's something that's happened in her past to make her think all men cheat? I understand her wall up to us. She's young, beautiful, and hardworking; she deserves the best.

Any man would be happy to have her. I've heard my teammates in the locker room talk openly about her, and it makes me sick. I have to grind my teeth together to prevent myself from growling, "*she's mine.*"

But for now, I just nod and open my hand to the table, ending the conversation on a good note. "Shall we?"

She dips her chin with a small smile. "Yes."

We walk over to the table together to take our seats, and she looks around at the name cards. My seat is directly next to hers, and if I didn't take much notice of her any spare second she's around me, I would've missed her furrowed brow. And the curse that fell from her lips.

When I take my seat, I see she's still holding on to the back of her chair, but not moving. It's like she's in a state of shock and doesn't know what to do.

"What's wrong?" I ask, holding back a laugh. "You don't want to sit next to me? Do I make you uncomfortable?"

I know I'm pissing her off.

Her eyes snap to me, and they are murderous.

Gotcha!

"No, I just, yeah, shit, I don't know...maybe." She shakes her head, exacerbated.

And I laugh at her response. I guess I can't tease her any further.

I try to lighten the mood, whispering to her, "I promise to be on my best behavior. If you sit, don't call me a player, or worse, a cheater. Then I won't poke the bear." I pull back and wink, but she frowns.

She nods and drags out her chair before taking her seat. Picking up her menu, she scans the catered options, and I can't help but watch everything she does. Every quirk and mannerism. Something about her has me endlessly mesmerized.

I turn my gaze to the table and pick up my glass of water, taking a big sip but needing a stronger drink to calm the sexual energy rushing through me.

I lean forward to whisper into her ear, and I stiffen. Fucking hell, I didn't think this through. I close my eyes and concentrate on my words, not on the way her breath hitched or the way the electricity between us seems to have ratcheted.

"Did you want another drink?" I grunt out.

She nods, causing her flowy locks of hair to hit my face. "A drink sounds perfect. Thank you."

Her coconut scent fills my nostrils, and damn, the sweet smell is unbelievably delicious. I want to taste her. I bet her skin tastes like coconut cream too. It's almost as if she's bathed in the stuff.

I pull my head back and watch as her eyes meet mine. My intake of breath is sharp, her gaze making me unsteady. "What would you like?" It comes out as a rasp.

"A tequila shot."

My mouth twists up. Of course, this girl drinks the hard stuff.

I lift my brows. "You need a shot to be around me?"

"Ah, no. I've already had a couple tonight. I like to stick to one type of drink. I don't like to mix. I've had too much experience to know the consequences."

I wish I was smart enough not to mix, but when I drink, I tend to go past the line of caring and just enjoy myself instead. Forgetting about the dreaded hangovers.

"Fair enough. A tequila shot coming right up."

I push my chair back and rise, already missing her intoxicating scent.

She turns toward me, and her eyes are glowing up at me as she bites her lip, hiding a smile.

My dick hardens from the sight. Grabbing the back of the chair, I widen my stance, holding myself back from taking a kiss

I haven't earned. They look so pouty and perfect, begging for me to savor them.

I shake my head; I need to get away from her before I do something right now at the table.

Fuck.

I stalk towards the bar, grateful she didn't offer to come. I don't have the restraint right now.

I'm almost at the bar when I get stopped on the way by John.

"How's she doing?"

"Who?" I ask, utterly confused.

"Natasha. How's Natasha doing tonight?" Disdain is evident in his tone.

"She's great. Why?" I clip, unable to hide my annoyance.

Where's he going with this?

His eyes flick between mine and then over in her direction at the table.

What's his problem?

"No reason. I'm just watching out for her. I'm not sold that she's a great fit for our team."

I grind my molars. Why would he come to that conclusion? What have I missed? Everybody on the team loves her.

"She's fit in effortlessly...better than most have. Why would you think otherwise?" I say, feeling my spine straighten.

"Because she's a woman. Totally distracting the team. Have you seen the way the guys are drooling over her. And frankly, she hasn't paid her dues."

I'm completely taken aback; this explains how he's been treating her. My fingers curl up in my palm, pinching my skin. I'm vibrating from holding myself back from hitting the asshole in the face. I really want to, but I just made quarterback. I won't jeopardize what I have dreamed about for so long.

"I haven't seen any of the guys look at her like that. And what are we in the 1950s, where women can't do anything? And she hasn't paid her dues? That's bullshit. The board hired her, and you're lucky she hasn't gone to them about you already. Maybe I should insist that she does," I sneer.

He leans back, eyes wide, totally shitting himself. He really shouldn't have said any of that to me.

I can't help but growl, "You should watch what you fucking say. I will not have people like you working on our team. Now that I'm the quarterback, I won't put up with this shit."

I uncurl my right hand and poke his chest. "I'm watching you. And I will report you. She shouldn't have to worry about her job because you're being a pig."

I see anger flash in his eyes at that, but I don't give a fuck. I couldn't care less if I step over the line. It's his words against mine.

The world is changing. He should be opening his eyes to see that she's fit for the job.

With a headache forming, I step away, muttering under my breath, "I need a fucking drink."

I walk directly to the bar, bubbling with anger. As I'm ordering her shot, I decide I need one too. Maybe it will help calm me. We can only hope...

"Hey, buddy. What's up? You seem stiff." I didn't hear Levi come up to me.

I turn to him, lifting my chin toward John. "Fuckin' John."

His curious gaze follows mine. John's now talking to another player, just where I left him. "What about him?"

"He said Natasha's distracting the guys. How she doesn't deserve the job. He's watching her because she's a woman who didn't pay her dues."

Levi looks murderous, clearly as angry as I feel.

"Yeah, you see what I mean?"

"Damn fucking straight. That guy's got some nerve." He wipes down his face with his free hand. The other one is in a sling for at least four weeks.

"Yeah, that's what I told him. I don't give a fuck. I warned him we'll not put up with shit like that on our team."

He nods. But the longer he stares at me with a curious expression etched on his face, I know what's coming. "And this has nothing to do with you having feelings for the beautiful blonde woman, who you just so happened to seat next to you."

I'll be shooting myself in the foot if someone overhears our conversation, because she won't give me a chance. And if John finds out, he'll probably use it as ammunition to get rid of her. And I can't have that. She deserves this job.

"No, don't be ridiculous." I scoff, stuffing my hand in my suit pocket, not daring to look her way.

The bartender sets the tequila shots down, thankfully breaking the conversation. I look over my shoulder at Levi. "Do you want one?'

"You're having fucking tequila?" His eyes widen in shock.

I dip my chin and pull my hand out of my pocket, grabbing the glass. "I need it after the conversation with John."

"Yeah, sure. I'll have one."

I turn to the bartender. "Can you make one more?"

"Sure."

Levi picks up the shot glass once it's placed in front of him, and we *cheer*, chasing back the liquor and sucking on a lime.

I point for another one, knowing I want one to *cheers* with Natasha.

"I better get back. Are you coming?" I ask Levi.

"No, I'll be back in a few." And he takes off, so I walk back to the table and retake my seat, holding out the shot glass and lime for her to take.

She looks at the shot and then back at me with a perplexed expression. "You like tequila?" she asks.

I smirk. "No, I actually fucking detest it."

She laughs loudly, and it reminds me of the day we met. "Then why would you order that?"

"Because you're having one and you shouldn't have shots by yourself."

"Oh, okay." She smiles, lifting the shot to clink with mine.

"Ahhh." I grumble as it burns my chest. This shit doesn't get any better. I suck the lime, desperate for some relief.

She coughs and splutters next to me.

I touch her back without thinking, stroking it gently. "Are you okay?"

She nods and chokes out, "Yeah, yep, yep, I got it. Just give me a second."

I'm still stroking her back in a reassuring rhythm. I can't seem to stop my hand from moving. She hasn't told me to stop. Instead, her skin prickles with goosebumps as if it loves the touch of my fingers.

It makes me feel connected to her in a way that feels normal. Touching her is easy.

As the minutes tick by, I expect her to snap at me, to tell me off. Shake my fingers away.

But she doesn't.

She welcomes it.

CHAPTER 13

NATASHA

COACH COMES UP BEHIND us, and Ben pulls away. I twist and see Chris's hand draped on Ben's shoulder, giving it a squeeze.

"You ready?" Chris asks. "Speeches are starting soon."

Ben's face lights up. "Yeah, I'm ready."

"Levi is going to do a speech first."

Ben nods. "Okay, Coach."

His voice is considerably lower, and as I search his face, I can see the sadness lingering there. It's so nice to see how much he cares about Levi. How hard it must be, to be in two minds right now. He's happy to be quarterback, but the cost was his friend's season. It's harder because there are no guarantees that Levi will ever return, as the injury could be career-ending. He wants to come back, but medically, we don't think it will happen. Even if Levi's mindset is strong.

"I better get up the front and start things off." Coach slaps Ben's chest and dips his chin with a smile toward me before he walks away, leaving us alone again.

"Are you prepared for your speech?" I whisper, bumping my shoulder with his, trying to be friendly. It pulls him from his blank stare and away from his thoughts.

He turns his head and peers down at me, tapping his suit pocket. "Yes."

My gaze follows the line, and I can't help but notice the bulge in his pants. If his tight suit isn't playing tricks on me, he's bigger than most. My thighs clench beyond my control, and swallowing roughly, I bring my eyes back up to his face.

His head is tilted to the side, his hard gaze staring back at me. I've totally been busted for checking out his dick. Grateful he says nothing, I shuffle in my seat, trying to ease the throb he's caused. As if he's a mind reader, his blue eyes darken, and when he licks his lips, I feel it as if his tongue is between my legs.

Oh my God.

He's being annoyingly hot.

I need to stop thinking like this. The shots are catching up to me. So, I grab my water glass, but accidentally tip it over.

Shit.

"Do I make you nervous?" he teases.

I glare at him, because I'd rather hide my feelings than show any evidence of the butterflies and warmth running through me from being beside him.

I roll my eyes and whisper, "Don't flatter yourself."

A chuckle leaves his chest, and the sound is so light that it sends renewed goosebumps over every inch of my body.

A tapping on a glass at the front of the room stops any further conversation. "Quiet please," Coach begins.

I turn my head to give Chris my full attention.

"Good evening, everyone. Thanks for being here tonight. Tonight's all about us coming together. So, behave yourselves. Thanks, Ben, for hosting. The house is amazing, and the spread of food looks delicious. I can't wait to dig in. But we're also here tonight because I wanted to officially announce you as the new quarterback."

The room erupts into loud cheering and whistling. Ben's face is beaming with pride. I know this is a dream come true for many players, but especially for Ben. I can't imagine the way he's feeling with all the love and attention.

As I'm concentrating on watching the excitement transform his face, his gaze fixes on me. He gives me a small smirk before he refocuses on the front of the room, where Coach takes a seat and Levi stands. My breath catches at the sight of his tight jaw and the tears building in his eyes. When he speaks, you can hear the wobble in his voice, and it's gut-wrenching. I wish there was something more we could have done.

And to make it worse, Mia can't console him because her dad still doesn't know about them. I peek over the table at Mia, who has a tear trailing down her cheek, quietly wiping it away before anyone notices. I look away, fearing I'll be a blubbering mess if I keep watching her.

Ben pushes his chair back and rises, walking over to Levi to hug him. I clutch my hands together, propping them under my chin to watch him support his friend. It's real and warm and totally infectious.

I wait eagerly for Ben to speak, standing next to Levi. For a moment, his gaze hangs on to me, keeping me breathless, until darting around the room and speaking to his team. I sit in awe listening to his speech, feeling the passion coming off him in waves.

"Good evening, everyone. Thanks for being here tonight. First, I want to say my deep condolences to my buddy, Levi. I'm sorry, man, and I can't imagine the pain you're in. You made us what we are today, have turned us into an epic team, and we're going to make you proud. Next, I want to say I'm honored to be the new quarterback. I'm fucking living my dream, surrounded by the best men a guy could ask for. I'm ready to take us to the win, and I appreciate your support."

The crowd erupts into more cheering, and I smile as I look around at everyone soaking in everything he has to say.

"I will bring this team to win the fucking Super Bowl."

The room claps louder now. My stupid smile can't help but also widen. He really can suck you in. He has a way with words and a natural aura around him. You feel pulled in whenever he's around.

He's smooth, charming, and, well...fucking handsome.

I sit and stare at him, which makes me feel hot and bothered. Taking another large gulp of water, I'm thankful I didn't spill the glass again.

He wanders off the stage, and I watch him over my glass, shaking hands with players before he walks back this way.

"How did I do?" he asks.

I close my eyes and soak in that deep voice that is speaking directly to my sex. It's the tequila talking...it has to be.

Snap out of it, you whore.

Tonight is about work, not play.

We've been tiptoeing around each other for a while now. But with all the crap being thrown our way. Adding to my already bruised heart. I know this is for the best. I couldn't offer a relationship without hurting him and I'm not a one-night or hook-up kind of girl.

Twisting to watch him slide back into his chair, I hold his eyes and answer him honestly. "You did great."

His eyes narrow, gazing at me intensely. "Should I believe you?"

I roll my eyes and shrug before looking away, mumbling, "It's up to you. I'm not here to stroke your ego."

I let out an audible gasp when his warm breath tickles my face, his mouth moving to my ear. I'm shocked at his sudden nearness. I didn't hear or see him lean in. Now, with his lips inches from my earlobe, breath skimming my skin, I quiver with a need for his lips on me.

"I'd be happy to stroke your ego."

"This is a work event," I say through gritted teeth.

I'm mad at my betraying body who likes him speaking so freely about what he wants from me. But the other part of me hates how he must view me as a walking, talking, sex object he can get his next release from. I'm not a toy to be played with. And I'm disappointed right now because I was starting to see him differently.

His face is two inches away from mine, amusement splashed across it. But his eyes have darkened and the heat staring back at me matches my own burning desire. "Well, it's going to be over soon. And then what will you do?"

Is he fucking serious? I stare at him like he's lost his mind. Rapidly blinking, I slowly enunciate every word. "Go home and go to sleep."

I shake my head at this ridiculous conversation.

How does he know how to get under my skin?

"I could join you."

I close my eyes, feeling the softness at what could be, but as I see John's face flash through my mind, I suck in a sharp breath and snap out of it.

"No. I want to go home alone." My response sounds more like a sigh.

"As you wish." He says it as if it's no big deal, and that sets me off. I'm pissed he thinks that's all it will take for me to be with him.

"Go find someone else." I swat my hand around in the direction of other women who haven't stopped staring at him the whole night. That only adds to my annoyance.

Another reason being with him wouldn't be a good idea. The women eyeing him constantly. Throwing themselves at him. I don't know if I would have the restraint to sit by and put up with that shit. I'd probably call them out. But lucky for me, he isn't mine. And with that thought, I swallow the lump stuck in my throat.

His smirk turns devilish. "You know I don't want them."

He places his hand on my thigh, just above the knee. With his other one on the table, his whole being closes in on me. I can practically taste his pine aftershave.

I mutter under my breath so only he can hear. "You and I will never happen."

He closes the last inch between us. At the same time, a tug on my hair has me gasping out loud. I can feel his body heat radiating off him, and mixed with mine, it's combustible.

"Why is that?" His eyes darken and his lips thin into a tight line. "Am I not your type?"

His question flusters me. Turning my head to check we don't have an audience, which we don't, I return my eyes to meet his hungry ones, and a chill snakes through me. He lifts a brow and drops the piece of hair. I know he's waiting for me to speak. But I just don't know how to answer him.

Do I tell the truth, or lie?

Deciding to do neither, I say, "I didn't say that."

"Then why?" he clips, and from the look on his face, I can tell he's getting pissy.

"I don't want to." I shrug. I know it's not really an answer, but I don't know what else to say.

His brows pinch together in a frown. "I see the way you respond to me. The way your breaths are quicker, your body flushes, and those wandering eyes are all over my lips and body." He matches his forwardness with a confident smile, and my mouth parts in shock.

I thought I was taking cheeky glances, but I'm getting called out.

"I can't," I mumble under my breath, looking at my clenched hands on my lap. I uncurl them and rub them over my dress. My heart rate skyrockets as he keeps pushing me.

"It's not a fucking answer." His snappy tone causes me to spill one of the reasons holding me back.

"This job is important to me. I can't do anything to jeopardize it."

Again, it doesn't answer his "am I your type" question, but I figure reminding him of why I can't cross the line will put a stop to his advances.

His eyes squint and he looks like he wants to push for more.

Please, don't.

Let it go.

I'm begging him with my eyes.

"Fine. I need another fucking drink." He stands with a huff, and I should be happy. So why is turning him down making me feel so sick I could vomit?

CHAPTER 14

NATASHA

A few hours later, I'm home, beyond tipsy, and my feet are killing me.

But deep down, I know that's not the reason I'm agitated.

No. That tall blond brooding asshole is the cause of my bad mood.

I try to remove my heels, but end up swaying, catching myself on the wall and ripping them off one by one. Tossing them across the room, they land with a thump. The feeling of my soft apartment carpet under my feet has a sigh slipping from my lips. I stumble into the kitchen, across the cold white tiles, making my way to my medicine cupboard. Thankfully, I find some Tylenol quickly, then grab a bottle of water and drink as much as possible. Before closing the lid and walking to the bedroom, the sound of my phone ringing pauses me mid-step. I spin around, seeing spots as I do.

Woah! Too fast.

When the room stops spinning, I walk to the counter where I threw my bag. But I'm not fast enough, hearing the tune telling me I missed the call. Seeing Mia's name across the screen, a stupid, lopsided smile splits my face, and I hit redial, bringing it up to my ear and leaning on the counter to hold my weight up.

"Where are you?" She hiccups.

"I'm home," I mumble drunkenly.

"God, you had me worried for a second." Her voice is a little slurry, matching my own drunken state. I hear the noise of the gathering in the background. She obviously continued to party, but I didn't want to. I had enough of the night.

"You should have stayed with me," she whines. "You were supposed to text or call me as soon as you got home."

I push off the counter and wander to my bedroom, ready to pass out and go to sleep. I feel heavy, and a yawn breaks out. "Sorry. But I'm fine. Home safe and sound. Ready for bed."

She hiccups again. "You sound like an old lady."

"An old lady with responsibilities," I say, and as I look at the clock on my bedside table, I'm reminded that I won't be getting as much sleep as normal.

"Your mom is a big girl. She can figure her own bills out. You shouldn't have to stop your life to help her."

I pinch the bridge of my nose, closing my eyes. "She's my mom, Mia. I can't let her suffer; she's been through a lot."

She sighs loudly. "And I'm not saying that. You still deserve to live a little, though. All you do is work and look after your mom. There is no time for you."

I drop down to sit on my bed with my head hanging. I can't argue with her there.

I'm getting a headache from thinking about this.

"Mia, go back to the party. I'm home safe, and thanks for a goodnight."

"Okay, Tash. I'll talk to you later."

I hang up and throw the phone on my bedside table, rolling over and face diving into my blankets.

My phone chimes with an incoming text.

I groan.

What now, Mia?

Moving back, I reach out and grab my phone to see an unrecognizable number.

I frown and open the message.

Unknown number: I'm sorry.

Natasha: Who's this?

Unknown number: Ben.

It's him. My heart jolts.

I pause, staring at the message.

He's apologizing.

My head is now pounding. I rub the side of my temple as I figure out what to do. I'm no longer tired. No, my body is wide awake. Dropping the phone and climbing off the bed, I decide a shower is in order. I need some time to gather my thoughts and preferably be free of alcohol, but that's not going to happen tonight. A shower will at least buy me some more time.

After a few minutes, I'm fresh and clean and in my pajamas, but I still have no idea what to say back. So, I stick with something simple.

Natasha: Thank you.

I save his number and see the bubbles moving, meaning he's writing back.

Benjamin: Are you home?

I bite my lip as I type my reply.

Natasha: Yes. Has everyone left?

Benjamin: Yeah. Not long ago. I'm glad to see you're not too mad at me ;)

A stupid smile sits on my face as I reply.

*Natasha: Well, I was mad. But hang on, how did
you get my number?*

*Benjamin: I was wondering when you were going
to ask me. Levi.*

Of course.

Does that mean Mia knew when she called before? No, she
would have told me. Mia can't keep her lips shut for one minute,
especially about men.

Natasha: Of course.

Benjamin: Do you live at home with your parents?

Staring at the phone, my pulse quickens. I start a message and
then delete it. I don't know if I'm ready to talk about my life.
He only messaged to apologize, yet now he's asking personal
questions.

Am I really ready for what can come from this?

The way he's acted toward me when he's sweet made it seem
he was genuinely interested in me...

I sigh and decide to live a little. It's not like I'm doing anything exciting right now. But also, it might be what Mia said still playing in the back of my brain.

Natasha: Yes. Do you live with anyone?

I don't want to say "only my mom," as we are chatting over text, and the story of my dad isn't a short, easy answer. And I have a feeling Ben would want to know every single detail.

Benjamin: God, no. I need space. We're super close, and I see them daily, but that would be too much.

I sink back a little farther into my pillows, not ready for the conversation to end as I type back.

Natasha: Fair enough. I love my mom too.

Benjamin: Just mom?

Shit. I slipped up.

My stomach hardens. After a few rewrites, I type out my response, deciding on the truth.

Natasha: My dad left us when I was a teenager.
It's been just me and my mom. I haven't heard
from him since.

I hold my breath as I wait for his text back. It feels like forever. When his text finally comes through, I release the breath I was holding.

Benjamin: Sorry to hear that. But you're close with
her?

As I think about my mom, I think about all that she has done for me since Dad left. The smiles, the loving hugs, and all the laughs. Mom made up for him leaving, but it doesn't mean that when he didn't come back, he didn't crush a little girl who now has trust issues and keeps men at an arm's length. Even if I wanted to give in, I don't know how, or if I truly could, let down my walls that surround my heart. I have built them over a long period of time, so it would take someone who is willing to be patient with me.

But who would?

As another text message comes through, I peer down.

Maybe Ben would.

I need to get rid of these stupid fantasies. It's not good for either of our careers...or my silly heart.

I try to reply, but I pass out.

———

A few days later, I'm strapping up a player's shoulder, ready for the game, when I see a set of eyes holding mine from the doorway.

"Is, uh, everything okay, Ben?" I choke out. I run my gaze over his fit body, then his right knee, before locking eyes again.

Ever since our night of texts, I can't help but have softened my hard exterior toward him. Maybe I could try to let my walls down for him.

His face has turned hard, and he shakes his head. "No, I just want to talk to you."

Oh. Talk...right.

What about?

Alarm bells ring in my head, but I push past the trepidation surrounding me and answer with a surprisingly even tone. "Sure. Give me five, and I'll be done."

I purposefully take the whole five minutes with the other player to calm my body down, knowing I'm excited by Ben, but also nervous. I need every minute to collect myself.

"All done," I say to the other player who wanders out.

Ben doesn't take long to stroll in, closing the door behind him. The click of the door sounds, and it sends my heart rate up.

I rub the back of my neck, trying to ease the stress building, and watch him step closer.

"What happened to you the other night?" he asks, his face a mixture of worry and anger.

"I passed out." I look at my shoes, and then back into his hard gaze.

How embarrassing.

His brow pops, but his face stays unchanged. He's reading my expression to see if I'm lying. "You couldn't have texted me the next day and told me you're okay?"

"You didn't text me the next day either." A smile creeps onto my lips. I'm trying to lighten the mood because him being all protective of me is too much to handle here at work.

He laughs. "Touché, Miss Blackwood."

His eyes lock onto mine, and I nibble one side of my bottom lip under his stare. "I'm sorry."

Silence.

He gives me a strange look as I realize his hand was close to touching mine.

"I was getting worried. I thought I pushed you too far in my messages," he says, running a hand through his hair as if he needs to do something with his hand other than touch me.

Staring into his warm eyes, I feel guilty about it. I debate internally if I should ask the question rolling inside my head. In the end, I go for it.

"Why?" I whisper.

"Because I care, and I want to be respectful of you."

My breath hitches. "Why?"

He falters, and I smile, knowing I stumped him.

He barely knows me.

Yes, there's a spark, and a small connection bouncing between us, but to care about me? I need to hear his answer.

"Next time, just let me know you're alive." He winks. But it's his bossy tone, mixed with his wink, that sets me off. I want the real answer, not his avoidance.

"I'm not yours—"

"Not if I had my way," he mumbles under his breath, but I catch it.

I stand still, clutching the medical bed in front of me to keep myself upright and stop me from crumbling. The way he's looking at me, it's as if I am deserving of attention and love. *But why?* I want to scream. He's all-consuming, and it's unsettling me.

I'm such a fucking mess.

I stand still, just watching him stare down at me. His shoulders are rising and falling with his deep, steady breaths while I am desperate for air.

We have a standoff.

Neither of us moves until he snaps, "I gotta get out of here," moving away from me.

Yes, you do, I say to myself. Before we do something we both will regret.

But before he leaves the room, I speak. "Yes, you do, before John comes barging in here and begins asking questions."

He stops in the doorway, turning to face me, his hand grabbing the frame. "Don't worry about that."

"What do you mean?" I question in a rush of panic. A dread-filled feeling washes over me. I don't like the sound of that.

"I gave him a warning."

I squeeze my eyes shut. This can't be happening. I'm going to lose my job. "Why? You're going to make it so much harder for me. He already wants me gone. You've made this worse."

How am I going to fix this mess? John is going to be wondering why Ben is sticking up for me, and even I can understand why.

"No. I refuse to have these types of men on our team. Times are changing. There's nothing that a man or a woman can't do. It's bullshit. He's bullshit. And he got called out. He knows that. I'm just telling him. He may be watching you, but I'm watching him."

My mouth opens and closes as I stare blankly at him.

What do I say?

The man stood up for me. He warned and threatened him. Fuck. Ben did that...for me.

I can't fathom why.

He's taking a huge risk, and I haven't had a guy do that, well, ever!

I'm in total shock. I'm sure I look like a deer in headlights, but I just can't believe what he just said.

"Thank you." The words are quiet. I feel like I'm trapped in a dream where real men exist.

He pushes off the door frame, closing the distance between us, and I suck in a sharp breath at his proximity. Reaching out, he traces a finger along my face. I shiver as the soft caress continues down my neck, then along my chest, ending just before my breast. I almost groan in protest as his hand pulls away. His handsome face is so close I can smell his minty breath and delicious cologne. My nipples harden under my bra, and my pussy tingles with desire.

"Ben," Levi's voice calls.

Panic rises inside me as I look over Ben's shoulder to see Levi watching us. I exhale heavily. I'm thankful it's not John here catching Ben and me.

But caught us doing what, exactly?

I recall the last few minutes.

An almost kiss?

Ben close to me...touching me.

Me practically begging him with my come-fuck-me eyes.

Yeah, I'm definitely grateful it wasn't John.

Ben steps away with a wicked grin. He knows exactly what he just did.

"Come on," Levi adds. "We better go."

"I'm coming. Relax, will you?"

CHAPTER 15

BENJAMIN

I WALK AWAY SMIRKING, leaving Natasha in a state of fluster. Her body reacts to me in a way that I love. The way her eyes glow, and the cute little pants that leave her mouth. Or the goosebumps that scatter her skin. I had to hold myself back from grabbing her chin and taking her lips in a heated kiss, right then and there.

She's so beautiful and she doesn't even know it.

If only she was interested in me the same way. She's got issues with dating a football player, or maybe it's just an issue with men in general. Then there's the hurdle about her wanting to stay professional, worrying that she'll lose her job.

"Two minutes, guys. Two minutes until we roll out," the strength and conditioning coach yells out, effectively snapping me out of my thoughts.

The words send an adrenaline rush pumping through my veins. I shake my hands out, as I know the game is about to start. Grabbing my helmet and putting it on, I head down the corridor through the stadium, with the guys beside me, in silence.

My first game as quarterback. Everything is falling into place. But I'm not gonna lie, I'm nervous as fuck. My palms are sweating and the way my heart's beating, it feels as if it's about to come out of my chest. As I get closer to the field, the crowd's roars become deafening. Swallowing my nerves, I try to focus on the part of me that wants to feed off the energy of the crowd. Allow it to pump me up. I've dreamed of this, and now it's fucking happening.

Our team is called out over the speakers and the cheers get even louder through the stadium.

My ears are ringing from the noise as I lead my team out onto our half of the field, stony game face in place. We take our positions, and my eyes hone in on my competition. The people who can prevent me from winning the game. But fuck that, I won't let that happen.

Dad and I have prepared for this day. I got my passion for the sport from him. I love it as much as he does. He shared his advice, wisdom, and tactics, which I will take with me and use today.

I know he is in the crowd watching. My whole family is here to support me. Mom, Dad, and my younger sister; the best cheerleaders a man could have.

We win the coin toss, and I choose to kick off. The whistle blows and the game starts with a deep kick, but it plays out of bounds, which results in stopping the clock. The first quarter is close, with only three points between us. At halftime, we head to the locker room, sweaty and sore, but feeling good about where the game is heading.

Removing my helmet, I grab a drink before heading to the training room for a few minutes of stretching. I feel her before I see her.

"Are you good?" she asks from behind me.

Turning around, I stare straight into her bright assessing eyes, knowing she's asking about my knee. "Yeah, I'm good." I keep it simple with a nod and a smile, not wanting to be distracted by her beauty. I'll have a chat with her after the game. Only one half to go, and then maybe I can convince her to have dinner with me.

In the first half, we made minimal errors, but it's still a tight game. I'm just glad we're playing well.

She offers me a smile in return and moves on to ask another player. There's tightness in my knee, but it's nothing worth mentioning to her. Instead, I stretch it out and rub it thoroughly. Thankfully, she hasn't noticed. I'm sure if she did, she'd be here asking to look at it.

Before the "three minutes" is called out, the coaches talk to me about a new play. Then, Chris delivers a boisterous speech to the team, recharging us for the rest of the game, sending us back out onto the field with the same energy we entered with the first time.

In the last ten minutes of the game, a defensive player hits me from the side, and there is a shooting pain in my knee. I drop the ball and crumble to the field instantly. When I try to stand, the intense pain has me falling again as a scream leaves my lungs. Fuck, the pain is unbearable.

I feel a hand on my back, then a loud booming voice sounds in my ear. "You okay, man?"

It's a guy from the opposition. His voice is pinched with concern, and other players surround me. My teammates. The noise around us is muffled by the pain taking over all my senses.

"Get me up," I grunt, frustrated, holding out my hands. A teammate clutches my right, and another teammate grabs onto my left.

They help me stand, but as I try to lower a foot down and walk, the pain strikes again. I can't even bear any weight on it.

The referee stops the clock.

"It's all right, buddy. John's coming."

I dip my head, unable to speak, my world crashing down before my very eyes.

This is a fucking nightmare.

It's been one game, for fuck's sake.

"We've got it. Clear out," I hear John's voice tell my teammates. I know who's with him and I can't get myself to acknowledge her yet. He then starts palpating my knee with his hands, and to distract myself, I lift my eyes to see her somber face.

My stomach hardens. I don't want to see her staring back at me like that. I lower my chin back down, avoiding reality.

She already knows that this isn't a good sign, just as much as I do.

I just hope they can heal me.

My goal is to finish the season and win the Super Bowl. I refuse to retire this way. I need to be quarterback of a winning team.

"It doesn't look like a fracture," John says, and I wish it would make me feel better, but it doesn't.

I limp off the field with her on one side of me, and John on the other. Her delicate arm around me keeps me warm, offering me support in more than just a physical way. But as much as I would normally crave it, I just can't think of anything but dread right now.

I haven't heard a word they've been asking me as we leave the field. The emotional turmoil is swirling through my skull, cancelling out everything else.

When I return to the safety of the locker room, I remove my equipment on autopilot and sit down.

As John asks me more questions, I don't even know if I'm answering coherently. "He tackled me," and then I add, "shooting pain in my knee. I tried to stand up, but I couldn't. The pain was too much. We need to fix this. I need to be back." The shakes are taking over my body as I speak.

Natasha's back a moment later with an ice pack, holding it gently to my knee. The pain and sadness in her glossy eyes match the way I feel inside my heart.

Please don't let this be the end.

"It's okay, son. You'll be back better than ever. Just give it a few weeks."

My dad sits next to me on the locker room bench. He's trying to give me a positive pep talk. He's the only person who's been able to cut through the noise in my head.

I've had so many teammates and even Coach try to talk to me, but I just sat here, unable to say anything.

But Dad gets the pain of an injury and how it feels to be me right now. How your dreams can be taken away from you in a blink of an eye.

I can't feel. I'm hollow and numb.

Wishing someone would wake me up and tell me it's all a fucking joke.

"I hope you're right," I mutter.

"Get up and get your x-ray done. Then I'll take you home. Come home tonight and be surrounded by your family. You need us right now."

As he says the words, I know they ring true. I need them. I can't be in a sad and sorry state alone. My family love me unconditionally, and they stand by me always, but I can't help feeling that, somehow, I'm letting them down.

He grips my shoulder and squeezes it. "Good. I'll be waiting for you out front."

I watch him leave and I sit in the empty locker room with my body curled over itself, my hands gripped together, and my head hung low, losing track of time.

"Are you ready for me to x-ray your knee now?" Natasha's soft voice calls from in front of me. I didn't even hear her come in.

I slowly lift my head and I see her kind face.

Am I ready?

No.

"As ready as I ever will be," I say, sitting up, before adding, "We need to fix this." I tilt my head back and my gaze finds hers. I'm breathing hard as my emotions get the better of me.

I should have listened to her. She cared about me and was able to read my body better than I could. And I was too fucking stubborn. This is my own fault.

Right now, I feel like the walls coming down on that happiness.

"I'm sorry, Ben."

I frown at that. "Why are you sorry?"

I'm confused. She didn't do anything, but I guess being a doctor she knows the devastation injuries can have to an athlete.

"That this is happening to you. I know becoming quarterback was your goal."

More than a goal...a dream.

"Yes, and to win a Super Bowl."

"Of course." She smiles and rolls her eyes, her playfulness coming back. "You can't win everything." Her teasing pulls my head from my downward mood.

"Oh, I know that." My double meaning hangs in the air. If I could win her, that might have me forgetting about the Super Bowl...which is craziness.

She rolls her eyes again, and the sight of it stirs something inside me. After how we left things earlier, my restraint is close to snapping. All I want is to kiss her.

"Don't roll your eyes at me, Miss Blackwood" I growl, and her eyes widen in shock.

I lift a brow as she bites her lip, and suddenly, I don't feel so numb anymore. Now, I'm heated with my desire for her.

She doesn't acknowledge my words but grabs my knee and gets to work. Her fingers touching my skin cause a tingle to travel down my spine. They are soft and delicate as they explore the problem area, like I might break.

"It's okay," I grunt through a clenched jaw.

She sighs, pressing on different areas of my shin, then knee, and when they reach my muscled thighs, I suck in a breath.

Fuckin' hell.

I want her hands on more of me.

The air shifts between us, but I keep focused on her fingers and what she's doing, too scared that if I look into her eyes, I just might beg.

Which is not usual for me. I never have to try. But with her, if I'm being honest, it's a fucking turn on.

When her fingers stop, I almost groan from the loss of contact.

I peer up into her glassy eyes and flushed cheeks.

"Examination is all done. Now I need to take you to get an x-ray. I'm worried it's an ACL injury. But first, you need crutches. Hang on, I'll grab a pair."

She returns after a few moments with a set of crutches, and I grind my teeth at the sight of them. This adds salt to my wounds.

"I'll help you up."

"It's okay, I got it."

But it's too late. She's already at my side, helping me stand. She's so close, I can smell her coconut shampoo, and the electric zing that rushes through me when we touch.

I wonder if she feels it too.

"Do you need a lift home?" she asks as she steps away, once I'm steady on the crutches.

I grin at her offer. If I didn't think she was perfect already, her kindness makes her even more so. "Thanks, but no, my dad has insisted I go home with them tonight."

I see a gleam in her eyes. "Aren't you cute."

I grumble. "Calling me cute isn't what I want right now."

"What do you want, then?" she asks with a puzzled expression.

"Honestly?" I know I shouldn't do this, but at this moment, I don't care. I want her to know what I'm feeling. Leaning forward, I whisper in her ear, "You screaming out my name." As I pull back, her face flushes crimson, and I chuckle. "You asked."

"I did, but I expected—something else."

I probably shouldn't have said it, but it's been an emotional last couple of hours, and I'm going to blame it on that.

"By the way your cheeks are flushed a deep shade of pink, and the way you're biting your lip, I can see you don't hate the idea." I smirk and tilt my head in a challenge.

She stops biting her lip and whispers under her breath, but I catch it. "Honestly, not as much as I should."

I rub the back of my neck at her confession. Her ass sashays away from me, leaving me to follow her, totally stunned.

I don't remember the drive home; it's all a blur since I left Natasha. I move slowly inside my parents' house, still figuring out the best way to use the stupid crutches.

"Oh, love. Are you okay?" Mom asks in a low, shaky voice. Her golden eyes look as sad as I feel. She grabs my cheeks as if I'm still a child, and I grimace.

"I've had better days."

"I bet. Well, go sit down on the couch with your father and watch some TV. I'll call you when dinner's ready. Do you want a drink?"

I smile. It's half-assed, but that's all I can manage. I feel gutted. "No, thanks."

She runs her palms down my face one last time and drops them and returns to the stove. As I wander into the living room, Dad sees me come in and gets up to move from his position in the corner.

"Dad, don't. I'm fine."

"No, please sit and rest your leg. Hopefully, with the added rest, you'll be back playing sooner than you think."

Unable to argue with him, I move closer and turn, lowering my butt down. Dad grabs the crutches, helping me get comfortable.

This was definitely the right decision. Coming here to be surrounded by my family. This house, full of good childhood memories and support and love, is better than sitting at home alone.

I lean back and focus on the TV. Only, I can't help my drifting thoughts, flashes of what happened, the pain, the humiliation of walking off the field, and last, how I'll fix this. My gaze moves down to my knee, the swelling noticeable even beneath my pants.

What results will the MRI bring? The x-ray cleared me of any breaks or fractures. What does my future hold if this is career-ending? Maybe I could coach like my dad...but truthfully, I'm not ready for that right now. Or is this going to be fixed with the help of John and *her*? My lips twitch at the thought of Natasha helping me. I can imagine us laughing, teasing, and trying not to be tempted to cross the line. The image of her is so vivid right now.

She makes me feel better, just by being around her. The kind of person who makes you hope and dream. A genuine diamond. She's so pure, so different from anyone else I've ever met.

But unfortunately, I can't seem to change her mind about me. Who can blame her? I haven't exactly given her a reason to see anything good. Therefore, I need to do something that makes her want nothing more than to give me a chance.

The attraction between us is palpable. When we are together, the room shifts with energy I've never felt before.

I've never felt this strongly, only with football and my family.

But I want her.

I need her.

I crave her.

CHAPTER 16

NATASHA

HOURS LATER AFTER THE game ends, my front door opens.

"Honey, I'm home." I turn to the sound of Sara's booming voice, waiting for her to appear in the kitchen. Stepping away from the stove, I meet her halfway.

"Did you grab the wine?" I ask.

Ever since I realized how much I haven't seen my friends, I decided to make more of an effort, even if it's just a dinner here after work, where I can cook for them. I figure it's a start, and Sara was more than on board when I asked her.

"Yes! Hello to you too. Why is wine getting more attention than me? Why do you need it?" Her eyes squint, looking around.

I laugh loudly, knowing my issues are nothing visible. No. I wish.

They are internal. My heart and feelings are the problems. I need to drink them away or at least have a drink before I unload everything on Sara.

"I will explain after I've had a sip. I just—it was a day."

She hands over the bottle, still wearing her work dress.

Going to the cupboard, I grab two wine glasses, and lift one up in an offer to her.

"Please," she says.

I carry the two glasses to the island and give us both a generous pour.

"How was work?" I ask, after taking a large sip of the fruity wine.

She shrugs. "Same old, nothing new. Working on the same projects for the last few months." Her gaze doesn't leave mine as she takes a sip too. I stalk past her to the table and sit down, folding one foot up underneath me, and getting comfortable.

"Fair enough. No other news?"

Her brows narrow, and she steps over, sitting across from me. "You're acting strange."

"Am not," I argue, but I know she's right, and I wish I wasn't so damn obvious. I want to tell her because I need advice. She's intelligent and level-headed and I need a friend right now. Mia is all for hooking up with a football player, consequences be damned, so she's no help. She would tell me to fuck him so hard that I can't walk straight the next day.

She's a dirty bitch. But I love it, and I love her dearly.

"You soooo are. Spit it out."

I sigh. "Fine."

"Is it work?" She leans back in the chair and crosses her legs.

"Yeah, kind of," I mutter while taking another decent sip.

"What do you mean? This is what you wanted."

She's getting it wrong.

"No, no, it's not the job itself—"

"Is it John?" she asks, cutting me off.

I hate John and his arrogant self, but it's not about him either.

Do I really want to say how I feel? It makes it more real. Do I want to know her opinion about Ben?

"No, John is John." I shrug, then decide to go for it. "You know Ben, the guy from the market?"

Her brows raise high, and she tries to hold back a smile. "Yeah..."

I rub my face and ponder how the hell I'm going to explain what is going on with him.

She's staring at me, waiting anxiously for me to spit it out.

"I just...this...I can't explain. I'm going to sound like an idiot. But there's just something between me and him. He just...I don't know. I just...but I can't, you know."

She drops her head back with a giggle.

And it irks me. "What?"

She stops laughing and returns her focus back to me. "That does not make sense at all. Rewind and start from the beginning. You're talking gibberish. Talk fucking English."

I sigh and try again. "Well, ever since I started working there, we kind of...I don't know," I mumble under my breath and rub my forehead, willing for the words to come flowing into my brain.

"You find him attractive?" She lifts a brow at me.

"Yes, obviously."

She rolls her lips. "Don't be smart with me. I'm just asking you a question."

I sag in my chair. "I know, I know. Sorry. Yes, I find him attractive. But also, there's this strange attraction that goes deeper than that. I don't know what to call it, but I shouldn't be feeling it. I don't want to be feeling it, but he was so close to me the other day at work, he has messed my thoughts up."

She opens her mouth to speak, but I cut her off. "And you know how much this job means to me. And I was so close to crossing that line. Way too close."

I drain the glass and look up at her.

And she has the biggest shit-eating grin on her face.

"Ben seems like a nice guy...well, from what I saw at the market and have read about him. But yeah, not at work. Just because John is John. If he wasn't there, I'd say go for it. But you're dancing on thin ice with him as it is. So maybe do it outside of work. That's my advice. I say, go for it. If he's a genuine one, he will accept your mom and the way you live your life."

I ponder her advice, leaning forward on the table and rubbing my temples. I wish it was easy; to block him out, concentrate on my job, and go home. But instead, he slams into my thoughts and rattles them, trying to get deep inside. My head is saying stop and think about it, while my heart is already beating wildly just for him.

I'm so screwed.

"Like, what if it doesn't work out?" I stop and drop my fingers, my throat dry. Getting up, I grab the bottle, topping our glasses off.

"You won't know unless you try," Sara replies.

"Hmm, I don't know. He's injured right now, so it's not like he's in the greatest headspace. I'll need to wait anyway."

I sip my wine.

"Well, I think...just be there as a friend, then. And if one thing leads to another, enjoy the moment. See where it goes. Don't put any pressure on it or yourself."

I smile at her. "That, I like the sound of. Just go with the flow, don't overthink. However, I'm worried about me. I fall too hard. I feel too strong. I know if we cross that line, I'm all in."

She drains her glass and leans forward. "I think that's great. When you're in a relationship, that's how it should be."

She rises to put the glass in the sink, and I follow suit to finish cooking as Mom comes out from the shower.

I hope I can just go with the flow and see where it goes.

But at work, it would have to be kept a secret.

A few hours later, I'm sitting in bed with the television playing football in the background because I'm still not tired.

The announcers talking snaps me out of my funk, and my mind drifts to Ben.

What's he doing?

How's his knee feeling?

How're the crutches going?

Has he taken any pain killers today?

Is he elevating and stretching and icing as directed?

All these stupid doctor thoughts run around in my brain on a loop.

I reach for my phone and open Instagram and Facebook, checking to see if he's online. It's nine at night, so I guess he could be asleep. But the green dot alerts me to the fact he is, in fact, awake.

I pause a second, before deciding to text message him. As Sara said, I need to go with the flow. And I need to check on him.

I type out a few different messages, none of them sounding right.

"Hey, Ben."

Oh, that sounds awful.

Delete.

"How are you feeling tonight?"

Ugh. That's worse.

Delete.

"What are you up to?"

Now I sound too fucking cheery.

Delete.

Why can't I just be normal? Why am I overthinking this? And I think back to what Sara said earlier.

Stop overthinking!

Natasha: Hi, Ben. Just checking in. I've been thinking about you and I wanna see if you're okay. I can't imagine the headspace you're in right now.

I hit send before I can change my mind, feeling good about sending a message from my heart.

I'm thankful Sara made me think that I can do this, that I can be a friend.

A friend is what he needs.

He may be looking at a career-ending injury, so he'll need everybody on his side.

Tomorrow, he'll have his MRI done. Then he'll find out exactly where his life will go.

I toss my phone on the bed and settle back into watching more TV. When my phone chimes beside me, it sends my pulse thumping nervously.

I can't pick it up quickly enough. Opening it, I beam like the Cheshire Cat.

Benjamin: Been thinking of me, were you? ;)

I can't help but laugh at the message and smile stupidly at the phone, knowing no one can see me right now. But before I have a chance to write back, he sends another message.

Benjamin: I'm as good as I can be, to be honest. I'm glad I'm staying at my family's house. I don't know how I would have done this being alone. And just thinking about what my future holds.

Reading that makes my heart ache for him. To be that passionate about something in your life makes me like him a little more.

It makes me think about my own life. I don't know what I would do if I wasn't a doctor. So, I can relate to him in one way. I wouldn't want that stripped from me. Which should be enough to deter me from my growing feelings for him, but I brush that thought away and reply.

Natasha: I feel for you. I don't know what it would be like to have your life change in a matter of seconds. I'm sure this sport is all you've known, or you've ever desired to do, and to have that maybe taken away from you is a lot to take in. I'm here if you need a friend to lean on.

A few moments later, a new message comes through.

Benjamin: It's a feeling that is definitely hard to describe. Almost like someone close to you dying...I feel numb. I feel scared. I'm glad you're my friend. Even if you know that's not all I want...

I stare at that last line and repeat it over and over in my head.

Oh, shit.

I pray that tomorrow won't be as bad for him, and that we get some good news to erase that dark cloud over his head.

> *Natasha: I'm sorry you feel that way. There really aren't any words that I could say to make that pain go away. But just know if you need me, I'm here.*

I hit send, purposefully ignoring his bit about wanting to be more than friends. And it isn't long before he responds again.

> *Benjamin: I like to tease. I know you just want to be friends. Just know that when you change your mind, I'll be here waiting. And thank you for taking my mind off my knee. Now my whole mind and body is filled with you and it's a much happier, warmer feeling. The numbness has subsided all because of you.*

I beam as I read over the text again, my chest warming.

He's feeling better because of me.

He, on the other hand, makes me feel achy, needy, and desirable.

No, I shouldn't think like this.

I swallow the lump that's formed in my throat, and type.

Natasha: I'm glad I can help. How's the knee feeling? Are you in pain? Have you taken pain medications? Is there swelling?

Benjamin: Calm down, Doc. If you're worried, you could always check on me in person. A visit wouldn't be a bad thing. ;)

It *would* be a very bad thing. There's no chance I will be going there. The friend zone would be blurred in an instant.

Like it kind of already is.

Natasha: A picture would do.

Natasha: Of your KNEE!

Benjamin: Dammit, how did you know I wanted to be naughty? I'm a very bad patient.

I giggle. That's something I can agree with.

Another message comes through and it's of his stomach down. A naked stomach, that is, and his green boxer briefs. Yes, his dusting of dark blond hair trailing from his navel leading into his boxer briefs is hot. I have seen his toned torso many times, and it's delicious every time. His thick thighs are dusted with the same blond hair, but the bulge between his thighs...that has me blinking rapidly. My eyes grow wide, my heart racing. He's so sexy lying there like that, truly every girl's fantasy. I can imagine myself sitting on top, riding him hard until I'm coming apart. The feeling of his hard muscles under my palms, and him—

I need to stop.

I feel flustered and tongue-tied. What should I write back? Oh yeah, look at his knee!

I drop my gaze and look at his knee; it's swollen, the bruising evident, even in the photo, but it's not as bad as I thought it would've been.

I rub the base of my neck, working out what to say, and then type a response.

> *Natasha: Your knee doesn't look as bad as I thought it would. Hopefully, it's a good sign.*

> *Benjamin: I hope you're right.*

It's time for the MRI results. I'm going through my studies with John, who's firing questions at me. He loves to play this game with me. It's as if he's waiting for me to mess up, so he can wear this ugly smirk and correct me like I'm still a student. He likes to remind me he's smarter than me. But he's also been a physician a lot longer than me.

I grind my teeth together and bite my tongue to hold myself back from retaliating.

I'm flicking through and reading parts of the medical book John let me borrow to "improve my knowledge," as he likes to tell me. He's unequivocally the worst part of my job.

I have my gaze down reading the book, when a knock on the door has my gaze flicking up. I find Ben standing there.

"Good morning," he says in a flat, sad tone. I'm becoming more sensitive to him the more we talk.

"Morning, Ben. How's the knee today?" John asks.

I close my book and stand to watch as John welcomes Ben into the room and into a chair to examine him.

He follows John's prompting. But his gaze holds mine, a softer hue to them when he looks at me. "Good morning," he says, holding my attention.

I smile back. "Good morning."

I feel John's eyes burning a hole through me. But I don't move or whither to John; I refuse to be bullied by him. I'm here to help, or in his eyes, to learn.

"Let's assess your knee while I wait for the results," John says. I go to grab my bag, but he stops me. "Natasha, you stay here. You have to finish your studies. I'll take Ben. We won't be long."

My entire body tenses.

Is he shitting me?

"I don't mind her coming, John," Ben argues, his voice unwavering. His jaw is ticking, and I can tell he is just as pissed at John as I am.

"No. She'll wait here. She can listen to the results with us, but for the assessment, there's nothing to see or help with."

Nothing to see.

CHAPTER 17

BENJAMIN

"It's okay. I'll see you when you get back," Natasha says lightly.

I stare at her face to make sure there's no hurt or pain. John is a real dick sometimes, but I have to hold my tongue and not say anything. I don't want her getting in more trouble with John, or worse, lose her job if her concerns about it are as valid as she thinks. The way she nods her head and smiles back at me, I feel content to let it go. We leave the office, and John escorts me into the next room.

I'm bouncing a leg up and down nervously. I want this all to be over.

He runs through his palpating inspection, something I would have preferred Natasha to be doing for me. He finds no further swelling or bruising, so it's not long and we go back to John's office.

When I walk in, I scan the room looking for her, sighing when I see her sitting in the exact same spot as we left her, reading a book.

I feel this magnetic pull from sharing the same air, so I move closer, needing to talk to her. She must hear our steps because her head lifts from the book, and I see her pretty face look up at me, concern shining in her eyes until I smile.

John's phone rings, so he walks into his office. I take that as my opportunity to move closer to her and sit on the edge of her desk. She leans back to watch me, a sexy smile sitting easily on her face.

"You're still studying?" I ask.

Her eyes flick in the direction of John's office, before meeting mine, and her lips thin as she offers me a small shrug.

"Good girl."

When her eyes meet mine this time, they twinkle. But just as quickly as it was there, it's gone. She reins herself back in.

"How was the assessment?" she asks quietly.

I rub my hands on my pants, clearing my throat. "The same. I just want to know the MRI results already. I want to know what's wrong, so I can make a return to play strategy."

Her hand lightly touches my thigh, and my muscles tighten in response.

"So, you still don't know. I bet you're dying for his phone to ring with the results. I can't imagine the anxiety running through you."

I stare back into her gaze, not even thinking about the call. I'm more excited her expert hands are touching me. I just wish it wasn't with pity-filled eyes.

"I'm okay. It won't be much longer, and I'll know what's going on."

"Guys, come in here. Doctor Taylor's on the line with the results."

She pulls her hand back in a rush and quickly stands.

It's time.

This is the phone call that determines my career. No backing out now.

Yes, I have an idea that coaching is what I'll probably do next, but I'm not ready to give up on playing yet. Just like I won't give up on the beauty in front of me.

I slide off her desk and walk into his office, promptly sitting down. Natasha sits next to me, crossing her legs and hands fidgeting in her lap.

Without warning, John speaks into the phone, "Hang on, Mike, I'm gonna put you on the speaker to Ben." He presses the button on his screen, holding the phone out to me.

"Ben?" Doctor Taylor asks.

"Hi, yes?" I say, nausea rolling in my stomach with anticipation.

"I've got your results here. And the good news is, it's not season-ending."

No way.

A sense of relief washes through my body instantly. The tense feeling that made my muscles ache seems to disappear.

A huge sigh leaves my mouth, and I lean forward, rubbing my face with my hands in disbelief. I thought I was a goner there.

"Ben?" Doctor Taylor says.

I sit up in the chair. "Yeah, sorry. Thanks. Just a little shocked."

John laughs.

"I know what you mean," the doctor says.

I feel a hand on my triceps, and I know it's her. Her hand is small, delicate, and warm. It immediately soothes me. I turn my head and give her a full smile, and she returns it with one that's bright and beautiful. It's clear how happy she is for me.

When she drops her hand away, I feel a loss.

"So, you'll need to ease back into it, but you could be back in a few games' time with all healing well. Just don't overdo it. I want you to follow John's orders. And when you're ready, take it easy. If there's any point that you get sore, take a week off. If you push yourself, you will lose the career you desperately want. But just know, it's probably a wake-up call. You don't have much longer in this game. Make every second count."

I sit there as if he just slapped me across the face. But it echoes my own thoughts; this is my last chance. I need to play every game as if they're my last.

"No pressure, Doc...no pressure," I say, with a chuckle covering my nerves.

"Good luck, and I just hope you guys win this year. You deserve it."

I smile, knowing we deserve it too. "I'll try to. I want to win this year." I scratch my temple and watch John hang up.

John explains he thinks it's a strained knee, and that I should be good to go in a couple of weeks. I need to keep on with the rest, icing, compression, and elevation regimen I've been given for another week. But otherwise, they'll get me back into the training room for small bursts. The other great news from today has to be losing the crutches. I hated every single second of using them.

We spend a few minutes discussing this week's rehab plan. I can't wipe the smile off my face. Even talking about rehab makes me excited. I can't wait to tell my teammates I'll be back for the season.

I'm back, baby.

As John talks, he discusses the days I'll be with the physiotherapists and the days with either him or Natasha. And I sit, nodding, absorbing the news. Deep down, I'm ecstatic at the fact I get to spend alone time with her. She'll probably see it as dangerous, but I'm fucking thrilled. I don't know how much more I can take being in the same room as her and not having her in the ways I truly want to.

Who's going to snap first?

Me or her?

I've taken the pain pills as prescribed and have stayed hydrated. I'm eating well and taking it easy. It's my first rehab session, and it's in the hydrotherapy pool. But unfortunately, I'm doing it with a physiotherapist and John.

I wish it was with Natasha.

But I can't argue. I'm here to work hard so I can return to the field to play.

No distractions.

And thinking about Natasha in a bikini is a huge one.

Getting to move around the pool feels surprisingly good. After some basic exercises, it has already been half an hour, and John tells me we're finished. I'm exhausted and my body feels heavy, as if I could sleep for hours. Dad insisted on driving me home today, and because the knee is still tender, I don't fight him on it.

Once I'm home, I nap for a few hours. A knock at the door wakes me, and I'm delirious for a second.

As I slowly rise from the couch, the knocking grows louder, so I yell out, "I'm coming."

Not using crutches anymore is awesome, but I'm still uncomfortable, so it takes me longer to get places. When I finally open it, Levi's there, holding a pizza box.

"Hey, man. Did you just wake up?" he asks.

I move back and he steps inside, kicking the door shut for me so I can return to the couch.

"Sure did." I smirk.

"What a life. I did too, and I bet the guys are all training their asses off while we're napping."

He laughs loudly, and I can't help but laugh too, knowing that's exactly right.

"I trained a little today. But not our usual twice-a-day sessions that kick my ass."

I take my seat on the couch as Levi lowers the pizza and takes a seat opposite me. Flipping open the box lid, he grabs a slice and takes a bite straightaway like the pig that he is. If we weren't training, he'd be the size of a house with the way he ate. And it's not just him. I'd be the exact same way.

"So if you're training, how much longer until you can get back to the game?" Levi asks between mouthfuls of food.

"John doesn't know; he's just taking it easy and we're just seeing how I feel in terms of pain. I don't want to push it. Otherwise, if I go back too soon, I could lose a chance of playing another game altogether. John has got me on a strict rehab schedule. One day with him, one day with Natasha, and when the pain, swelling, and bruising are gone, he'll talk to Coach. And I guess they'll roster me back in. Until then, I'm just working with them. I feel good, though."

He looks at me and nods. "Thank fuck, it wasn't a bad injury. I'm excited for you. At least one of us can get back this season."

I get up and grab us both a bottle of water, talking on my way to the fridge. "Yeah, me too. I thought I was screwed. I'm sorry this has happened to you, but fuck, I don't know what I would do without football."

"Find a real job," he jokes before a deep chuckle leaves his chest.

I laugh and walk back into the room, pretending to swat him over the head with his bottle, tossing it in his lap.

"Ha-ha, dickhead," I say with a smile, before lowering my tone to a serious one and taking a seat on the couch again. "No, but seriously, have you ever thought about what you will do after football?"

His face screws up, and he shakes his head at me. "No, why would I? I'll be playing football forever."

I twist the bottle cap and take a decent drink before screwing it back on. "You wish. That would be a dream, but we're in our thirties now, and unfortunately, even if we want to, we can't do it forever."

He grabs another piece of pizza, talking before he has finished his mouthful. "True."

"I'm leaning toward coaching," I say honestly, knowing I hadn't given much thought to this until recently. Events like this remind you that you can't keep going on forever. That life has different directions for you, different challenges, different life lessons. You either take the bull by the horns or you fail. And I don't fail, I win. I compete and give my very best at whatever I put my mind to.

"Yeah, you'd be a good coach. Are you talkin' about high school, college, or NFL?"

"I've only just started looking at new opportunities, but maybe college."

He nods, and we fall into more casual conversation as we finish eating, watching some football and moving on to COD. (Call Of Duty video game.)

"How's Mia?" I ask.

I'm happy he's found someone to settle down with, despite knowing that when the coach finds out it's his daughter, he'll want to chop Levi's dick off.

"She's good. Same old, really. Sweet and kind of crazy. But I love it."

I choke on my water before swallowing to speak. "Yeah, she's fun."

"I don't know how she puts up with my shit sometimes. I've been such a grump since this shit happened." He points to his shoulder with a grim look.

My lips thin at his honesty. But also, I wonder what that feels like? Having someone to be there even when you're being a moody prick.

"What about you and Tash?"

Deep down, I have thought a lot about a certain blonde. Probably a little too much.

I'm definitely not hooking up with her.

I fucking wish!

Telling Levi more about my little infatuation is a waste of time because Natasha and I are only friends. Even if a part of her wants to explore, there's something holding her back.

And I should keep focused on myself and my goal; getting back on that field and winning the Super Bowl. But of course, I can't bite my tongue.

"Nothing to report."

Two days later, I'm in the training room with her. She has me sitting down and doing basic arm exercises. It seems a bit ridiculous. I feel like I'm stretching, and I fucking despise it.

On the plus side, we're talking and getting to spend one-on-one time together. I can openly gawk at her, and it's all for *work*.

"Come on, you've got this," she encourages. "You want to be back out there soon, right?"

"Yes. Fuck, I have to. I need to win the trophy." I snort as I think about almost fulfilling the other one.

"What?" she asks with a puzzled expression.

I wipe the sweat from my brow as I explain. "My two goals were to become quarterback and to win the Superbowl. I almost got the first goal, but I didn't even make it through a whole game."

She touches my shoulder. "Don't be like that. You did it. It doesn't matter for how many minutes. I know that you've worked hard to get back on the roster and you'll be quarterback for the rest of the season...there's really no one else."

A deep laugh leaves me. "Ouch."

She removes her hand, but still stands close to me. "I'm playing. I just mean, I believe you'll be back out there, grabbing your goals with both hands." The sincerity of her voice reminds me that if I wasn't injured, this time with her wouldn't exist. I've been tempted to send her another text, but haven't, as I'm trying to respect her boundaries. Pushing is only going to drive her further away.

"Press up five more times," she says, and the joy on her face makes me grin with contentment. She loves her job, and I love seeing her in her element. It also makes me realize fully why she wouldn't want to lose this opportunity. I understood before, but she's so good at what she does, and it's obvious how much she enjoys working for the team.

Now, I can see why I'm such a risk.

Fuck.

I just wish I was worth that risk.

"That's it. Great work."

"This is easy."

"It's not on your muscles. Just because I'm not letting you lift heavy weights doesn't mean your muscles and tendons aren't working hard right now."

"I can't really argue with you there. This is your speciality."

"Exactly. So shush, Mr. Chase, and keep going."

I chuckle. "Yes, Doc."

We're almost finished stretching, thank fuck, because my patience is dwindling with it. No matter how hot she is, it doesn't help me enjoy stretching any more. I go to stand, and almost topple over, trying to get up too quickly.

"Shit."

"Gotcha," she says, coming to my side and wrapping her arm around my waist. There's not an ounce of hesitation in helping me. I possibly weigh double what she does, yet the thought hadn't crossed her mind. No, her first thought was to help me. And fuck, that wobbles me further.

The sudden closeness of her body under mine has my senses on overdrive. I take a deep breath of her, the air that's filled with her beautiful coconut scent, and it causes my nostrils to flare. She inhales sharply when she realizes what I'm doing, and it sends a hum through me.

Gotcha.

Oh yeah, she feels the tension too.

"You having a good feel?" I joke.

Her mouth pops open, and she rolls her eyes, slapping my shoulder playfully. "Hey!"

"I'm only joking. Thanks for saving me, I mean," I say, staring down into her mesmerizing eyes.

"I don't know about that. I think I helped you get a little bit steady, but you..." She pauses for a second. Her cheeks turn pink under my stare before continuing. "Um, you're kind of big."

Now her cheeks turn crimson.

At her blushing, a grin spreads on my face. Her hesitation means she didn't want to say the words, but I love to stir the pot and make her squirm. Leaning forward toward her ear, I whisper, "Yeah. I am. But hey...try not to be dirty at work."

I feel her body shudder lightly. And my mind suddenly shifts to the bedroom.

What would she be like naked underneath me?

Would she shiver?

Would she arch her back?

Would she scream?

Or would she be quiet?

God, how I would love to know.

Strip her bare and sink my teeth into her, see what she would do.

"You're going to get me in trouble," she whispers, staring at me with these come-fuck-me eyes, and I don't know how I'm supposed to deny her.

And I simply can't anymore.

So, fuck it. Here goes...

"I want you," I say huskily. "I fucking really, really need you."

Her mouth slacks into an O.

And I fucking snap.

CHAPTER 18

NATASHA

I KNEW RIGHT THERE and then I was a goner. The moment my hands touched his body during the stretches, to the way our eyes held each other's in such a close proximity. Then, to top it off, his genuine words hitting me much harder and deeper in the chest. One second, I'm sucking in a deep breath, and the next, his mouth is on mine.

The way his hands clutch my face is such a contrast to our kiss, which is ravenous and desperate. Our teeth clash as he walks me back until I hit a wall, his hand cushioning my head. I groan in pleasure at his ferocity. How he can't hold himself back. When he swipes his tongue through my lips, I open wider and tangle my own in the mix. At the feeling, he groans into my mouth, and my hands grip his shoulders even tighter. I wouldn't be surprised if my knees give out from the daze he has me in.

I've always wondered what it would be like to kiss him. My answer: it's even better than I imagined. Even though I swore off men, and definitely no football players. Yet, here I am, ravaging him with my mouth and enjoying every single blissful moment of it.

My legs are quivering, sex throbbing for more. He's such a good kisser. The feel of his lips is so soft, velvety. His tongue is warm, taunting and controlling.

One of his hands trails over my face and down my back to cup my ass, pushing me forward against him, so I'm flush with his hips. I can feel his hard cock pressing into my stomach, and I can't hold back a moan.

God, I'm totally screwed.

In this moment, I want him. I don't have any smart thoughts about how wrong this is because everything feels so right.

I snake my hands up around his neck and find my way into his hair, curling my fingers and gripping. Pulling him closer, even though I don't think I can, as we are already swapping air.

He lets out a little grunt. It's deep and feral, and my sex clenches at the sound. I pull his hair again, just to hear it once more. And the grunt is louder this time, and so much hotter.

I want more, so much more.

I should stop this.

I'm at work. We've been close to being busted by Andrew and Levi before...

Right now, I'm jeopardizing everything.

I pull back with closed eyes, my forehead touching his, and I whisper against his lips, "We shouldn't." But my voice is weak, betraying me.

"But do you want this? Do you want me?" His breathing is labored, telling me how much he wants me to feel the same.

His tongue slowly runs across my lower lip, causing me to shiver.

I'm breathing hard and fast. "God, I shouldn't," I reply in disbelief.

But I can't hold back.

He chuckles and captures my lips in another kiss, but this time it's less urgent and more exploring.

I'm enjoying how much he towers over me, yet at the same time makes me feel safe. His hard muscles feel amazing against my soft skin. When his hands squeeze my ass cheeks roughly, I grind against him.

God, I want more. More. More.

But a noise causes me to snap my eyes open and take a step back from him. "Stop."

And he does.

My heart is pounding so hard it feels like it's about to come out of my chest. He drops his arms and his heavy desire stares back at me. I have to close my eyes for a second and gather my thoughts before I reopen them from the sound of his voice.

"Why?" he asks, still trying to catch his breath.

I glance around, hugging my body as he stands still.

"Why, Tash?" he presses, his eyebrows furrowed.

"This can't happen here. I need this job, Ben," I plead, wanting him to let me go.

No matter how tempted I am right now, I need to remind him what's important.

His hand reaches out and his thumb brushes my cheek. "Please...I know your body wants me."

I inhale sharply.

God, it does.

It's traitorous, and the way he's looking at me like I'm the only food to cure his hunger, it kills me. My eyes roam his face, down to his obvious, large erection tenting his pants. I grow wetter at the sight, and it's hard to resist relief when it's been a long time since I last had sex. And to have it with someone who wants me this badly is making me cave...

Fuck it.

"Okay," I whisper. When I bite my bruised lips together, they feel swollen and thoroughly kissed.

My heart is in my throat as he takes my hand, walking us out of the headquarters.

I can't believe I'm doing this.

I'm about to cross the line and hit the end zone.

When we're almost to my car, his cursing makes me wince. Realizing that by being swept up in the moment and trying to avoid bumping into anyone of importance, I'm moving way too fast.

"Maybe—" I say, slowing down my pace.

"No. I've waited for you long enough. Get that sexy ass in your car now."

One look at his blazing eyes, and I want the hot sex he's silently promising.

I snort at his order, but also, I'm amused. "Bossy, Mr. Chase."

"You have no idea," he growls.

His voice sends heat spreading up my spine, and I have to concentrate on not begging for sex in my car right this minute.

"I can't believe you're driving me. This is humiliating. If I'd have known this would be happening, I'd have driven in today."

I smirk. "Get over it."

He looks up at me, and I bite down on my bottom lip to prevent a groan from slipping at the hunger staring back at me. I can't wait for his hands to be all over my body.

As soon as I put the key into the ignition, his hand is on my thigh. I gasp.

I take off and try to focus on not crashing. His fingers grazing the inside of my thigh is making me crazy with arousal.

"Are you listening to me?" His voice is firm, but there is a bit of a waver. He's struggling to control himself too.

"Sorry. What were you saying? I promise to listen this time." And not be distracted by your thumb tracing my thigh in circles.

He chuckles. "I said, turn right at the next street."

"All right, got it."

As we get closer, I recall I'm wearing the world's most boring bra and panties. The soft cotton isn't the least bit sexy. And to add to that, they don't match. This is a dead giveaway that I wasn't planning to have sex today. I'm wearing this for comfort, not to seduce. Let's hope the ravenous state we were in doesn't stop and they are off before I have to feel self-conscious about them.

The drive is only another five minutes, and the rest of the way, his hand causes me to sweat, the music and the tension in the car building up. By the time we park, my heart is hammering in my chest. I try to help him, but he's hobbling toward the steps before I can.

When his smoldering eyes stare down at me, my knees nearly buckle. "You ready?" he murmurs softly.

I don't hesitate choking out, "Yes."

His eyes darken. "Let's go."

He takes the stairs slowly and unlocks the door to his house with ease. No nervous energy comes from him. However, I'm so wound up with anticipation, it's killing me. I worry one touch, and I'll...orgasm.

Holding the door open, he waits for me as I step across the wooden floors. When the door clicks shut behind me, I jump. Before I can spin around, I'm pushed against the staircase railing.

His lips find mine, and we kiss passionately again, only this time our feral noises are loud, with no care in the world. My hands gripping his shoulders move to his pecs, and when they contract under my hand, I moan. The feel of him is better than my dreams, and lately, I'll be honest, he has appeared nightly.

I move my hand lower, over each ridge of his abs, feeling every one and dying to trace them with my tongue. His hands run over my neck and down to my heavy breasts, where he rubs his thumb over my nipple, finding it immediately even though I'm wearing a bra.

I pull back from the kiss, heavily panting and gasping for air.

"Fuck, I've been dreaming of this."

I bite my lip at his raspy confession, not wanting to tell him he's been featured in mine.

He leans down, kissing my neck, and I tilt my head back to give him better access. Nipping his way to my collarbone, he pinches my nipple, caressing the sting away and repeating again.

"Oh, god," I pant, watching his big hand over my breast.

"You're so responsive." He moves to my other nipple and rubs and pinches that one too.

My back is hard up against the railing, and I'm grateful I have something to help hold me up. I'm feeling like jelly the closer my climax is climbing.

"Or just really horny," I breathe.

"Mmm...maybe, but how long has it been?"

I swallow the embarrassment. "A while."

"So, you're nice and tight, then. I'll need to warm you up."

Before I have a chance to ask him how he plans to warm me up, he stands back. Turning me around, he whispers in my ear. "Hold on tight. Don't let go."

I gulp down air as my legs tremble from anticipation.

Holy fuck.

"Do you understand, Natasha?"

I grip the railing with white knuckle force, and I wait for him, unable to speak. I can feel him behind me, but I don't know what he's doing. I feel vanilla compared to him if he's thinking of fucking me here against his stairs. I've only been touched on a bed before.

"Natasha?" His husky voice pulls me out of my thoughts.

"Yes, Ben. Yes. I understand."

He hums. "Good girl."

I hear a small thud, but I'm distracted as his fingers graze my neck, moving my ponytail to the other side, his breath tickling the exposed skin there. I'm now shaking uncontrollably from adrenaline. So much so, that when his warm lips hit the skin on the nape of my neck, I moan.

The idea of not knowing or seeing what he's doing is adding to the intensity. My panties are already soaked from his presence.

"Do you know how much I have wanted this?"

He's breathing harder in between his kisses.

I shake my head, and he nips my neck in response.

I feel his arms snake around my waist on either side and pop the button on my pants. He glides them over my hips and pushes them to the floor, and I step out. As he kicks them to the side, goosebumps rise on my legs from the cool air. He trails his fingertips on the outside of my thighs, and the feather-like touch is nice, but I'm so eager for him, I'm about to beg for those fingers to move somewhere else.

He doesn't touch me where I want him to, though. Instead, he moves on to my top and lifts it off, and I stand in my mismatched bra and panties.

I can't see him, so I have no idea if he is still fully dressed or not. I turn my head to get a glimpse of him, but he catches me.

"I'm still dressed, baby girl. One thing to know is, you'll always come before me. And if I'm lucky, I'll get you coming twice before I fuck you."

I squeeze my eyes shut.

"Fuck," I mumble under my breath. His words speak directly to my sex.

His hands unclasp my bra, freeing my tits, my nipples already in tight peaks from arousal.

Kissing my shoulder, he reaches around to grab my breast, squeezing and then rubbing his fingers together to roll my nipple.

"Ah." I tip my head back, still sensitive from his earlier touching.

"Are you wet for me, Natasha?" he asks with a growl.

I nod.

"Let me check."

I lift my head up and my eyes widen, knowing he'll find me *very* wet.

As he slowly pulls my panties down my legs, I feel my wet slickness running down my inner thighs.

"Jesus Christ," he chokes out as he runs his finger up and down through my opening before he circles my swollen bud.

"Ben," I moan.

"Baby, you're dripping...spread your legs."

I do.

"Wider," he instructs firmly.

Again, I follow his order.

"Better."

His injury dawns on me, and I rush out, "Ben, your knee."

"Fuck my knee. It feels amazing on the wood."

I frown.

The wood?

What the?

I feel his hands grip my hips and pull me back. I'm hinged forward and before I have time to think, he swipes his warm tongue along my clit to my pussy, and I moan loudly.

This is a lot.

"Too much," I mumble, but it's unconvincing even to my own ears.

His mouth pulls away, and my body shivers. "Do you want me to stop?"

"No," I whisper-shout.

"Does it feel good?" he asks before doing it again.

The warmth of his tongue on my pussy has my legs quivering all over again, and I drop my head. He has taken my breath away with the vision of him between my legs.

"Ben," I say desperately. Feeling the pressure building inside me, I know I'm close. He promised to pleasure me first, and it's working.

The doctor in me wants to yell at him for not elevating his leg, but the whore in me wants his tongue to keep going.

"Yesss. That's it. Just like that," I pant out.

And he answers me by pulling his tongue out of my core and licking me slowly again over my swollen clit, letting the whore win.

"I'm so close," I moan.

"I know. I can feel it on my tongue."

I've never had a guy who openly enjoys eating my pussy. They've always made me feel like I had to shower beforehand. But with Ben, my insecurities have left, because he's loving every second of it.

"You taste better than I imagined. Remember when I said I wanted to hear you to scream my name? Well, be a good girl and scream."

His mouth returns to my core before moving to my clit, and I feel his fingers at my entrance.

"Please," I beg.

He enters two fingers slowly inside me. It's tight, and I scrunch up my face from the biting intrusion, but he then begins to pull out, and my pussy clenches around his fingers, intensifying the pleasure.

"Such a greedy pussy."

"Faster," I beg.

But of course, he doesn't comply. He just continues at his slow, torturous pace. His other hand is gripping my hip hard, keeping me as still as possible. I'll bruise there tomorrow, but I don't care in the slightest. It'll be worth every bit of tenderness.

His lips find my clit again, and I refuse to open my eyes in fear I'll ruin the moment with my doctor brain seeing him in a compromising position. I let the feeling of his tongue and teeth on my clit, of his fingers thrusting in and out, deeper every time, to consume my thoughts instead.

"Ben!" I shout in warning.

My orgasm is about to hit me at full force.

"Now. I want you to come for me," he whispers on my clit.

The warm air and him pumping in sync have me screaming out his name embarrassingly loud, and coming hard on his fingers.

"Fuck, yeah, baby. That's it."

I convulse as it takes over my whole body. I'm breathing hard, trying to collect myself, but Ben doesn't let up. No, he picks up the pace with his fingers, driving me into sensory overload.

"Oh, fuck."

And he enters another finger.

"Ben. It's tight." It stings a little, but after a few pumps, it feels good again.

"I know, but I need you ready for me. You want my cock, don't you?"

"God, yes!"

"Well, I need to stretch you. Trust me, even me stretching you now won't be enough. You'll be so full of my cock. Is that what you want?"

The promise of him fucking me sends me wild.

"Yes. God, yes."

"I can't wait to fuck your pussy."

He doesn't say anything else. Instead, he kisses the backs of my thighs and keeps pumping me harder.

And without warning, I feel his thumb on my clit, causing my heart to somersault.

What is he doing?

But as he rubs lazy circles over and over in a rhythm, my body heats up again. Telling me I'm about to hit climax once more.

"Good girl, that's it. You're so close, I can feel it. You're so fucking tight and perfect."

His fucking words.

I can't hold on anymore.

"Ben," I moan out his name.

And as I come again, he adds his tongue, making me cry out louder. And doing exactly what he wanted, screaming his name.

I'm thankful to be still clutching the handrail of his staircase, as it prevents me from crumbling to the floor when I shudder uncontrollably above him.

After my orgasm, I stand, unmoving, just trying to collect my breath from that out-of-body experience. I definitely need to be more adventurous, because that was surprisingly fun.

"Natasha?"

"Hmm?"

"Are you okay?"

I slowly straighten and blink my eyes open. "Yes. Mmm." I can't even think.

"Come here."

I peel my fingers off the railing and shake my hands out. Turning around, my gaze hits his naked chest.

When did he lose his top?

His chest is rising and falling in labored breaths, and when I look up and meet his gaze, it's darkened and heavy. Full of lust. I swallow and continue to stare back, and like he's been starved of my lips, he leans in and kisses me hard. I open my mouth, and his tongue enters at my welcome, tangling with mine. I can't get enough when he kisses me like it's our last.

When he pulls back, I groan. I'm about to protest and kiss him again, but he grabs my hand and turns us toward the stairs. We climb them, careful of his knee, but still moving with haste, until we reach a bedroom,

Ben has money—a lot of it.

His room alone is the same size as my house, and my house isn't small. When I see his wooden bed sitting in the middle, my nerves come back. But it's as if he knows, so he yanks on my ponytail, tilting my chin up to face him.

He brings his lips to my ear. "Don't overthink this. Let yourself enjoy it."

The hair pinches on my scalp, causing an ache between my thighs. He lets go of my pony and comes to stand in front of me, pressing his lips to mine. I kiss him back with everything I have. Brushing my hands over his chest, I feel his athletic build and dusting of blond hair under my palms. Ready for more, I lower my hands to his pants, popping the button and pushing them down.

He breaks the kiss to watch me shove off his briefs. As I glance at his face, I see he has a brow raised and a gleeful grin. When I run my gaze over his body, it's like my eyes can't wait any longer to see his cock. I moan when I look at it, hard and pointing at me, precum at the tip.

"Fuckin' hell," he gruffs, as I reach out and wrap a hand around him. Or try to.

I stay focused and watch my hand with fascination. I smear the liquid over his tip with my thumb in lazy strokes, then glide my palm down his length, feeling his prominent vein throb.

His breathing picks up, chest rising and falling rapidly. I lift my gaze to see his drunken, satisfied gaze, and I can't help but smile.

Leaning in, I capture his lips in a brief kiss before returning to watching my hand move up and down, and as more precum forms, I hear him grunt out, "Stop, baby. I want to fuck you."

I can't disagree. I want that too. "Yes. Please."

He walks me backward to his bed, and I fall to my ass on the edge as he steps closer.

Both of us are naked, breathless, and desperate for relief.

"Lie back and open your legs for me. I want to see your pretty wet pussy."

"You kill me, Mr. Chase," I say with a smile as I lie back.

"Don't you like my mouth?" he asks with a raised brow.

I shake my head. "No, that's where you're wrong. I fucking *love* your mouth."

His face lights up, and he bends forward, licking my pussy in one long stroke.

"Ben," I choke out from the unexpected toe-curling feeling.

"And I fucking love your pussy."

I moan and arch my back. I'm pretty sure I've died and gone to heaven.

A tingle begins in my lower back, and I know I'm close. And so does he, because he stops. Before I can protest, he moves up to hover over me, his eyes boring into mine. Then he kisses me. I groan as I taste myself on him again.

"You will come on my cock; because I want to watch your face when you come."

Oh my God.

"Yes."

He leans over and grabs a condom from his drawer, and I watch him tear the packet and sheath himself before lining up and easing inside me. My body welcomes him, inch by inch, and the fact I have come again already doesn't make it easier.

"You're so tight," he grunts.

"Mm-hmm."

When he's all the way in, he pauses, and our gaze's lock. "Are you ready for me to fuck you?"

"Please."

He doesn't wait. Pulling out, he slams back in, filling me with him.

Oh, fuck, this guy is ruthless in the best fucking way.

With every thrust, I climb closer to another orgasm. The energy between us is unlike anything I've ever experienced.

"I'm close," I pant.

"Not yet. Hold it, baby."

"I don't know if I can." My legs shake with how hard I'm holding back.

He growls between thrusts. "You fucking will."

And then he lifts one of my legs with one hand to get a better angle and enters even deeper. I shudder.

I can't hold it.

"Come. Now," he growls, eyes locked on my face.

I moan loudly, and he joins me with his own loud groan. His cock jerks as he empties himself, slowing to a stop. I look up in awe at his post-orgasm face.

Leaning down, he kisses my lips, then my forehead, before pulling out and saying, "I'll be back."

I watch his bare ass disappear into the bathroom to dispose of the condom. Then he returns from the bathroom and slips beside me, his large frame cocooning mine in a surprising cuddle. This football player is ready to spoon after sex?

What is happening to my life?

This is going to end badly. It's too perfect.

But I'll just lie here for a minute before I need to get home.

"How are you feeling?" He kisses my hair and then snuggles his face into my neck. His warm breath tickles me, and I wiggle against him.

"Thoroughly fucked." I laugh, and he grips me tighter as a roar of laughter leaves his chest.

CHAPTER 19

NATASHA

I'M DRAPED ACROSS BEN, his warm, hard muscles underneath my cheek. The sheet has fallen down, exposing my naked back, and he runs his hand up and down over every curve and crevice. His warm hand feels incredible on my body, drawing lazy strokes over my back. My skin prickles with goosebumps.

He stirs, and I open my eyes as he wakes up slowly. Tilting my head up, he smiles down at me, until horror takes over. I sit right up, thrusting the covers off me, and scramble to grab my clothes off the floor.

He sits up with a frown, though, he looks also slightly amused. "What's going on?" he grumbles with his sexy morning voice.

"I need to go," I mumble frantically.

He watches me re-dress into last night's clothes and dash out of his room without another word. Getting out of his bed, he follows me out the door, realizing it's the morning. I feel a tightness in my chest, not liking the fact I didn't let my mom know I wasn't coming home.

"Is everything okay?" he asks, squeezing the back of his neck, wondering what he's missing.

"I need to get home," I say on a breath, briefly looking at him before I take the stairs down to his door.

"Why? Please stay."

I finish dressing haphazardly, grabbing the door handle. "I can't. I'm sorry, I don't have time to explain. I have to go. Thanks for a good time."

He stands butt-naked in his entryway, at a complete loss. I don't have time to explain right now. I need to go. I pause to take one last glimpse of his mouth-watering body before I leave with my stomach full of regret.

I wish I was ready to tell him about Mom. It's been years since someone stirred something inside me, yet he does it easily. He's so different from any other man I've dated. We couldn't just be a fling. He makes it so difficult to resist when he gives me the attention I've been craving for what seems like forever. Making me believe that he might be worth risking my job for.

I drive away with a million thoughts running through my mind. Arriving home, I park and jump out of the car, dashing inside. I'm surprised to find Mom sitting in her spot on the couch with a cup of tea in hand, perfectly happy.

"Natasha," Mom's voice cuts through the noise in my head.

I shake my head, clearing the fog of thoughts. I had stopped in the middle of the lounge room, trying to catch my breath.

"Sorry, Mom. I'm a little tired. I can't believe I didn't get home to put you to bed."

She walks with her stick from the couch to the table and I go about making us our morning tea.

"It's okay. Patty next door helped me."

To hear that she had to call the neighbor makes me disappointed in myself. I should've been here doing it.

"I'll bake her something and take it to her to say thanks. I'm so sorry—" I cease talking, knowing I don't have an excuse worked out. And I'm not about to tell her I was too busy fucking Ben in his bed and, oh, I fell asleep.

"Unnecessary. You had a late night at work. Patty and I had a great night chatting—it was nice."

When she says the word work, my stomach knots. I sure took *work* a little too far when it stopped being work, and I crossed over to be intimate with Ben.

I rub my eyes and finish making our tea. "I still should've been here."

She takes the cup and cradles it. "Look, you're tired. You need some time off. Patty said she would be happy to come hang out anytime. And maybe you could go on a couple of dates."

Is she serious?

I take a sip of tea and I say with a soft shake of the head, "No. I don't date."

Mom leans forward, capturing my hand, and her gaze burns into mine. It's the serious mom talk.

"You need to think about it soon, love. You know your body clock." Her gaze travels to my stomach before meeting my gaze.

I grimace. "Mom, you're making it sound as if I'm old. Thirty-one isn't old and I have plenty of time to have kids."

She squeezes my hand.

I hate that she feels guilty about the accident and now depending on someone to help her. But I don't mind. I love her for being there for me. Supporting me with school and giving the love of two parents. I didn't feel like I missed out because she made up for both. She's the best mother and father a woman could ask for, and I'll be forever grateful. I wish she knew how much I care for her and don't view her the way she views herself.

Like a burden to me.

I put my other hand on top of hers and smile, "Mom, I do live."

I avoid talking about my fear of being alone to raise a child or that the child is left feeling like they aren't good enough to stay for... aren't good enough to love.

"How? You won't even think about Patty looking after me for one weekend."

Done with this conversation and before I think, I say, "Fine! I'll go out on one silly date so you can have Patty care for you."

"A date with a man."

I laugh, "Yes, of course, a man. Who else?"

"It's just a question, love, no need to get defensive. What's really going on? This isn't like you."

I scratch the back of my neck, knowing talking about men, dates, children, and my past, leave me feeling vulnerable and weak. Two things I don't like feeling, let alone allowing anyone else to see.

"Nothing, Mom. Sorry. I'm just tired." I rub my eyes to avoid her questioning gaze.

It isn't a complete lie but definitely not the truth, but mom needs less stress. Tension will only cause more pain in her back.

"I'll call Patty today and you can go out this weekend. Any guys you can ask? How about anyone you work with?"

I pop my mouth open in shock. Trying to think quickly.

What do I say?

I decide on a lie for now until I get a second to collect my thoughts. I'm still coming down from the high of leaving Ben.

"I haven't thought about it, Mom. You just backed me into a corner by agreeing to a date. And don't you even think about weddings or babies after this one date. I'm doing this is to appease you. Not to discuss my aging ovaries." I smile, knowing she'll show me wedding dresses after the date. It's no secret she wants grandbabies and I'm her only hope of bringing it to a reality.

I peel my hand away, returning to drinking my tea and see my mom's shit-eating grin, and I can't help but giggle at her. "Settle down."

"What?" she questions, holding back a grin.

"You know what." I retort.

I sip my tea and think about how to ask him out on this... *date.*

CHAPTER 20

BENJAMIN

"COME ON!" I SCREAM at the TV. I'm hanging with my friends I've known since high school. It's been a couple of hours since Natasha left.

The team scores a touchdown, and we stand up excitedly. The whole bar crowd is cheering. Clapping their hands, shouting, and whistling; everyone's going crazy for the close game.

"How's work, James?" Joshua asks.

"Same shit, different day, flying here and there, signing more contracts, building new places. I wish it was more exciting. But it's not."

"What about your parents?" I ask James.

We didn't have the same upbringing, which I sometimes feel guilty over. When you have parents who love you, and your only issue is wanting to make them proud, it's vastly different to James's lack of caring he grew up with.

"Still a work in progress. I wish I had more to update you guys with, but you know they're in a different rehab. I'm hoping that this one works."

"How much is this one costing you?" I ask, knowing he would foot the bill, and private rehabs aren't exactly cheap.

"One hundred thousand each, so it should work, but that's what I said with the last one. And look how well that lasted."

I almost choke on air...*one hundred thousand for each parent. Fuckin' hell.*

I shake my head, at a loss for words.

But if I was him, I'd do the exact same thing. I love my parents and I'd give them anything I could to save them.

"But anyway, what can I do?" He shrugs.

"And how's what's her name?" Joshua clicks his finger until he remembers. "Abigail. How come I couldn't think of her name for a second?"

James's face lights up with humor and we wait for his answer.

"You must be getting old dickhead." He laughs at Joshua before continuing. "She's good...Real good. Her brother Rhys is due to fly in soon. So, she's super excited about that. I'm not so sure he is. I don't know how he's gonna do in a city. He seems a little stiff."

"What does that mean?" I ask, wondering why her brother won't be able to settle here.

James sighs and sips his drink before saying, "He's a police officer in a small town. He's very quiet and calculating. I don't know. I've only met him a few times, but I don't know what to think of him."

"You're so judgmental." Joshua slaps his shoulder and continues, "Be nice."

Before an argument breaks out, I interrupt. "And what are you up to Josh?"

"Well, I've finally broken my millionaire status and chasing James, so I'm planning a holiday with Ava."

I whistle. "Where to?"

"I'm thinking of the Caribbean or Bora Bora. Somewhere tropical and relaxing for me. I'm not working on this trip."

"No work?" I ask shocked,

"Yeah, I work too much. Ava tells me she needs more play-time." He winks.

I choke on a laugh.

Lucky bastard.

"She's always been a little wild," Joshua says.

"A little?" Thomas says, joining us at the table with a beer. Ava is Thomas's assistant, so he knows her very well.

"I worry about Jennifer when she's around," Thomas teases.

"You have nothing to worry about," Joshua says, annoyed.

"Jennifer is exactly like you Tom," I say and continue, "Quiet, smart, nurturing-"

"Your perfect person," James says.

Thomas smiles. He's the only dad of the group.

But if I had my way, I would be one too.

I haven't mentioned this to anyone, but I've always wanted kids...sooner rather than later.

I just want to grow up with them and not be the old dad.

But I've never found the right person to settle down with. They always wanted fame, the paparazzi, social growth, and that has nothing to do with wanting *me*. They want the things that come with me. But not me. But being with Natasha, though, I see she's different.

She makes me feel different.

"And how's everything going in your world?" Thomas asks me, pulling me from my thoughts.

"Yeah, all right. I'm still in the rehab program but looks like I should be back in a week or two.

"No way." Joshua claps. "Is there a game they think you might return in?"

I shake my head. "No exact date, just taking it week by week, but I say another two weeks and I should be back on schedule."

I ultimately want to start at a home game. So, I'll probably be scheduled for our next one.

"Well, you better get us tickets. We want to come," James says.

I smile from the support of my high school buddies.

"Of course. For you guys, anything," I answer honestly.

Their food arrives, and I sit with nothing while they eat their burgers and fries. This is a small sacrifice I don't mind making for my dream job.

All this talk about their partners makes me wish Natasha would let me in. I would do anything to have her. I just have to keep convincing her I'm worth letting her walls down for.

Her ears must've been burning because I get a text from her.

> *Natasha: Sorry for leaving in such a rush this morning. Thanks for a good night.*

Benjamin: It's all right. Maybe you can make it up to me by meeting up with me this afternoon for coffee?

I watch the bubbles bounce for a bit until, finally, I get a text back.

Natasha: Sure. What time and where?

I check my watch and then type back.

Benjamin: Say 2 at Bean Café?

————

Walking into the cafe where I told her to meet me, I step in and scan the shop. I pull down the brim of my hat to hide more of my face. It doesn't make me feel good. I want to be able to walk her in here with me, but I have to use my head and not my heart, knowing she has to make the right decision for her career. And being seen with me would only piss off John. She's still too new to be able to do that.

I'm grateful she agreed to have coffee with me. Not that I would have given her much choice, but it'll be nice to get to know her more, and she can finally get to know me. The real me.

The family man, the one who wants a future. The one paparazzi doesn't take photos of. The one she doesn't know about.

I spot her in the back corner, and I smile, just as I'm met by a waitress giving me fluttery eyes.

No, thank you.

I put on my fake smile.

"Hi," she says in a seductive tone.

But this little blonde doesn't do anything for me.

Not like the woman waiting for me in the back corner.

No...that one turns me into putty.

"I'm just meeting a friend," I say to the server, not wanting to slip up in case she gets interviewed by the paps later.

"Sure. Are they already here?"

"Yes, *she* is."

"Oh, oh, ah." Now she gets it.

"I can see she doesn't have menus. Can you please bring some over?"

"Yeah, sure."

I walk off in the direction of Natasha.

Her head is down, and she's looking at the menu. Fuck, well, we're about to get double of them.

"Hello. Fancy seeing you here." A stupid smirk forms on my face.

Her eyes flick up to mine, and there's a twinkle in them. A small grin forms on her lips.

It mirrors my happiness.

"Well, hello, nice to see you. How are you feeling?" Doctor Natasha is out, and I'm even more excited.

"Extremely good."

She pops a brow, not understanding. "Extremely good?"

"Yeah, I had a really good sleep last night." I wink and take the seat opposite her.

"Did you now?"

"But then you left..." I tease with a playful grin.

She bites the corner of her lip. And I see it in her eyes that she won't talk about it today. I don't want to push her for personal information; I want her to let me know when she's ready.

We stare into each other's eyes until the waitress comes over with menus, interrupting.

"Can I take your coffee order?" she asks, and her eyes flick to Natasha.

"Oh, yeah. I'll grab a latte. Thanks," Natasha says with a smile.

"Sure." But of course, the little blonde waitress is too concerned with me.

"And what would you like?" she purrs.

"I'll have a non-fat latte." My eyes return to Natasha, not giving the waitress any more attention.

"Sure. Did you need more time for your food?"

I feel her eyes on me. I'm not the only person sitting here, but she doesn't seem to care.

"Do you want something to eat, baby?" I ask.

I look up at her, and she's nodding with horror-filled eyes.

"Well, you go first. I can scan the menu while you order, and then I'll be ready when you're finished."

"I'll have a chocolate chip muffin."

"And for you, sir?"

"I'll have poached eggs, a piece of wheat toast, and turkey bacon."

I didn't eat with the guys. Avoiding deep fried fat foods.

The waitress repeats the order, then, "Okay, won't be long," before practically running away.

My eyes go back to Natasha, and I lay my hands across. I go to take hers, but she jerks them back to hide them under the table.

Crap.

"I didn't mean to do that. Sorry."

"It's fine. Accident," she whispers, tipping her head back.

"I'm so hungry. I had a busy night last night."

She giggles. "I thought you might have been full. You ate a lot."

My mouth drops open.

Dirty Natasha—I love it.

I rub my finger over my lips. "That dessert was the best I've ever eaten. I could feast on it for breakfast, lunch, and dinner, and never be sick of it."

Under my stare and words, her face turns pink, and she looks down for a moment as if to collect herself.

"You're so beautiful," I whisper so only she can hear, and she lifts her chin. Her eyes are glowing. If I thought she looked beautiful before, she looks even more stunning now.

I just wish I could capture her lips in a ravishing kiss. Not sit here, talking code, as if we're friends.

"You're cute when you blush."

She nibbles on her bottom lip, something I notice she does whenever she's nervous or shy. "Thanks. You're cute too."

"Another compliment. I should write this down or record you."

She rolls her eyes and chuckles. "Don't be so silly."

Our food arrives, and we eat. My eyes drift to watch the captivating woman tearing into her muffin. She lets a moan slip.

"Is it that good?" I ask, lifting my brow.

"Amazing. Here, try it," she says, grabbing a piece and holding it to my mouth. Chocolate chip muffin and her fingers an inch away from my lips. Fuck the diet. One piece won't kill me.

I open my mouth and let her feed me. My eyes stay on her face. When I feel her fingers touch inside my mouth, I bite down and run my tongue over her fingertips. Her eyes flash and she lets out a gasp. Then purposefully, I suck on her fingers before letting them fall from my mouth. She blinks and stares at me, utterly perplexed.

"Good?" she asks in a strangled voice, dropping her hand and shuffling in her chair.

"Delicious," I say, and I'm not just talking about the food.

We sit for a moment, staring at each other again. Then, clearing her throat, she breaks and looks back down at her muffin and resumes eating. I force myself to stop staring and eat my food before my stomach chews in on itself.

My phone buzzes in my jeans, and I pull it out to check it. Seeing it's an email about a coaching opportunity at a college in Seattle, I put it away. It's not urgent. I'll deal with that later. Right now, I want to soak in every second Natasha gives me when we're out of work. It's hard to deny the chemistry now we've fucked. If anything, it's heightened shit for me. I'm more sexually charged and right now, I'd love to take her home and bury myself deep inside of her again. But I can't, so I'll take this opportunity to learn as much as I can about her.

"Have you ever tried to have a relationship with your dad?"

She looks down at the table, pushing her muffin away, and brings her hands together. "When it first happened, I tried a few times, but then I gave up. He didn't want me in his life, and I didn't want to be in his either." She shrugs, but I know she'll be hiding her pain.

"I can't relate as my parents are still happily together, but I can only say it's wrong. How can a so-called man leave his wife and daughter? Never keep in contact or stay a part of their life. To then move on to a new family. No. That's not what a man does. I'm truly sorry he has made you feel less than, but you're better off without him."

She's silent for a beat and when her eyes meet mine, I notice how glassy they are.

"I kept thinking, how could he leave us? Why would he leave us? Am I not worth loving? Maybe I had done something wrong. The number of tears I used to shed for him until one day I woke up and realized he was the problem. Since that day, I made a decision that I would make something of myself, not rely on another person."

"To prevent being hurt."

Her lips part. "Exactly."

Time stretches between us. As I sit here, I don't want this to end. "Do you have anywhere to be now?"

She checks the time on her phone and her brows pinch together. I'm half expecting her to say yes, so I'm surprised when she asks, "What are you thinking?"

I lean over the table to bring my face close to hers. "Go for a walk?" I tilt my head to the exit.

"Are you sure that's a good idea?"

"I'll keep my head down, but we'll be fine."

She hesitates before nodding. We stand, and I pay the bill before we leave. I have to shove my hands in my pockets to keep myself from holding her hand.

We stroll side by side along the shops, avoiding the crowds of people. Occasionally, I move closer to her as people come toward us, keeping my head down or focused on her to avoid any fans spotting me.

"I can't remember the last time I went shopping," she whispers sadly.

Her face turns to the glass windows as we amble past a clothing store. A part of me isn't surprised. She's responsible with her time. I couldn't see her roaming the shops on the weekends, wasting money. She works hard. It's what I've come to like and really admire about her.

"Why? You don't like clothes?"

"Of course, I do. Clearly." She waves her arms over her floral dress and brown sandals.

I take in her white flowy dress, enjoying the way it cinches in at her waist.

I fucking love her body. I'd give anything to have my hands or my mouth on her again.

"I do too, but it would be way more fun without them," I tease.

"Of course. You're such a b—man." She slams her mouth shut. It's so fucking adorable, but I know what she was about to say.

"Nice save. But I still heard it. And for that, I'm thinking, I should punish you."

"Is that so?"

"Uh huh." My mouth tips up in a *you wait and see* smirk. I love playing these cat-and-mouse games. Bringing my head down to whisper in her ear, I breathe, "And what a man does to his woman in a dress like this."

Her whole body shivers. As we both slow our walk, peering in a department store window, a tight, short, figure-hugging red dress captures our attention. With her blonde hair, it would bring me to my knees.

Our hands brush, and I don't hold back. I interlace our fingers and drag her into the shop.

She squeals. "What are you doing?"

"Getting your sexy ass in here to try it on." My voice is all gravel as I picture her in the dress.

"Why? I can come back later. It's busy in here."

Fuck no. I step in front of her, our gazes locked, and I reach out to skim my finger along her jaw and down her neck as I speak. "Because I want to see it on you."

Her throat bobbles as she swallows. "Fine."

I smirk at the rasp in her voice, struggling with the sexual tension too. She squeezes my hand. "Let's go."

"Can I help you?" a shop assistant asks.

"I'd like to try on the red dress in the window." I'm grateful when she keeps her hand in mine.

"Can we get another couple to try on too?" I interrupt.

The shop assistant's eyes light up, but Natasha's expression is pinched with confusion.

I want to enjoy a show of her trying on dresses—for me. If she hasn't been shopping in a while, then I want her to have an experience to remember.

"Sure. Have a look around for a couple of minutes, and then I'll bring them all into the changing room."

I nod. The shop assistant leaves us, and I lead us around the store.

"What are you doing?" she whispers.

I turn my head and kiss her temple. "Letting you shop."

"You actually want to do this?" she asks with a frown.

I kiss her temple again. "Mmm...so fucking much."

"You're so weird."

"Only for you." I wink.

She gives me a shy look before turning and scrolling the racks. I follow behind until we've grabbed a few outfits and now we move our way to the changing rooms.

"I've set you up in here," the store assistant says, pointing to the open curtain.

I take a quick glance inside the fitting room and spot a chair in the corner. It's bright from the store lights, with mirrors all around. I stand to the side as Natasha enters. She pulls the curtain across, and the assistant is called away to serve more customers.

"Call me if she needs a hand."

"Will do."

Will fucking not. If Natasha needs a hand, I'll be helping.

"I'll wait here if you need me."

She nods before closing the curtain and leaving me picturing her removing her dress only a few feet away.

I stand to the side for what feels like forever.

What the fuck is she doing in there?

Checking the time, I see ten minutes have passed, and she hasn't said or shown me anything. I rub the back of my neck and ask, "What are you doing in there?"

I hear rustling and a sigh.

"Nothing looks good," she huffs.

Bullshit.

The annoyance mixed with sadness sets me off. I pull open the curtain and quietly slip inside.

My heart beats wildly.

It's like a spotlight shines on her. She stands there with a dress halfway up her body, sitting mid-thigh. Her round full ass is unable to fit inside the dress.

It's fucking hot.

I step forward, my shoes making noise on the floor.

She turns and shrieks.

"What are you doing?" she hushes and tries to cover her body with the dress. Which is a fail.

I chuckle.

"Natasha, I spent half a night between your legs and you want to hide yourself from me?" I shake my head and tsk. Moving closer, I stand face-to-face with her. "Don't hide from me. Ever. You got it?" My hand slides down her hips and over her ass, and I slap it.

"Keep trying on the dresses, and I'll tell you what doesn't look good."

She sucks in a sharp breath.

I sit down in the chair. Whereas she hasn't moved, she's still clutching the blue fabric to her chest. Or at least, trying to. I lean back and cross my leg.

"You're seriously going to sit there and watch?" she asks, flabbergasted.

"Yes," I deadpan.

She rubs her forehead and blinks.

I think she realizes fighting will lead to nowhere because she's quick to walk to the clothes that are hanging and shuffle out of the dress she's unable to get into. Adding it to the pile of clothes in the corner I hadn't noticed before.

Her curves are on full display in cute navy boy-short panties and a cotton gray bra. Her lack of impressing is what draws me closer. She's so fucking sexy, yet she doesn't even know it.

"The red," I grunt.

She peeks over her shoulder at me and my dick twitches. I lower my leg and widen my legs, accommodating for the growing erection. I can't see this ending well.

"This feels strange with you watching."

"Turn around and face me. You'll feel better if you were looking at me. You can see how much you turn me on."

Her lips part. "Are you serious?"

I squint. "Is that a challenge, Miss Blackwood?"

She shakes her head and lowers the dress to step into it. I watch her dance to get the dress over her hips and when it's on, I swallow a growl.

It's short and tight and the way it pushes her tits up and out, I don't see myself wanting her to wear this out.

No fucking way. This is only for me.

She's facing the mirror and grabbing the bottom, trying to pull it down to cover more of her luscious ass. But when she lowers it there, it pulls the top down, revealing more of her cleavage. So then she pulls the top up and huffs. Spinning to meet my gaze head on, her hands land on her hips. "Nothing fits."

I raise my brow. "It fits perfectly for me."

She frowns, running her hand over the fabric on her stomach. "Where? I feel like I'm falling out of the dress. And look..." She twists her body to show me her back. "My ass is nearly hanging out."

I can fucking see, and fuck, I'm not complaining. Not one fucking bit. In fact, I crook my finger and wave her over.

"Come here." I pat my lap.

CHAPTER 21

NATASHA

THE WAY HE'S DRINKING me in, I can't help but move closer to him. How could I not? The hungry look and the glimmer staring back at me tell me he doesn't see the flaws in my body under this harsh lighting.

No, instead, his desire is etched in his face and body, making my restraint snap.

Remembering the way he made me feel on the stairs, letting him take control, gave me the best orgasm of my life. So why wouldn't I say yes? *Because you're in a fucking change room in a shop.*

The tension swirling in the room right now doesn't make my feet pause until I'm right in front of him. Making my decision.

Letting the whore in me win again.

I stand in front of his knees, staring down into his lust-filled blue eyes. His chest is moving slowly while my breaths are short and shallow. I'm panting with raw need. My panties are soaked, and I want to beg him to touch me. To take the ache away from me.

Suddenly, he sits up in the chair. His hands touch my outer thighs in a gentle grip, then he skims his hands upward. My skin prickles with the roughness of his hands as he pushes the fabric high on my hips. When he's happy, he yanks my hips closer. With our eyes holding each other's, I step forward inch by inch as he leans back in the chair.

"Sit," he demands.

I straddle his thigh.

He shakes his head. "Sit on my cock."

I move up, so I can line up my pussy directly over him and lower down. My panties and his boxers and jeans are the only fabric stopping us from fucking right now.

Grabbing his shoulders for stability, he hisses when I grind over his erection. The friction sends a lightning bolt up my spine.

He grabs my neck and brings my lips to his, claiming my mouth. My hands slide up to grip the sides of his face and kiss him back harder. He deepens the kiss in response, with a swipe of his tongue.

He groans in my mouth, and it spurs me on. The kiss is frantic and bruising, and we can't get enough of each other.

My hips continue to grind down hard over his thick erection, the sensation making me wild. I want to feel him with nothing between us.

His hand touches my panties. "Soaked," he grunts, as his finger teases the edge of them.

I whimper into his mouth.

"Is this what you want?"

Do I?

"Yes." I nod frantically.

"Good, because this dripping pussy is mine."

Before I have time to think, he tugs at the sides of my panties, ripping them off. Pulling them free, he tucks them into his jean pocket.

"Should I be worried about you?"

"Yes. Because remember when you called me a boy?"

I gulp, knowing I'm getting my punishment now. Even though I was talking about him stealing my panties. He's talking about tearing me apart again.

I nod. "I didn't mean it."

"I need to show you what a man does, so that word *boy* doesn't even enter your mind."

His fingers touch my bare clit, and I buck.

He draws lazy hard circles, and my head lolls to the side in ecstasy. I flutter my eyes, trying to keep them open.

My hands on his shoulders grip tighter, trying to keep myself steady.

Without warning, he thrusts two fingers inside me.

And an involuntary loud moan leaves me.

"Shhh, or they'll hear you."

I pant heavily but swallow my moans as he continues. I'm focused on his fingers entering in and out of me in a delicious rhythm.

My legs tremble with pleasure as I feel my impending orgasm.

"Is everything okay in here?" the sales assistant sing-songs behind the curtain.

Oh God.

I squeeze my eyes shut, wishing this wasn't happening and that she would go away. I can't form words right now. I'm so close to coming. Something about her there and about to walk in on us adds to the thrill.

"Answer her," he growls in my ear.

His command has me snapping and finding my voice. "Yep," I squeak.

"Are you sure?" she calls out.

He draws in a frustrated breath.

"Yes," I say again in a high-pitched voice.

"All right." Then she thankfully walks away.

I let out a shaky breath.

After a beat, he speaks. "You liked that, didn't you?"

"What?" I ask, looking at him, puzzled.

"I felt the way your pussy milked my fingers. The sound of her about to catch us. You fucking liked that."

I feel the heat on my cheeks. I pinch my lips together as I nod shyly.

He hisses, "Fuck. Unbutton me. Now.

My fingers grab his button and undo it, scrambling to unzip him, and then frantically pulling him free.

"So fucking desperate for my cock, aren't you?"

I don't wait another second answering him with my actions, not words. I sit on him and fuck, the biting pain as his thick cock fills me.

"Fuckin' hell, babe. You're so damn tight," he mutters through gritted teeth.

His hands on my hips guide me up and down. The intensity growing in my lower back has me bucking harder to chase my release.

"I should stop you from coming just to punish you."

"No!" I gasp, horrified he's thinking of doing that. I think I'd cry. The heaviness in my pussy and the tingles in my lower back tell me I'm so close.

"But I'm fucking selfish, and I want to watch you come. After watching you wear the hottest fucking dress, I couldn't possibly not come."

I ride him hard and fast. My body is so hot and sweaty.

The feeling of my peak slams into me, and I crumble on him with a hushed whimper. His hands dig into my hips to keep me moving, and when I feel him jerk inside me, I sigh, lowering my head down to his shoulder and sucking in his masculine post-sex scent. Getting drunk off of him.

He rubs my back. "Are you okay?"

"I don't know. I'll tell you when I stand."

He chuckles.

I wiggle off his lap to stand, my pussy a tad sore. But in the best possible way.

I peel the dress off, and he takes it from me.

"I'm buying that in every fucking color."

He tucks his cock in and buttons himself back up. Then walks out holding the dress, leaving me there, speechless, in a bra and nothing else.

CHAPTER 22

NATASHA

The next day

"What's up, girl?"

I jump at the sound of Mia's voice. I clutch my chest and close my eyes and then reopen and turn to her.

"You scared the crap out of me, Mia," I say, taking slow deep breaths to slow my heart rate down.

She giggles and takes a seat inside the room.

"Are you on a break?" I ask.

"Yeah, I was coming to ask if you wanted to grab lunch together."

"Levi said he'll meet us."

"Just us three?" I'm wondering if Ben will come along too.

She leans back in the chair. "Yeahhh. Unless you want me to invite a friend. I'd be happy to ask him—"

"No, it's okay," I say before she finishes her sentence.

I'm nervous about asking him out today. I just need a moment to calm the butterflies.

"Jeez, you're awfully jumpy today."

I shake my head. "Sorry, I haven't been sleeping much."

Which is true. The ache between my legs is unbearable. It's like I unleashed my sex drive with his cock. Not that I'll be sharing this information with Mia or him. I'm glad he'll be happy to repeat our romp from the last two days. But that wasn't all I was running from...

The changing room...him eating me out at his house...he's all about my pleasure. He makes me feel desirable, sexy, and wanted. It's beyond any fairy-tale book my mom ever read to me as a child. I know he could push through my hard barriers because I was so close to letting go with him.

Letting him know about my mom. Maybe on the date, I can.

I need to get out of here. Away from the noise. Everything here reminds me of him. He makes it hard to concentrate.

"Same. Must be the weather."

I grab my purse and jacket. "Yeah. Let's go, I'm starving."

We walk out together. Of course, I don't get far, and I see Ben. If he isn't on my mind, he's right here in front of me. All I do is think about him, and I've got no place to hide while working here with him.

We pass *him* talking to another player. His gaze meets mine. I watch his Adam's apple bobble, and I tingle. The heat from one look between us is too much for me to think about right now. I dart my gaze to the door and don't stop until I hit the fresh air and gasp. Welcoming the fresh cool air in my lungs and body, there's no need for the jacket now. I'm burning up.

"Ben wants you baddd," Mia says behind me.

And it seems I want him too.

I squeeze my eyes shut, trying to block her out for a minute while I recover from my body's reaction to him.

"What do you mean?" I ask, unsure if she saw our exchange and not wanting to seem transparent.

"As soon as we walked out of the office, he watched you, totally ignoring his conversation. He has wanted you since you started here. I'm pretty sure the whole team knows." She giggles, but I don't find it funny.

The whole team knows.

"I hope that means John doesn't know."

She shakes her head. "No, I didn't mean him."

My shoulders sag with relief. "Good. I like him, and I need to ask him out this weekend."

She claps excitedly and I narrow my eyes at her embarrassing reaction. "Calm down." But her face looks like I said the opposite.

Why in the world does this woman insist on not listening?

"Don't hold back on the deets. Give me it all. Where are you going?" she questions.

"I don't know. I blurted it out when Mom was accusing me of not having a life."

She pops a brow and is about to talk before I cut her off. "Don't you start. I have a great life."

She pulls a face. "If you say so. I've been telling you to go out with him since day one."

I smile at her words. "Oh, I know. You've made it loud and clear."

I see Levi sitting in her car, so I grab her arm and she stops and turns, a frown on her face.

"Don't say anything to Levi. I need to ask Ben first, and I'm freaking out—seeing the way you're reacting."

The bottom of my stomach twists in guilt.

"No, go! Please. It's a wonderful opportunity to get to know him outside of here."

My pulse increases as we jump in Mia's car. I've seen one side of him outside of work and that's what I'm afraid of.

Stepping into my office after lunch, I look around, smiling. There's a gift in the middle of my desk. I know it's from him.

I expected him to be around somewhere.

But he's not.

And I'm disappointed.

Moving closer, I touch the chocolate chip muffin. The same one I had at Bean Café with him.

It's such a sweet gift, and I feel stupidly giddy.

I need to ask him out. I'm running out of time. But I can't bring myself to do it. The anxiety of putting myself out there scares me. I know he won't say no. So why am I hiding out in my office with a swarm of butterflies in my stomach at the thought?

A knock on my door has me looking up from my fixation on the muffin.

"So, you like my gift?"

"I do," I say, lowering the muffin back to the desk.

I know the heat from my chest is rising onto my cheeks. The intense way he's staring at me makes my breath catch. There's this shift between us, and I can't help but be absorbed in.

"Good."

No words seem to form in my brain. I lean forward to hold myself up, using my desk as support.

He hunches forward, mirroring me. The only thing between us is my desk.

"You're trouble," I say, smirking.

He chuckles and there is a gleam in his eye. "Me? No." His eyes drop to my mouth.

I'm struggling to keep my words in. I want to beg him to kiss me.

A voice in my head is telling me to stop this right now.

You're at work.

But of course, he makes me ignore it by leaning across and crushing his lips to the soft sensitive flesh on my neck. It's just under my ear. The flick of his wet tongue as he laps at my skin and then he sucks hard makes soft whimper escape me, and I shudder from the incredible gentle touch.

It's torture, wanting more, but knowing I can't right now.

"Trouble with a capital T," I rasp.

A low chuckle leaves his chest. "And the way your body is responding right now, I'd say you fucking love it."

"Oh God." I shake my head.

He pulls away and holds up his hands, wearing a sly grin. "I'm sorry for interrupting you."

I'm not.

My chest rapidly rises and falls with the quick breaths I'm taking. If it wasn't for the way he's pupils are a shade darker and dilated, I'd not have known he was affected.

"You're not, but—"

"Ben, do you need help with something?" John's voice calls from behind Ben. I jerk back a step and sit down in my chair to put distance between us.

John's eyes narrow, and he looks at me and then at Ben's back.

Ben winks at me before spinning to face John. "No, I don't need help. Natasha helped me."

I pinch my lips together, knowing I didn't help him at all.

Ben retreats out the door. I move my gaze to focus on John.

"You two seem close. There's nothing going on between you, is there?" he asks, crossing his arms over his chest.

I swallow hard. And lie through my teeth. "No. Nothing at all." And my stomach drops at saying that. Because the truth always has a way of coming out. And will it be worse that I've lied?

Probably...

But admitting my feelings for Ben when we haven't spent enough time together doesn't seem right. I don't want John to put a stop to it before it's really begun.

"I'm watching you," he says and walks out without another word.

It's time to stop dragging my feet and approach him. After finishing my work for the day, I walk out, looking for Ben. I hope I'm not too late because the gym looks quiet. I head out to the field, but he isn't out there practicing either.

Just when I'm about to give up, I walk back past the locker room to see him changing. I swallow the lump that's stuck in my throat.

His naked broad back is begging me to trail my fingernails down over his warm skin. There's a droplet running down the middle of his back and my gaze watches it. I lick my lips, my mouth suddenly dry. But I'm firmly planted on the spot, unable to move closer.

You've seen him naked before. Why are you flustered?

I shake my head and step towards him. The sound of my heartbeat is in my ears, and I'm feverish from the stupid fantasy.

His head turns, and I suck in a breath.

As his crystal blue eyes lock with mine, I recover and clear my throat. I rake my gaze slowly down over his chest and stomach as he stands in only a towel. Averting my gaze back to the safety of his eyes, I pray he doesn't decide to dress now.

His brow raises, and I realize I haven't said a word.

I clasp my hands together in front of me and I say, "Um, so, I..."

When his mouth curves into a smug grin, I internally roll my eyes. I know he caught me checking him out, and what did he expect? I find him only wearing a towel. I'm only human and I have eyes.

"Natasha."

The sound of my name on his tongue is sensual, and I need to get out of here before I start moaning again, or worse...begging for him to take me.

"Hi, Ben. So, I need your help."

His brows rise in surprise, and his arms fold over his chest with a cheeky grin. "How can I help you?"

I blow out a shaky breath. "Well, I want to go out on Saturday night, and I was thinking—"

"Are you asking me out, Doctor Blackwood?"

Yes.

No.

Dammit.

Give in.

You want to.

"Yes," I say shyly.

His whole face lights up, and I can't help but giggle at his reaction. I roll my eyes. "Calm down."

"Can't help it. You're gonna see how perfect we could be."

"Don't get ahead of yourself. I did see you asking me out, not the other way around. But I need to appease my mother."

"Your mom?" He asks, a deep frown set in between his brows.

"Yes."

"I guess I should thank your mom—"

I shake my head. "No."

He chuckles, the sound echoing in the room. And the tension around us is back. He leans in close to me and speaks into my ear where he was earlier. This time, his lips brush my ears as he says, "Mark my words, baby, you'll be with me by the end of the night. You belong to me. Actually, no, we belong together. We are two magnets who always find each other...equally."

I shiver from his words.

Why is he making it so hard to fight *us* here at work?

His lips graze my jaw and my eyes close from the unexpected sensation. The soft feel of his lips sends a tingle to my core, lighting it with a pool of desire.

I finally speak, even though he's peppering kisses that are driving me crazy. "We can't. I need to go. I can't be caught at work. John is watching us."

He pulls back and the cool air hits the areas his warm lips were, and another shiver runs down my spine. "What time will I pick you up? And send me your address now, so I know you won't do a runner."

My gaze locks with his, and I smile. "How do you know I'll run?"

He smirks. "I know, because you always run. But I know you're worth fighting for...worth chasing. I will always follow you. Wherever you go, I'll find you."

The beat of my heart doesn't feel like my own, it's running on its own beat.

"Should I be worried?" I ask jokingly.

"Maybe." He pokes my nose, and I stick out my tongue.

We laugh together, and then he asks, "So, do I get to plan the date?"

Shit. I hadn't even thought about it.

"Uh—"

He chuckles again. "I'll take that as a yes."

I shrug. "I guess, if you want."

"Yes. I want to. I'll pick you up at five."

I have to help Mom and then get ready.

"That's a tad early. How about seven?"

"Too late. I want as much time with you as you'll give me."

I roll my lips to stop myself from beaming. "Fine, let's meet in the middle and say six."

"Deal. But send me your address now." His smirk causes my smile to break wider on my face.

He's so light and easy to be around; he makes me feel young and free again.

I pull out my phone and quickly type my address and hit send, muttering teasingly, "I'm going to regret this, aren't I?"

"Falling in love with me...Never, baby."

CHAPTER 23

BENJAMIN

I PULL UP TO the address she gave me. Not wanting to scare her away, I've avoided messaging her, worried she'll bail.

I walk the couple of steps to her door, noticing how much better my knee is. I'm getting stronger every day, working out longer and harder.

My nerves are front and center as I press the doorbell, but I'm more excited now I'm finally here.

The door opens, and my breath catches. I run my gaze down over her, starting with her long wavy blond hair, her pink stained lips, and down over the black top and tight blue jeans and boots. I smirk. Just how I remember her at my house—perfect.

"You look beautiful."

She drops her chin and runs her hand over her jeans. "Will this be okay for where you're taking me?"

Her shyness is adorable. The normally confident and controlled Natasha is now replaced with a shy sweetness that I could easily get used to.

I nod, and she meets my gaze, her teeth catching her bottom lip, and my smiles widens.

"You look perfect."

"Okay, I just need to grab my jacket and bag."

She turns, and I step inside the house, following her down the hall across the tiles. Until we reach a kitchen. The television is on, and I move closer and see a woman who looks similar to Natasha, but older, and I can clearly identify her as Natasha's mom.

"Hi, Ms. Blackwood, I'm Benjamin Chase. It's nice to meet you."

I move closer, noting a walker and stick near the couch. I lean forward to shake her hand, and she does the same with a large smile that reaches her eyes. At least her mom looks happy to see me.

"Hi, Benjamin."

I step back and straighten. "Sorry, you can call me Ben."

"Okay, well, Ben, I'm Teresa. Please take care of my daughter, but also have fun and stay out late," she says with a wink.

I chuckle, getting the hint she's insinuating. I love her already.

"I promise to look after her and give her a great time."

I hear her shoes click on the tiles before her sweet voice speaks. "I'll be the judge of that. Now where's Patty? I'm not leaving until she gets here," Natasha says as she walks to stand behind me.

Her mom rolls her eyes and mimes, "Bossy."

I slam my lips together to prevent a roar of laughter. Her mom is a fucking hoot.

I'll feel sad to leave. I kind of want to sit on the couch with her and Natasha. It's probably something Natasha would love, but I also want alone time with her.

"Yoo-hoo! I'm here."

The front door slams closed.

This must be Patty.

Natasha moves past me, and I get a whiff of her strong scent. The coconut smell is something that I now crave. I'm aching to touch her, so I cross my arms and wait as Natasha kisses her mom and says bye. I wave and smile at Teresa. She winks at me, and when I turn, I greet Patty, but then Natasha is quickly ushering me out the door.

Once we step outside, she pauses mid-step, pointing at my black Bugatti parked in the drive. "This is yours?"

I frown, not understanding. "Yeah. What's wrong with it?"

She shakes her head and walks again. "I didn't predict this car."

"What did you expect?"

She shrugs. "A Porsche or a Ferrari. Like the other guys. Just not that."

"You don't like it?" I ask, my frown deepening.

"No. I actually like this a lot. It's nice," she says, still staring happily at it.

A smug grin opens on my face. She keeps surprising me and looks like I keep doing the same.

"It's roomy inside, if that's what you're worried about."

She turns when she reaches the passenger side, and I walk up to her, standing so close, and I reach out to the handle before she can grab it. She stills and backs herself against the door. I hear the hitch in her breath, and it turns me on.

If I didn't want to push her and come off too strong, I would kiss her right now. But I want to take her out and show her she means more to me than just this sexual attraction we share.

I tug the handle and it seems to shake her, her gaze hardening at me. "That definitely didn't cross my mind."

Now I know I'm sure she has thought about our time together. I know I have.

I whisper, "That's a shame, baby. I've missed you."

I run my gaze over her and watch as her chest rises and falls rapidly before I step back, and she slides into the car. I almost laugh at the urgency, clearly needing the space.

Tonight is going to be fun.

I close the door once she's tucked in. I walk around and jump into the driver's seat.

"Where are we going?" she asks.

I turn on the ignition and look at her with a smirk.

"It's a surprise, baby."

"Can you stop with the baby."

"No."

"No?" she retorts.

"No, sweetheart."

She huffs and sits back in her seat, eyes in front of her and her arms crossed.

Man, I love to piss her off. It's such a fun game now.

The drive to the location is quiet.

Half an hour later, I park, and she edges forward, peering in the windows to look around. I know she won't be able to guess where I'll be taking her.

I get out and quickly walk around and open the door, holding my hand out, and I half expect her not to take it and fight me like she always does. But to my surprise, her soft hand hits mine and my fingers curl around hers. She climbs out of my car, and I hold her hand. She looks down at our unison and then back at my gaze, and I raise my brow as a challenge.

I'm not letting you go.

We walk to the Italian restaurant I had booked earlier, making sure to get a private area. I don't want any pictures tonight with fans or the media. Opening the door, we step inside, and the delicious aromas hit me. Sucking in a deep breath through my nose, I enjoy the smell of garlic, tomatoes, baking bread, oil, and cheese.

"I'm allergic to gluten," she deadpans.

My back tenses.

Fuck.

"I didn't even think to ask you about allergies. I'm so sorry."

She laughs and tugs on our hands, shaking her head. "No, I'm kidding. I'm not allergic to anything, but you should've seen your face. It was priceless."

My jaw drops and my mouth forms an O before I laugh. "You had me." I lean in to peck her cheek, whispering, "Cheeky," before pulling back and walking to our seats.

If this is the tone of the evening, I can't wait to see how the rest of the night plays out.

I'll be sure to win some brownie points with her mom.

The soft lights hitting the tan chairs give the room a warm glow. It's one of the most romantic places Chicago offers. The waiter stops at one of the white tables that look out the windows and onto the river.

The waiter pauses at one of the tables, and once we sit, he hands us each a menu and leaves. I'm relieved to have made it to the table without being approached. If this wasn't a date, I wouldn't mind, but tonight is important to me.

To us.

"I've heard the best things about their cheesy crust," she says, opening her menu.

I smile, peering up at her over my menu. "Same. I think I'll get the three-cheese pizza."

One corner of her lip tugs up and she closes her menu and lowers it to the table. "Exactly what I was thinking."

"Great minds think alike." I wink, closing my menu too.

She giggles.

"Did you want to order a large to share?"

Her brows pinch together. "I thought you guys were always hungry. And don't you have to be careful about what you eat?"

"Yes, that's why I thought we could share. But I also want room for dessert."

Her face flushes, and she drops her gaze to the table, grabbing her water and taking a sip.

I didn't mean it to come out dirty, but now I wonder where her mind is drifting. And if dirty is something she wants, then I'd be happy to give it to her.

Before I have a chance to tease her, the waiter is back, so we order.

After I hand over the menus, I sit back in my chair and ask her, "So no allergies..."

I rub my chin, trying to think of anything else I want to ask her.

"Oh, that reminds me, I really have to call and check to see if she had her medication—" She pinches her lips together. Obviously, she wasn't supposed to say that.

"You help your mom on your own, then?" I ask gently.

She looks down at the table, unable to meet my gaze, as if embarrassed. I lean forward and wait, giving her the space to open up when she's ready.

She lifts her head slowly, and her eyes meet mine. The sadness staring back at me kills me. The way she cares for her mom only makes me admire her more. Not only is she beautiful on the outside, but it matches on the inside too.

"Yeah, since my dad left when I was a teenager, it's been really tough on her and me."

"What happened?" I ask softly, hoping she won't close up on me like she usually does.

She sighs, peering down at the table and then back at me before answering. "It wasn't always this tough. She worked as a waitress, but had an accident, and ever since she hasn't been able to work."

I sat there as if I could sense all her pain and sadness, as if I was experiencing it. But I know I have only scratched the surface. There's more to her pain than I see in her eyes.

"Do you have any brothers and sisters?" I ask.

She shakes her head. "No. I wish. I'm an only child."

"So, you're alone?"

"Very," she answers, and it's quiet for a second.

She picks up her glass of water again to drink, and I do the same. The food arrives, and she grabs a slice of pizza.

"Enough drilling me with questions. Your turn." She takes a big bite of her pizza. And I love how she doesn't care about counting calories or not eating carbs.

I smile, grabbing a slice for myself. "Fair enough. Hit me." I bite into the pizza, enjoying the cheesy goodness hitting my tongue.

"What about your parents? What do they do?" she asks between bites.

"My dad, as you know, is an ex-football player. He's now the offensive co-ordinator. He doesn't really have to work. He was smart with his money. But both him and mom love having a purpose."

I feel like the bite of pizza I just took is stuck; this is my worry—what will I do after this year? What's my purpose? Could a coaching job give me that?

Thankfully, she asks me another question, pulling me away from my worries for a second.

"What does she do?"

"She's a pharmacist."

She nods and takes another bite and so do I.

"And do you have any siblings?"

"Yeah, I've got a younger sister. She's pretty cool."

"Oh, I didn't know you had a sister. Should I be worried?"

I lift my brows in shock, and I wiggle my brows. "Why are you planning to meet her?"

I haven't brought a woman home in a very long time. Not since my high school girlfriend. Meeting my parents is a big deal and the next girlfriend planned to bring home to them is my future wife.

She shakes her head and laughs. "I was just asking."

I chuckle at her reply.

Maybe she'll meet them one day soon?

"It's fine. I would love you to meet them. They would love you. And I think you'd love them. My sister's sweet and such a good kid. Super smart too. Probably a little too good. But I could see you being very similar to her."

"She sounds really smart." Her face radiates with pride. "Except I seem to have lost my way recently."

I tilt my head, not understanding, waiting for her to indulge me and explain.

"I met you," she says through a laugh.

This has me laughing with her. "Am I corrupting you?"

"Yes, I said I'm only focusing on my job. And definitely not dating anyone. And here I am, having dinner with you against my better judgment."

"Do you regret that?" I ask, holding my breath, waiting for her answer.

She shakes her head, and our gazes lock. "Not for one second."

And I let out the breath I was holding, a broad smile taking over my face with relief.

"Are you ready to get out of here?" I ask her after we've finished eating our meal.

She inclines her blonde head. "Yes."

When I see her grabbing her purse, I grit my teeth. Reaching my hand out, I stop her. "No," I say sternly, my hand on her arm.

Her big blue eyes met mine with a curious look. "I asked you out on this, so I pay." Nervously, she moistens her lips, and I continue, "You know I've wanted you from the first day I met you. It's my honor to pay for this meal. I was raised well, and a gentleman always pays."

She opens her mouth, but I finish before she can argue with me. "I know you're independent and things have changed, but please. It would hurt me if you even paid half."

She bites her lip, trying to stifle a grin. "Fine, we can't have your heart broken, can we?"

A low, throaty laugh leaves me from her words. She can be as playful as a girl or as composed as an intelligent woman. "No. It's currently beating with joy."

She meets my smile with her own infectious one. Both of us stand to leave. I offer my hand and she takes it. Her fingers are warm and smooth as they touch mine.

We leave the restaurant hand in hand, and I really can't take this stupid grin off my face. I've never been happier in my life than I am right now. Even more than when I became the quarterback.

"Gelato?" I ask, not ready to end the night without dessert.

Her mouth curves into an unconscious smile. "Sure." Outside, the way her skin glows under the moonlight sends a familiar shiver of awareness through me.

The touch of her head when I kissed her passionately the first time. Or the vision of her soft, smooth skin when I bent her over my stairs and in the dressing room. It makes me desperate to do it again.

We grab gelato cones, both of us choosing vanilla, and walk around the pier, eating them. The fact we share so many similarities is confirming that I knew she was perfect for me.

My person.

I spot the Centennial Wheel, where I'm taking her next, and I gesture for her to take a seat on the park bench. I sit close and she tries to take her hand away, but I resist.

"I need to swap hands. It's dripping on my fingers."

"Fine, let me." And before I can stop myself, I grab her hand and lick up the droplets. The mix of vanilla and her salty skin is the perfect combination of sweet and salty. A growl rumbles from the back of my throat as I lick her fingers clean. When I finish, I straighten back up and stare at her from under my heavy lids. Her gaze burns darker than before and her pretty mouth gapes wide open. After a beat, she clears her throat and looks out across to the pier.

I stare at her profile a moment longer before sitting back. We finish our gelatos quietly, but it doesn't stop the sound of my heart from beating loudly in my ears.

When she finishes, I stand in front of her, holding my hands out for her to take. She accepts the offer with a questioning look.

"Don't ask, just trust," I say.

Rising to her feet, she leans lightly into my body, tilting her face toward mine. I stare at her mouth, noticing her lipstick has worn off. Now her natural pink lips are begging to be kissed. I groan. She's so fucking irresistible. We're both inching closer to each other. Our lips are so close to touching that I can hear the way her breath hitches.

She whimpers when I pull away, causing my dick to twitch. But this isn't about him. Tonight's all about her. I turn to take us to the wheel.

"I have always wanted to go on the wheel," she murmurs, staring up at it in awe.

"Me too. I'm glad to be taking you to all these things for the first time."

She's smiling wider now and the excitement that we're about to go on it is heavily displayed on her face. Adding to my excitement.

Arriving at the entry, we're guided into our own gondola where we take a seat. I sit close to her, so our bodies are touching. I'm not gonna lie. I'm a little fucking nervous about going to the top, but I don't want to sound like a pussy. So, I don't say it out loud. Instead, I wrap my arm around her and snuggle her in close for support. When she doesn't pull away and sinks into the cuddle, I relax.

The speakers come on and soft music plays as the wheel moves. I hold my breath as we go up. Her hands hit my chest and I finally release the breath.

"Are you okay?" I ask as I peer down at her.

"Yes," she breathes, staring out of the glass at the view. But to me, no view can be as breathtaking as her.

The whole evening has been perfect. I knew it would be with her, but I want more. I'm greedy as fuck. And I take what I want.

Her head turns to face me as I peel myself away. The lights around us reflect in her eyes, making them gleam. I reach out and trace my thumb over her cheek and lift her chin, then I lean in and claim her lips with my own. I swallow her whimper as my tongue enters her mouth. Sweeping my tongue along hers, our lips and tongues move with a perfect rhythm.

Running my hand up her smooth neck, I pause when I feel her pulse under my palm. I gently squeeze her neck, and it sends it beating wildly.

She likes that.

A lot.

And fuck.

So do I.

Moving my hand to her face, holding her in my hands and kissing her with every part of me, her moans spur me on as we kiss. My teeth nip her bottom lip and her sexy sounds let me take charge. She melts into me, pleading with her body to keep going, so when we pull apart, I'm breathless and she releases a whine. I'm surprised when she leans in and brings her lips to mine again.

When she pulls back, we're both gasping for air. I watch her eyes flutter open, and I love how glassy they are. My own heavy desire reflected in them. I'm glad I'm not the only one feeling this...*us*.

CHAPTER 24

NATASHA

IT FEELS LIKE A dream. The one where a real prince exists. The whole evening is going by way too fast, and I know it's coming closer to the end of our date. But in a deep part of my heart, it feels real. I've never had a normal childhood, so to have him give me a date that feels so carefree is more special than he could've ever realized.

The kiss we shared on the wheel was better than the view of the water or the city lights. He leaves me breathless and searching for more.

I have my head laying in the crook of his neck, and we're almost at the bottom of the ride, only I don't want to get off.

I could stay like this forever.

His pine scent fills my nose, and it brings such a calmness I didn't know I needed.

The halt of the gondola wakes me from my lost thoughts. I lift my head up and away from him, stretching out. We wait in silence as the door opens and we are let off. As we walk along the path by the riverside, we hold hands, making our way back to the car. He's closest to the river to keep me safe. Him being cute and protective makes it hard not to fall for him.

Our stroll is lit up by the stars and the moon, making it even more romantic. And the cool night air and music coming from the restaurants we pass make this night more memorable. There's no awkward silence, just peace.

"Thanks for tonight. It was really nice. I had a great time."

He squeezes my hand. "Mmmm, me too. And it was my pleasure." He kisses the side of my head, then we both jolt at the sound of fireworks. We pause and turn ourselves to watch the show, in awe at the surprise to end our night. He chuckles and leans into my ear. "I didn't plan this, I swear."

I say with a grin. "Sure, you didn't."

He moves behind me and wraps his big arms around my middle. I tense for a moment before my body sags against his, the back of my head dropping to his chest as the fireworks continue into the sky.

I can't lie. To have him hold me for a few more minutes is something I'll treasure. It's not every day I let a man hold me...support me.

As we watch the show, he whispers in my ear. "This has been the perfect date. I could only ask for one more thing."

I frown, wondering what he wants. "And what's that?"

"Will you be mine?"

My heart skips a beat, but I don't hesitate. "Yes," I say and turn in his arms, linking my arms behind his neck and standing on my tiptoes, crushing my lips to his.

His soft lips part, and I don't hesitate, sweeping my tongue inside his mouth to taste him. He's still sweet from the vanilla gelato. He groans. And that same yearning need takes over my body. My fingers skim through his hair to the back of his head and bring him closer. Our bodies press flush against each other. My lust for him drives the kiss harder and longer. His chest rumbles with approval, and he swallows my moans.

When the show's over, we pull our lips apart, still holding each other close. We stay like this for a moment before we know it's our time to go.

As if reading my thoughts, he sighs loudly. "I guess I better take you home now."

I'm glad he can't see my face yet. I'm sure the sadness I feel inside is written in every feature.

"Yeah," I whisper sadly.

I peel myself away from him, and we walk back to the car holding hands. It's quickly becoming one of my favorite things. His large, calloused hand tangles with my small one like the perfect puzzle pieces connecting.

"I wish I didn't have to drive you home right now."

I roll my lips, staying silent. Because what do I say...

No?

Take me back to yours?

No, that's not my life.

I have responsibilities to get home to, even if the temptation is strong. I can't run away and be selfish for the night.

Mom's expecting me home. I can't let what happened last time happen again, leaving her alone when I was supposed to be there for her.

I stare out the window as he drives me back, and when he turns the ignition off outside my house, the car fills with tension.

Will he kiss me again?

The anticipation is killing me. My leg bounces up and down. I wonder if I should just jump out, but it's as if he knows. His hand snakes across my thigh, causing it to quiver under his touch. He squeezes as he asks, "Are you okay?"

Too scared to look into his dark blues filled with lust and promises, I whisper, "Yes."

His hand creeps higher, and I breathe through the temptation to close my legs and stop the ache in my sex. The memories of his mouth on me earlier and his hand on my neck hit me at full force.

His breath tickles my face. And an "oh" slips from my mouth while my heart races from the unexpected closeness.

When did he lean in closer?

I shiver in response to his warm breath and soft sounds.

It sets me off, and I have to kiss him. It's a need.

I turn my head and capture his lips once more, moaning as our mouths melt together. He kisses me back with a longing that I feel all the way in my toes. It's an all-consuming, passionate kiss, one I wish I could have every day of my life. I move my hands to his hair to tug him closer, and he groans against me, making me want to get closer. The car is harder than standing under the stars.

I squeeze my eyes tighter, knowing I need to stop soon, otherwise I'll be risking my mom and Patty watching me dry hump, or worse, fuck him, naked, right here in his car. And thankfully, I still have some brain cells left that prevent that from happening. I put a hand on his chest, feeling the fast beats against my palm, and push him back, separating our mouths.

I gasp, trying to catch my breath. And when I open my eyes, his blues are now staring back at me with adoration. I pinch my lips together, suddenly feeling overwhelmed. I need space.

"Thanks again for tonight. To say it has been amazing wouldn't do it justice, but it's all the words I can form right now." I feel heat rising from my chest, and I scratch the base of my throat before I turn and begin opening the car door.

"No, let me," he says in a rush.

I pause as he exits the car and walks around to open my door, helping me out.

I dip my head with a small smile. "Thanks."

We walk to the door in silence. I stop and turn when we arrive, pecking his lips and pulling back with a shy smile.

He runs his hand down the side of my face, grinning. "Night, baby."

"Goodnight."

Once I'm in the safety of my house, I lay my head against the door and let out a deep breath.

"Is that you, darling?" Mom's voice calls.

"Yeah, it's me." I squeeze my eyes closed briefly, needing a minute to collect myself.

When I'm calm, I push off and walk into the kitchen, dumping my purse and joining them in the lounge, ready for the interrogation.

"Where's Ben? I expected him to come in. It's still early," Mom says, wearing a frown and moving her head to look around me. As if I could hide an over six-foot quarterback behind me.

Patty is sitting beside her, nodding her head.

I try to hold back a smile, but I struggle, and it slips out. "I was gone for hours. I went on the date I promised." I walk over and take a seat on the couch.

"I didn't expect such a handsome man, but I guess from your work, I don't know why I didn't expect a hunk?" Mom adds.

I laugh. "Who says hunk now?"

"We do," they say in unison.

"But other than him being a hunk of a man, tell us more," Mom presses, rubbing her hands together.

Seeing her face lit up makes me happy. But I don't want to share too much. I love her, but some things are for friends' ears only.

"There isn't too much to say. I had a good time." I shrug, trying to act unaffected, even though inside I'm still jelly from the most romantic date I've ever been on.

"Will you see him again?" Mom asks, sitting up more on the couch.

"Of course. At work," I reply with a smirk.

She shakes her head but laughs. "No. Outside of work, like another date?"

"Yeah, I know that's what you meant. I was just playing with you. Yeah, I will."

She looks at Patty, both beaming.

"You two would make some pretty babies," Patty adds.

I groan, shaking my head vehemently. "Not a chance."

These women and my ovaries need to stop. It won't be happening any time soon.

"That's my cue to go get ready for bed. I'll help you when I'm done that, Mom."

"No, we haven't finished our movie yet. I'll stay and help your mom," Patty replies.

Getting up from the couch, I look at Mom and say, "Wake me up, and I'll do it. Don't let Patty do it."

"Yes, Doctor," Mom says with a wink.

I kiss her cheek and say goodnight to Patty. As I get to my room, my phone's flashing.

It's Ben.

My heart rate picks up as I quickly open the message.

Benjamin: Thank you for taking me on this date. It's my turn to take you out next time. ;)

Natasha: You organized the whole night so I'm pretty sure it was a joint date. I had a great time too.

Benjamin: When are you free for another one?

Natasha: Someone's eager.

Benjamin: And desperate...

I giggle at his message. But then I sit down on the edge of my bed, staring at his message with a sigh.

I don't know what to reply. Despite having a great time, I need to give myself time to think. When am I free? I can't expect Patty to help every weekend.

I take my time to shower, dress, and blow dry my hair. Then I wander out to check on Mom before coming back and texting him the truth.

Natasha: Sorry, but this weekend I'm busy with Mom.

Benjamin: Fair enough. I'll never interfere with your mom. I know she's number one, even if I'd like to be in that spot secretly.

Natasha: Not a secret when you tell me, silly.

Benjamin: True. So, the weekend after that?

Natasha: You're pushy, you know that.

Benjamin: Is that a yes? You agree to another date?

Natasha: I'll think about it. I could ask Patty if she can help me next weekend.

Benjamin: I promise to plan a better date than the last.

Natasha: Not sure that's possible.

Benjamin: Wanna bet?

Natasha: No, I'm not a betting person.

Benjamin: Because you'll lose? You know I love to compete and win. :P

Natasha: OH, I know! Anyway, I'm going to sleep.

Benjamin: Wish I was with you. I'm lonely here. It's not the same without you in my arms. I know you remember...

I laugh to myself, but then sigh once more. Yes, I do, and it was nice. So nice, I fell asleep, forgetting my responsibilities.

> *Natasha: I do. So much it was nice. But it's hard with Mom. Anyway, I should go to bed now...*

> *Benjamin: I understand. If you need help, I'm here and I'm not going anywhere. I'll see you tomorrow, baby. Night.*

My chest swells.

He won't give up on me.

"I need you to go work with Ben and not on paperwork," John says, standing over me the next day. It causes me to stop writing. I stiffen and twist to face him, anger seeping into my veins. For a second, I was worried he found out about my date with Ben.

"I'm writing in my plan. I like to track the progress of each player," I tell him in the best controlled voice I can muster.

"Don't be smart with me, Doctor Blackwood. Just go set up the gym. Ben should be here in fifteen minutes."

He walks off before I can answer. I watch his back leave the office and go fuck knows where, but I'm glad it's away from me. I have no idea how much more I can take of that jerk.

Ignoring him, I finish my plans and decide on the exercises I can get Ben to do today that'll test his readiness for the upcoming game he's scheduled for.

I finish and carry the papers out, seeing Mia talking to Levi.

I walk over to join them. "Mia, be careful. Your father is around. You don't want him finding out, do you?"

She shrugs, and there's a new brightness in her eyes. It almost looks like determination.

I frown, totally confused.

"I don't care anymore. It won't change how I feel." She twists back to face Levi, who's sitting down, grinning like a lovesick puppy as he looks up at her. If they don't calm down, I'm going to need a trash can to vomit in.

"What's changed?" I ask, trying to understand.

Levi meets my gaze and answers instead. "Since the injury, I realized work isn't everything. It can all be taken away at any moment. I want to be happy, and Mia here makes me so fucking happy."

I stand still, unmoving, in a state of shock. Surely, he isn't serious?

I scratch my temple with my pen. "B-but you're not giving up on coming back?" I stumble over my words at their confession.

He can't give up his dream.

For what?

Her?

That seems crazy.

He shrugs. "I don't know. I'll see what the next couple of months brings."

A football player professing his love. I'm going to need to get my ears checked. Everywhere I'm turning, they keep pushing me to think about love and it causes a tightness to form inside my chest. I feel like I'm struggling to breathe again.

"Are you okay, Tash? You're awfully pale?" Mia asks, frowning.

I rub my chest and nod, even though I don't feel okay.

The date, and now them...

It's all too much.

"Yeah, sorry, I need a drink of water."

I move to get my water, and I chug as much as I can, until I feel myself relax again.

"Here you are."

I jump at the sound of Ben's voice, and the water pours over my chin and down my chest.

Great.

"Shit, Tash. I didn't mean to scare you. You're just late, and I came to see if you're okay," Ben says in a rush.

I turn to face him, finding him in navy shorts and a white top. His eyes drop down to my stiff, peaked nipples. Thanks to the cold water I just spilled down my top. He bites down on his bottom lip hungrily, and I wish I could feel his lips on mine again. The only thing I'm holding on to right now is the reminder I'm at work. Even though the only thing I want to hold on to is him.

He comes over and wipes my chest with the gym towel he had slung over his shoulder.

I clear my throat and speak with a raspy voice. "I can do it." I'm surprised I didn't let a moan slip out.

Quickly grabbing the towel, our fingers brush, and I shiver. He quirks a brow at me, smirking. I know my voice is betraying me and giving him the ultimate win...knowledge that I want him right now. But I ignore it.

I shake my head and finish dusting the water off, then hand back his towel. "Let's get in the gym. I have a plan for you."

"Well, don't let me stop you. I'm ready for you to be on top—of my plan."

His double meaning is obvious and the sexual tension screaming through me is going to make this hour session torturous.

CHAPTER 25

BENJAMIN

I ENJOY THE VIEW of Natasha's ass as I follow her. I wish I could give in to the temptation.

Arriving in the gym, I sit down at the bench she's pointing to. And I *try* to behave....

Watching her move to explain each exercise I'll be doing is a turn on. I can't help but be mesmerized by her. She's devoted to her job, and I should be listening, but I'm too enthralled by her pouty lips to hear a word she's saying. Her mouth is taunting me with memories. I want to kiss her hard and make her forget where she is because she feels so right in my arms—

"Are you listening?" she asks with a frown.

I blink and shake my head. "Sorry."

"Are you okay?"

The concern lacing her voice causes me to confess. "I'm more than fine. To be honest, when you're around, I get lost looking at you. I'm totally distracted."

Her mouth opens and closes a few times before she murmurs, "Oh."

I laugh and give her a shrug.

She wanted to know.

She clears her throat, scratching the base of it, and I expect her to say more, but she doesn't. "Let's start with our usual warm-up and then get into the session."

"Whatever you say, Doc."

She smiles at that, and I focus on getting myself back into gear by following our usual warm-up stretching exercises.

I kick back my leg, and she stands close, causing a vibration of energy to rush through me with her hand on my hamstring and the other on my shoulder. The stretch loosens my body, but I enjoy her hands on me more. I fight with myself to keep my thoughts on the reps and not the sensation of her soft, delicate hands on my body.

Every rep, every exercise, is like a bolt of heat meant to send me to hell.

This session is hard in more ways than one. By the time we're finished, I'm exhausted and ready to relax at home.

During the cool down, when there's distance between us, and I'm not thinking with my dick, I can't help but ask her, "Are you free for dinner tonight?"

I want to spend more time with her, where we can be free and not worry about work or family responsibilities.

She looks around the gym to make sure we're still alone. "No, I can't. I have Mom, remember..."

"You don't want to think about getting help?" I ask, because surely, she has options.

She shakes her head. "No way. She's my mom, and I'm a doctor. It's my job."

My brows furrow at her words. "Doesn't mean you can't have help."

"You sound like Mia," she grumbles.

"I don't think that's a compliment. But if she's saying this too, then I'm agreeing with her."

"I don't want to be rude, but—"

"You're gonna," I cut her off with amusement.

She ignores me to finish. "It's how I feel, and I don't really care what you or Mia say."

I smile easily. "You're rude, but it's kinda hot. You're my stubborn sexy blonde, and that seems to be my weakness."

"So, I'm not as attractive when I'm nice?" she teases, crossing her arms over her chest.

I tip my chin up and tap my finger on my jaw, then look back at her, grinning. "Nah, I like the edge. It makes me hard."

She rolls her eyes and playfully pushes me. "I'll make sure to only be nice, then."

I step closer so there isn't much distance between us, and her chest rises with a big intake of breath, urging me on.

I love how her body responds so easily to me.

"Nothing you can do will turn me off," I say huskily, our breaths now racing in unison.

I run my finger down her temple, skimming her cheek, dusting it across her jaw and down her throat, gently pausing on that now racing pulse, before moving to the middle of her chest.

Stopping at her heart, I feel the frantic beat underneath the pads of my fingers.

"This in here is mine. It beats for me."

Her wide-set eyes are killing me. I want her mouth on mine to confirm the attraction, but I can't, so I peck her cheek and I breathe into her ear, "Thanks for a killer session, baby."

I watch her mouth drop wide open, and I turn and walk out, leaving her standing there in a state of fluster.

"How're things going with Tash?" Levi asks, as we're about to enter the local children's hospital to volunteer.

We are visiting fans who are sick. I love to do this because it keeps me grounded. There's nothing better than putting a smile on a kid's face. You'd be surprised how a handshake can lift their spirits. This is an honor. It's a small thing to us but a huge deal to them.

As we walk inside the creamy-walled hospital, I explain. "I took her on a date the other night. She seemed to have a good time."

"So, you're not going to give up?" he deadpans.

I shake my head. "I can't."

It's not the first time Levi has said this, or should I say warned me, but I simply can't. The soul crushing feeling just thinking of not having her is too much to bear.

"But maybe you have to." His tone is harsher than I've ever heard before.

"Underneath that hard exterior is this sweet, soft woman who loves her mother unconditionally, and if she can give up her life for her family, that woman is worth walking across fire for."

"Yeah, I can see that side being attractive. Are you sayin' that's it? No other women?"

"Nope. No one else has ever held my interest. I get bored quickly, but with—"

He cuts me off to finish the sentence and I hear the amusement in his voice. "Her it's different."

Exactly. No one will compare. She's the start and end of my universe.

"We've been getting to know each other outside of work and it's working. We are exclusive. She keeps opening up to me, little by little."

"If you think she's worth it, then I totally support you."

It doesn't feel like work when I'm with her, it's easy.

"She is."

We arrive at the ward, so the conversation ends.

The in-charge nurse takes us around to the first room where a little boy lies in his bed. He looks so small. It never gets any easier doing this. It's hard to see a young boy with a drip in his arm and the color of his face almost matching the bedsheets. I wish I could fix him.

Levi and I stand beside his bed, talking to him and his parents. Laughing and answering all of his questions. Before we leave his room, we jump in and get some photos, then sign some old sneakers that we hand him. And fuck, the way his little eyes water as we gave it to him fucking killed me.

———

I leave the ward with a heavy heart but a smile on my face. The mix of sadness and happiness wiping me out today.

It's late afternoon and Mia picked up Levi to take him to dinner. I walk outside, back to where I parked my car in the lot, and pause.

It's her.

I squint to double take, but that sloped nose, those pouty lips, and blonde wavy hair are unmistakable.

It's Natasha.

I move faster and confirm it's her with her mom, so I call out, "Natasha." Jogging up to them, I take in her luscious curves in her white singlet and blue jeans. Her hourglass frame is so much nicer out of uniform. I'll never get sick of it.

Her body flinches, and she looks up, meeting my gaze. I smile from ear to ear.

"Hi, Ms. Blackwood. Sorry, I mean Teresa," I say to her mom with a smile. She gives me a wide one back.

At least someone is happy to see me. Poor Natasha looks like she's seen a ghost and may need a hospital bed herself.

"Natasha, where's your manners?"

Her mom's voice seems to shake her, and she says, "Sorry. Hi, Ben. What are you doing here?'

"Darling, don't be so rude."

But I know she wasn't being rude. She's just shocked to see me.

"No, it's fine. I was visiting the children's ward. We volunteer here regularly. Mia picked up Levi, but he was with me. I was just heading to my car when I spotted you."

Her mom's face lights up and she lays a hand on her chest, the other holding her stick. "What a lovely thing to do."

I wave it off. "It's not a big deal, really. I love to see their faces when we come into their rooms and talk to them."

I peer over at Natasha, whose gaze is glassy, but she looks away, blinking repeatedly.

I point at the building where they came from. "Are you on your way somewhere?"

"No, we just finished. I had an appointment at the pain clinic and now we're on our way home. But speaking of dinner, you should totally join us. We're going to grab some tacos. Please come over and eat with us." Her eyes are bright, and she almost looks giddy.

"Mom, I'm sure he's busy tonight," Natasha says, probably feeling like her mom is being pushy.

"I'm not. So, that would be great. How about I pick the food up and meet you back at your house? That way, you guys can get settled at home after your appointment."

"That's a great idea, and so thoughtful." Her mom smiles up at Natasha, who rolls her eyes.

I bite back a chuckle.

"Natasha, can you please text me your orders, and I'll meet you at your house?"

She turns to face me, but no words come out of her mouth. The shock melts from her face, and she finds her voice. "You can't be expected to pay for ours. There's only one of you."

"No. Please. Let me do this," I say softly.

Let me help you.

She exhales heavily. "Okay."

The way she's staring back at me with admiration and awe. Fuck, it makes me want to help her more. Those doe eyes are every man's wet dream.

CHAPTER 26

NATASHA

THE DOORBELL RINGS, AND Mom and I peer at each other. I push up without a word and walk to the door, my pulse in my throat and my knees going weak at the thought of him in my space again with my mom. It's so personal to me and allowing him into it is strange. I'm trying not to overthink what he will think this means. It's not like I have had deep conversations about my feelings about him with my mom, but he doesn't know that.

I suck in a deep breath, filling up my lungs with fresh air before I open the door and his masculine scent hits me in the face.

He stands there in his casual look of a black hoodie and blue jeans, holding out two bags of food.

"Hi," he says with a panty-dropping grin, and my nerves pick up.

"Hi, uh...is that all for us?" I ask, pointing at the numerous bags.

He lifts them in the air. "Yeah, I picked up a few extra things. I do like to eat."

I shiver at his words.

Oh, how I know.

His face is playful, and I know he can read where my mind just went.

Dammit.

Play it cool, woman.

I clear my throat and smile. "Come in and let's eat."

I feel the heat on my back and sense him following close.

We reach the table, and he lowers the two bags in the middle. Mom comes over to join us.

"Hi, Teresa."

"Hey, Ben, it's nice to see you again."

They share a laugh, and I watch him kiss her check. I'm kind of jealous I didn't get one too. I know that's stupid, but I can't shake it.

The way Mom looks at him, it's like he's a damn prince. I can't blame her, though. He's definitely charming.

I stand in awe, my gaze flicking between the two.

Mom takes her seat at the table, and it gets my brain working again. "What would you like to drink?"

"Water is good," he says, as he unpacks the food from the bags onto the table.

"Same," Mom says.

I grab bottles of water for us three and sit.

He notices the spare plate across from me and sits down. I really didn't think this through. I should have sat him next to me, but at least from here I can look at him during dinner.

I can't help but laugh as I take in all the food on the table. "I can't believe you brought this much food."

"I'm a guest. It's the least I can do. God, I love your laugh."

I pause and look up at him shyly. Our gazes lock, and I feel my heart skipping a beat.

"Me too, Ben. However, she doesn't laugh much anymore," Mom states with a sigh.

"Hey, I'm right here. And I do laugh." I narrow my gaze at Mom.

She smirks, but of course, challenges me. "No, darling, not as much as most people your age."

"Wow, this is a depressing dinner," I mumble, wishing the ground would swallow me up.

This time Ben laughs, and I feel his calloused fingers graze the top of my hand. I glance up, meeting his tender gaze. The lightness in them has me taking deep breaths to calm me down.

He doesn't remove his touch as he speaks. "It's a perfect dinner. Thanks for letting me come."

I don't move my hand from under his. I'm stuck; it's like his touch helps ground me.

But his words sadden me. Why does he feel like he has to thank me for allowing him here?

I want him to know I want him here. I hold his eyes and say, "I'm glad you came."

Mom's clapping reminds me we have an audience, and I wince, squeezing my eyes closed and wishing we were alone.

Oh, is Mom going to give it to me for this.

I pull back my hand and grab the container of chicken tacos, refusing to make eye contact again.

"How's recovery coming along, Ben?" Mom asks.

That has me peering up under my lashes at him, waiting for him to answer as I eat.

"Really good, thanks to your daughter. She has helped me so much."

I swallow the food I was chewing to say, "It's my job."

"One you're very good at," he adds with a wink.

The food feels like it's wedged in my throat, so I grab a drink of water to wash it down.

"I agree," Mom says.

"You haven't seen me work." I scrunch my nose up and return to eating my taco.

"You're my daughter. I know you're smart."

I shake my head, but I can't help but smile.

"What will you do after you retire?" My mom asks between bites of her food.

He reclines back in his chair. "Truthfully, I hadn't thought about it until this injury. Now I've decided that I'd like to become a coach. I enjoy talking to kids, and mixed with my passion for football, I think I'd be good at it."

I nod. He would make an amazing coach. And seeing his face light up as he speaks about it humbles me.

"What type of coaching?" Mom asks, taking the words right out of my mouth.

His head turns, giving me his sexy profile. I wish I could rub my hands through his scruff and up into his blond hair.

"High school or college. I think I could make a real difference there with troubled kids."

I feel my body warm, his soft side melting me in my chair. "I think you could really make a difference."

He turns to me, and the current between us is palpable. I roll my lips and look away from the intensity.

"You're a special one, Ben," Mom says.

That, I agree with.

After we eat, Mom goes to her spot on the couch, and he helps me clean up the kitchen.

"You don't have to do this," I say.

"I want to."

We move around each other, me avoiding bumping into him and him trying to get closer. It's a funny dance.

"Every time I see you outside of work, it attracts me more."

"Ben," I warn, checking over my shoulder to make sure Mom can't hear.

I load the dishwasher, and when I stand back up, he is towering over me. "Oh."

He leans his face closer, his lips hovering over mine, causing my lips to tremble with anticipation. His arms snake around each hip to grab the counter to lock me in. I take a step back, but my lower back hits the counter's edge.

Nowhere to go.

Shit.

He has me pinned.

My body heats at his dominating presence.

"Darling, can you make me tea, please?" Mom calls out.

"Yep!" I yelp, then squeeze my eyes. I sounded like a strangled cat.

He chuckles and moves to my neck. "I love how you respond to me. I want to take you home and rip these clothes off your body, leaving you naked and dripping wet. Then I'd spread your pretty legs and sink myself deep inside of your cunt."

I feel my eyes bulging and my sex aching with need. "Ben..." I breathe.

He kisses and nibbles over my neck, up to my ear, lifting a hand to trace a finger over my collarbone and down between my breasts. I'm trembling under his touch.

"You'd try not to scream my name. I'd be fucking you so hard you'd come apart, leaving your come all over my cock."

"You're so—"

"What?" he cuts me off, and chuckles against my flushed skin.

"Dirty. Filthy. Wrong."

"And you fucking love it." He steps away, smirking.

I do.

Fucker.

I sag, clutching the counter behind me so I don't slip to the floor as I collect myself.

When I can use my legs again, I bring Mom her tea.

We all sit down and watch TV together, flicking stations, until we opt for a movie. I'm spent from the night of up and down emotions running through me, so I'm utterly exhausted. The overwhelming calm feeling his presence gives me causes me to drift off...the next minute, I wake to darkness.

Shit. Mom. I need to put her to bed.

I hear voices coming from her room. I push up and follow them in a hurry. They get louder with every step I take, and the hair on my neck rises as I see them.

"What the fuck are you doing?" I say in disbelief.

Mom gasps. "Natasha, mind your language."

Ben turns around and stiffens from my tone. His hand on her back stops moving from the sound of me, the smell of medicated gel filling the room.

He pulls his hand back to walk toward me. I'm vibrating with anger.

Why didn't he wake me?

"I'm sorry. She wanted to go to bed, and I knew she needed help, so I offered." He says it softly, obviously aware of the fact that I'm not happy about this.

But I don't care, because he overstepped. Even if I opened up to him, it doesn't give him a right to do this.

It's *my* job.

"I'm over here, I can hear you," Mom calls out, breaking through the fog that's filled with confusion, and anger.

"He should have woken me," I spit out.

"I'm sorry, you just looked tired. When I saw you curled up fast asleep on the couch, I wanted to help—"

"And I told him to not wake you," Mom cuts him off, and her tone sounds like she's pissed at me.

What for?

I rub my face with my hands, not knowing what to do. He feels too close now, and all this is just too much.

I need time to digest this information.

"I need you to go," I say, just wanting space to think without him around.

"If you want. I'll just wash my hands, and I'll leave."

I simply nod without saying anything.

He walks past, while I keep myself tight and unmoving. When he's in the bathroom, I finally move, walking over to Mom. Her face is taut.

"Don't," I say, my voice laced with confusion.

"What? I didn't say anything."

"I know you're wanting to say something. It's written on your face."

The corner of her lips rise, confirming my suspicions.

"See. Well, hold your tongue until he's gone," I whisper.

I hear his footsteps down the hall, so I turn around and walk back to the entry without looking at him.

"Thanks, Ms.—Teresa. Goodnight." He sounds sad, but I can't think about that right now. I look up at him, now ready to open the door.

"Night, Ben, and thanks for helping me."

His gaze flicks to mine, but I don't soften. I walk to the door, pulling it open, and he steps out. I pull the door closed behind us.

"I'm sorry if I overstepped," he says quietly.

"It's my mother. My responsibility is to help her. I don't need you pushing into my life and taking over."

He winces, and I am hit with a pang of guilt.

"That's not what I was trying to do. I only wanted to help. You know it's okay for you to get help with her." With his hands stuffed in his pockets, he stares at me with pleading eyes.

But his words make my back stiffen. I hold out a hand. "Just stop. I don't need you telling me what I should be doing."

He doesn't say another word, even though his mouth opens and closes again.

"I need to get back in and get Mom into bed."

"Okay, I'll go. Just know I'm very sorry."

I dip my chin, but don't say anything else, my mind on overdrive. I watch him walk to his car, hopping in and offering me a wave. I don't wave back. I just stare as he drives away.

When I can no longer see his black car, I suck in the cold night air, then head back inside, returning to Mom's room.

"You are way too hard on him."

"He shouldn't have done that. It's weird," I reply, trying to hide my shaken state.

"No, it's a bit of gel on my back, getting my pills from the containers, and then he would've returned to the couch to you."

"It's my job. Not his."

"Is this what this is over?" She narrows her eyes at me, as if trying to read something on my face.

"No. I don't know...I guess I'm not used to help."

I feel lighter, sharing what's eating me up inside. But I'm still overwhelmed.

"I'm not your job, darling. Maybe we should look at hiring a caretaker for different hours."

Her words are like a stab to the heart.

I shake my head vehemently. "No. Sorry, I didn't mean it like that. I'm happy doing it."

I feel sick at the thought of her hiring outside help for when I'm supposed to be the one doing the job, as if I'm not able to.

"I know, but you don't have a life here with me. And you're pushing Ben away because of your father, aren't you?"

I stare blankly at her.

Am I?

CHAPTER 27

BENJAMIN

WHAT A FUCKING MISTAKE. I draw in a frustrated breath and rub the back of my neck.

Her venomous look is still taunting me, even here in the safety of my car.

Fuck, I was only trying to help her.

I pull in my drive and realize I don't want to go inside, because there's no one waiting for me. I'll be alone with my thoughts, and I know I'll replay the night repeatedly in my head.

No, I need to talk this out.

I call my friend James, knowing he will give me good advice, even if he throws shade my way.

"Benny boy, how you are doing, man?"

I snort. "Could be better, if I'm honest. You free to chat?"

"Want to swing by my office and talk it out? Everyone is out and Abby isn't home until late tonight. She has a project to finish for design school."

"Yeah, sounds good. I'll be there soon."

Twenty minutes later, I park and arrive at James's office. The gnawing ache in my chest has increased with more time that's passed.

I check my phone for the millionth time, wishing I'd see a text from her. But once again, despair fills me.

She hasn't reached out.

I take the elevator up, watching the lights of the numbers until they reach the top. When the doors open, I step out and notice his door has been left wide open for me. I'm about to be vulnerable to James, which I hate, but I need to talk it all out. I need the mess of jumbled thoughts out of me before our next game, and the only way to do that is speak it out and get advice.

I step inside and see James working on his computer until he spots me. When he does, he finishes typing and then stands to walk toward me.

I meet him halfway and pat his back in a man hug. "Still hard at work?"

He returns to his chair, and I pull out the chair opposite him.

"Yeah. With Abby coming home late, I may as well take the opportunity to work. Going home alone sucks." He sighs.

Don't I know it.

"Yeah, it does," I mumble.

"Is it Blondie?" he asks curiously.

I look away from his quizzical gaze and I shuffle in my seat, trying to get comfortable. "Yeah."

"What's happened now?" he asks.

"That's half the problem. I'm not totally sure."

I sit up and lean my elbows on my thighs and continue to explain what's running through my head. "When we're together, she's just—present. Things are so good."

He frowns. "So let me get this straight. She wants you, but doesn't want to commit?"

"No, I don't think commitment is her issue. Because tonight it was about me helping her mom."

James leans back in his chair, his brows rise as he asks, "What happened?" Getting up, he walks to his drink trolley. "Do you want a drink?"

"No," I say as I watch him grab a glass, then pick up the bottle of whiskey and pour a two finger thickness of the liquid and walk over carrying it back to his desk.

"Long story short, I'm over for dinner, and afterward we watch a movie with her mom. Natasha falls asleep on the couch. Her mom needs help going to bed, since she had an accident at work and there are issues with her back. She even goes to a pain clinic."

"Must be serious."

"Yeah, but anyway, the mom struggles to get up from the couch, like it was hard to watch, truthfully. She has a frame and stick, but even with her frame, she struggled to walk. She shuffled. So, I asked if she wanted me to wake Natasha and she said no."

"Hmm," James muses.

"I watched her walk, and she was seriously struggling, so I got up and she told me not to wake Natasha because she needs to sleep and that I could help her. So, I helped her get into her bed and she asked if I could rub some medication on her back."

"That's fucking weird," he says with a concerned expression. "Your girlfriend's mom wants you to rub cream on her back. That's so fucking weird, man. Is she into you?"

"Hell fucking no." I rub my forehead. "God, that sounds bad. It wasn't like that, though. It was just to help Natasha. Fuck."

He holds his hands up in surrender. "I'm just asking."

"Anyway, I'm rubbing the cream—"

James claps and yells, "And Natasha fucking walks in."

I nod, and he bends over, laughing.

I shake my head and my anger rises. "This isn't funny, moron."

"As if you wouldn't be killing yourself laughing if this was me?" he says, raising a brow at me.

I shrug. He got me there. "Yeah, true, but it sucks. So Natasha was pissed and told me to leave."

"Well, fuck. I would never guess you were coming here tonight and saying that. That was—"

"A lot." I finish his sentence, knowing exactly how crazy it sounds.

I need to move. I'm suddenly feeling twitchy, so I pace his office, running my hands through my hair. "But now I have, and I need to fix this. Help me." I pause and glance at him.

James leans farther across his desk, clasping his hands together and his glare turns hard. "Take a break and focus on you. Fuck, focus on winning the Super Bowl. She sounds like she's not ready for a relationship. What's that saying, if you love someone, set them free? Well, do that, because you can't keep chasing a dead end."

"I kind of thought that maybe we need a breather. And I should stop chasing her. But I don't want to, because deep down, I know she's worth it."

"Yeah, man, but it looks desperate from where I'm sitting. And that's not fair to either of you. You're both supposed to want to be in it. And at the moment, all I see is you wanting her."

"Thanks," I scoff, my ego getting kicked. I can't blame him. I wanted the kick up the ass, and I'm getting it.

"You know I'm only being honest."

I nod. "I know. It's why I came to you."

"Then listen. Come hang out with the guys, focus on you, and distract yourself."

I wish it was that easy, but I don't have much of a choice.

"Are you ready to train?" Dad asks.

I turn away from my locker and peer over my shoulder at him. I just did my exercises in the gym, and I was about to head home.

I can barely sleep with my mind wandering to Natasha. Some part of me wanted to get up and message her. But I promised myself I wouldn't.

"Sure. Give me a sec."

Dad nods and leaves the room to meet me on the grass.

I walk out with my bag slung over my shoulder, planning to head home as soon as I tap out with Dad. I see him tossing the ball to himself, so I whistle as I get closer.

He turns and smiles, tossing the ball to me. "How are you feeling?" he asks.

Like death...

But that's how I feel in my heart. My body for the game, well, that's a different story.

"Better. So ready for the game," I say proudly.

My dad's face beams under the sunset. "That's good, son. We need you out there. The team needs you and Levi. The experience is missing."

Hearing that is like music to my ears. I'm needed. I love to help with the younger players coming through...some willing to learn, and others thinking they know better. Either way, I'm happy to teach anyone who's eager for the information.

I know I shouldn't, but I push myself a little tonight. I want to show Dad how ready for the next game I really am. But of course, he notices...

"Benjamin, I think you're pushing too hard." His voice is stern, and my body halts at the command.

"I feel good," I argue, wanting to feel exhaustion instead of heartache.

He shakes his head. "I get that, but I don't want you pushing before the game. You're better off taking it easy and resting."

"I have. We—" My phone rings, breaking the conversation.

I see Joshua's name flashing, my other friend from high school.

I look up at Dad and explain, "It's Josh. I'm going to grab it and head home. I'll see you tomorrow."

He nods, but I don't wait for an answer. I hit accept on the call and speak, "Josh, how's it going?"

"I'm good, just sitting in the office finishing up an email. Thought I'd check in and see if you're free to hit Thomas's house for the basketball game?"

I walk back to my bag and scoop it up and walk to my car.

I look at the ground in front of me weighing up my options. I really can't be seeing anyone right now. I'm in such a shitty mood, and I can't drink, so I'm best to get home and get the rest Dad ordered. He's always right.

"Nah. I've got my game this week, and I need to rest. Can we take a raincheck, and I'll come next week?"

"Pfft, we're watching your game this week. No way we're missing out on your first game back."

I smile at his response. I really needed that support. I didn't know how much until he said that.

"Thanks, man. That means a lot." I sigh.

"You, okay? You sound...off."

I choke out a laugh. It's not funny, it's just how well he knows me.

Do I tell Joshua what's happened or not?

Deciding I don't want to unload the whole story, I keep it brief.

"Woman troubles."

He laughs in my ear. "Ah, I get it. I've been there. Especially if she's special. I'm going to assume she is."

I swallow the lump that's formed from the next words that leave me.

"She was," I say quietly, arriving at my car and throwing my bag inside and taking a seat inside my car.

No rush to get home and be alone.

"Was? What does that mean?" he asks.

"She's pissed at me...I'm feeling rejected. Fuck, I sound like a pussy." I try to laugh it off, not wanting to sound as sad as I really feel.

"It's all good, you don't. Maybe a kitten, but it's hard when you love someone, and it isn't reciprocated."

My stomach knots from the realization that Joshua is referring to his parents, and I feel guilty for whining about Natasha.

"Sorry, man. I shouldn't be like this. You had serious shit with your parents, and I'm sulking because a girl doesn't like me back," I say, squeezing the phone.

"I'm over that, and hey, you need to talk it out. It's better to talk to your friends about it than to hold it in. We can help. Bottling that shit it up isn't good for you...or your upcoming game."

"Yeah, I think this is it," I confess.

It's been weighing me down, holding on to the knowledge I won't be playing past this year.

"What is it?" Joshua's tone picks up with worry.

"My last year playing."

"Means you'll have to get a real job. You can always come work for me," he teases, and it causes me to chuckle.

"No fucking chance. I've got a coaching job offer."

I couldn't work for any of my friends. Their jobs are their passions, but I don't have any desire to work in an office in real estate or electrical.

"Just know I'll always make room for you if you need it."

"Thanks. I better get home. I'm sitting in my car like an idiot, talking about my life. I swear I'm turning into a bitch."

He laughs. "Women do that to you. But get going and I'll catch you at your game. And hey."

"Yeah?"

"Call me anytime, about anything, okay? I got your back."

CHAPTER 28

NATASHA

"DOCTOR BLACKWOOD," JOHN BARKS behind me. The tension in me has me pausing. I look up into the eyes of Andrew, assessing his readiness for the upcoming game.

I plaster a fake smile. "Sorry, let me see what he needs. Do five more on this side and then repeat on the other. I'll be right back."

I straighten, trying to rein in how pissed off he's made me.

Why bark like that?

The look on Andrew's face made me flinch. He felt sorry for me. I don't want anyone feeling like that for me.

I'm not weak.

I walk into the office. John's sprawled out in his office chair, tapping his pen on the desk. I wish I could reach over and snap it.

I smirk, imagining it. Yes, now that would be fun.

"Is something funny?"

I wipe the smirk off my face and answer. "No. I'm seeing if everything is okay, or can I get back to my job?"

I know I probably shouldn't speak to him like this, but he maddens the heck out of me. And I've been running on fumes with no sleep, so my tolerance is low.

"I'm making sure you know Ben requires a full assessment. I moved him last so you can spend as long as required."

Great.

My mouth drops open, and I stare blankly at John.

"Is something wrong?" He looks down his nose at me.

I shake my head, realizing I'm probably giving away how much the word *Ben* affects me.

I haven't reached out to Ben, and he hasn't either. I want to, but I'm scared to admit to him how much his help frightens me. I've never been able to depend on a man before. Therefore, for him to cross that line without asking me, had me pushing him back.

"No, that makes sense."

"Then I'll meet you here for a meeting at the end to talk about each player. I need to write a report of the findings. The selection of players can be chosen accordingly."

"I'm happy to tell the coaches directly, then it saves me repeating it."

"No. You'll meet me here after all the assessments," he says in a louder voice.

I pinch my lips together, reminding myself I'm just touchy because of my fight with Ben.

"If that's all, I'll return to Andrew, whom I was currently assessing, and see you later."

"Watch your tone, Doctor Blackwood," he says, ceasing the tapping of his pen.

Finally.

The silence is amazing.

He looks down at his papers on his desk and ignores me.

I straighten my back and return to Andrew, apologizing for leaving him. Quickly and thoroughly, I finish his assessment. Then I continue on to the rest of the players until it's lunchtime, and I see a text from Mia.

> *Mia: Meet me for lunch? Sara is coming too. Usual spot.*

Looking at the message, I realize I could use some fresh air to get rid of the headache forming from the busy day.

I type out a message and grab my bag.

> *Natasha: Sounds good. See you soon.*

I walk inside the restaurant and see the girls in the back booth. Mia waves as if I didn't spot them. I giggle to myself as I head over.

When I arrive at the booth, I sit down and slide across. "Hey, girls."

"Hey, Tash, we're going to order margaritas. Will you have one too?" Sara asks with a sparkle in her eyes.

"I shouldn't—"

Mia cuts in. "Stop. You're having one. You need to loosen up. I can see the frown lines causing you wrinkles already." She points to my forehead.

"Mia, I have lines because I'm thirty-one going on thirty-two, you idiot." I shake my head, laughing.

She brings her finger to her lips. "Shhh. Don't say our age. Some people don't like others to know."

I lean forward to whisper, "Why would you care? You're stunning for thirty—"

"Shhh." She looks around at the fellow patrons within earshot.

I roll my eyes, sitting back in the chair. "Mia, you're acting ridiculous. Anyway, I'm happy with my lines and age."

Sara nibbles her lip. "I'm with Mia. Sorry, Tash. I need the Botox and all the creams to keep young. The fashion industry wouldn't want me much longer if they knew my age."

"You can't pretend to be in your twenties forever," I argue, picking up my menu.

"I know. I'm just waiting on a big offer overseas. I need change." Sara glances at the table before sitting back in the booth.

"Don't you dare leave me," I say, lowering the menu with a warning tone.

"I barely see you," Sara argues.

I wince as the thought freezes my brain.

"Sorry, Tash, but it's true," Mia mumbles her agreement.

I rub at my brow, thinking about their admission. "I know. It's hard. I'm trying to juggle everything. I don't have a life outside of Mom and work."

"If you keep this up, you'll be forty before you know it and still single. No kids, because you still haven't met someone," Sara adds, reaching out to cover one of my hands with hers.

It's not that I haven't met someone. I have...but I tuck the thought away and don't voice it. Instead, I stare down at her nice gesture, even if her words feel like a slap to the face. I know they're coming from a kind place.

"Wow. Talk about needing a margarita. You girls are brutal," I say on a deep breath.

"Brutally honest. And you'd be the same," Mia says, with a small grin.

That's true. But it doesn't mean this doesn't hurt.

The server comes and takes our order, setting down tortilla chips and salsa before walking away again.

"Levi said something interesting to me last night," Mia says.

I look up. She has my attention now.

"Levi said he was offered a job at another team after the season's over."

"Is Levi going to take it?" I ask.

"Not Levi. Ben, silly."

I pause mid-chew.

Another team?

Where?

I clear my throat and swallow before speaking. "If he wants to do that, and it's a good opportunity, then I'm happy for him."

Mia and Sara exchange a strange look, and it annoys me.

"What?"

"Are you really happy for him?" Sara asks.

"Of course I am. How else would I feel?"

"Oh, I dunno. Sad?" Mia rolls her eyes.

"Why would a good opportunity for him make me sad?"

I know I'll miss him.

"Come on, don't play dumb," Mia says.

"What she's trying to say is, how would you feel if Ben wasn't around anymore?" Sara questions.

I hesitate, flicking my gaze between them.

"See," Mia sighs.

"Yes. I'd be sad, but I don't want to hold him back from a good work opportunity."

"Don't be ridiculous. You're not holding him back. He likes you; you like him. You're dating, for God's sake," Mia says.

I stare at her, wordlessly, knowing she's right, but it doesn't completely fade the noise in my head. To really be in a relationship with Ben, I need to let go of my dependency issues and welcome him into my life without holding back. I don't want to hurt him anymore. Which means I need to let him go until I can give him all of me.

"All right, enough. Let's talk about something else," Sara says with a smile.

I nod as a silent thank you. Our drinks finally arrive, and I pick up mine straightaway. Sipping the frozen alcohol, I love the refreshing taste, but I'm also eager to calm my nerves at the thought of seeing Ben soon.

How are we going to be around each other after I kicked him out?

Thankfully, after lunch, I'm straight back to assessments with no time to let myself think about *him*.

I wipe down the equipment and prepare for him, when the player I've just seen calls out, "Hey, Ben. You going in now?"

"Yeah, man. First week back this weekend." His voice is like smooth silk across my skin.

"You've got it. Tash will sort you out. Anyway, catch ya."

My heart rate kicks up a notch at the knowledge he's here, and a minute early, of course.

I draw in a sharp breath and spin around, my gaze cutting to his. A pained look mars his face, and I know it's me who put it there. A silence envelops us until I find my voice. "Did you want John?"

I don't want him to feel forced to have his assessment with me.

He shakes his head. "No, I want you."

Heat burns my cheeks, and I squeeze the cloth tighter in my fist.

"Okay...uh...just give me a second. I'll set up." I turn quickly, needing a few minutes to settle the waves of nerves, attraction, and heat running through my veins.

"Sure," he mumbles.

When I finish up, I see in my peripheral him peeling off his jacket and tossing it onto the nearest chair. Leaving him in a light gray top and black workout shorts.

I swallow hard and move my gaze back to clean the equipment, but I stub my toe on the workout bench as I do. "Shit."

"Are you okay?" he asks.

I look over to him and see him biting his lip, trying not to laugh at me. "Yes. But you're laughing at me," I say with a small smile.

His lip pops out between his teeth, and his smile broadens, reaching his eyes. "I'm trying not to."

I roll my eyes playfully. "I see you're really trying."

"Let me see," he offers, moving closer to me.

I hold up my hands, not ready for him to be too close to me, let alone touch me. "No. I'm fine. We're here to assess you."

"Doesn't mean I don't care about you. I'm still sorry for what happened at your mom's."

His apology hits me hard in the chest. He steps closer, ignoring my hands and, in this moment, I forget my left and right. I try to lean on the equipment but end up falling. I squeeze my eyes and take a deep breath.

Give me a fucking break.

He moves quickly to offer me his hand to stand up, and I take it, staring into his intense gaze. I'm upset at myself for being such a mess in front of him. He makes me feel like jelly.

He doesn't say anything, just stares at me. It makes my mouth move on its own to explain. "I'm a little protective of my mom."

"A little?" he teases.

I bite the corner of my lip to prevent a broad smile. "You're leaving the team?" I whisper. Letting go of his hand, I cross my arms over my chest. I stand still, not trusting myself anymore.

"Where did you hear that?" he asks as if he's shocked I found out.

I flash him an amused grin. "Have a guess."

"Mia."

I nod.

He pinches the bridge of his nose. "Levi and his big mouth."

"That I can't disagree with." I smirk.

Dropping his hand away from his face, he rests it on his hip and looks at me with a sad expression. "It was an offer, but it's in another state."

"Where?"

"Seattle."

"That's...um...exciting." I try to keep my voice even, so he doesn't hear the panic I feel.

"If you think so. I don't know what I'm going to do yet. I have some things to consider."

His eyes narrow, probably seeing how I feel about this. But it's not like I can tell him there is a new anguish searing through my heart from the thought of him leaving.

I need to get his assessment started because I still have to meet John.

Fucking John.

"Let's get started. I have a meeting after this."

He nods.

I point to the first exercise and set him up, adding weight and reps to push him a little.

His exerting breaths are sexy and speak directly to my sex. It feels intimate being this close again. Beads of sweat form on his forehead, and as I watch a trickle of sweat drip onto his eyebrow, I don't know what comes over me, but I swipe my thumb along it, swatting the droplet away. He hisses, and my skin prickles from his warmth under my touch. I drop my hand and step back, trying to control the feelings swirling through me. I just want to let go and forget everything and hold him.

Our gazes lock, his blue eyes darkening and his pupils dilating. It reminds me of...something I shouldn't be thinking of. He has my body humming for his, and the craving for his touch is becoming unbearable. His chest heaves, and I drop my gaze down to see his hands gripping his muscled thighs with force.

I wonder if this is hard for him too.

"Baby."

I squeeze my eyes and shake my head in a no. "Don't," I breathe.

I'm begging. I need him to behave.

I sense movement, and when I blink, he's moving his hands up and down his thighs as he croaks out. "I can't go without you."

"Don't. Please. I can't," I rasp as tears spring to my eyes.

I can't fucking what...

I don't know, but I need to keep myself in check.

For a moment, his eyes hang stay on mine. Fear clogs my throat at what he's silently telling me, and I have to swallow to wet my mouth, ready to get us back on track and refocus. "Let's finish out strong. You have outperformed every exercise. You are more than ready for this week."

"Thanks. I couldn't have done it without you."

"Well, you could've had John."

His eyes give me a death stare, and I chuckle. This light mood makes the tension fall away and puts me at ease. I can think clearer, and it's a safer zone.

"He isn't fun or beautiful."

I go to open my mouth to speak, but he holds his hand up. "I know. I know."

"Good b—" I slam my lips shut, knowing what happened the last time I called him a boy.

He raises a brow. "You aren't going to say what I think...were you?"

"Oh, no. Of course not."

"Good, because I thought I did a good job of showing you, how much of a boy, I'm not."

His tone is gravelly and oh-so sexy. I check the time before I get distracted all over again.

"I have to go meet John, so let's do this last exercise and you're done."

He nods, giving me his million-dollar smile, and my knees shake. "Deal."

We finish up, and he begins re-dressing into his jacket. Raking his fingers through his blond hair. "I'll see you at the game."

"You will. I can't wait to see you back out there."

"Thanks." He dips his chin and turns, leaving me breathless and trembling. When he's out of sight, I grab a bottle of water and sit down for a second. Being around Ben is unnerving. I know he's holding on to me, but it would be selfish of me to hold him back from future opportunities?

I'll be fine if I lose him, right?

CHAPTER 29

NATASHA

I SIT ACROSS FROM John and run through each player's assessment, leaving Ben for last. "How was Ben?"

With flashes of how he looked, all sweaty and perfect from training him hard, I look down to where my nails are digging into my palms.

He worked hard despite his injury; he didn't let himself go. His body is all muscle and minimal body fat. And those sweet words he said to me, they're making him even more irresistible.

I clasp my hands and look up to John. "He passed with flying colors."

That makes John beam with happiness, leaning forward on the desk. "Thanks for the update. I'll go let the coach know."

"Are you sure I can't come?" I ask one last time, with the hope he hears the plea lacing my voice. I want to come and listen in.

"No. I'll be fine. You can go home now," he dismisses me.

"But—" I sigh.

He sits up, waiting.

I drop my gaze and mutter under my breath, "Because I'm a woman."

"Natasha, that's untrue," he denies with a hint of anger.

My gaze flicks up to meet his hurt expression.

There's no backing away from the truth now. I need to lay it all out now.

"John, you've been awful to me since I started. I know it's a male-dominated industry, but times are changing."

He crosses his arms, staring back at me. "I'm not upset you're female. Now, I won't lie. When you started, I wasn't happy they hired you without paying your dues."

I scrunch up my face, not understanding. "I went to school. In fact, I had a scholarship during college where I received the highest scores. And worked at a hospital. I've worked hard to be standing here today. Sacrificed more than you'll ever know. So, tell me, what do you mean when you say I haven't paid my dues...because I'm having a hard time understanding?"

"Most of us paid our dues by working at the college level before we got the chance to move to the big leagues."

"John, surely, you've seen my high scores and work history before I even started here. And I've been one of the hardest workers since day one. Even though you blatantly ignore me."

"Yes, you work very hard here and have proved me wrong. I'm not happy we started off on the wrong foot. I'm a grumpy old man, and I'm too old to change. But don't for a second think I haven't seen you outperform any other physician. You've caught the eye of many of the players...they are very protective of you."

I hold back a smile. "I've worked hard with each player. And I think I've proved I deserve my spot. Even if I haven't paid my dues." My gaze doesn't leave his in a silent battle of standing up for myself. Dropping my shoulders or looking away would be like cowering, and I'm not.

"Let's agree you deserve your spot. Don't think it's about anything else when I don't need your help. Trust me, when I need it, I'll ask."

"But please include me from now on. I don't feel part of the team if I'm constantly on the sidelines."

He dips his chin. "That's fair enough."

I stand from the chair with a small smile. "Have a goodnight, and I'll see you Sunday."

"Night," he replies before looking down at his papers.

I turn and leave, happy I got everything off my chest with him. Now we can move on and begin to work together. Well, at least, I can hope.

It's Ben's first game back. I amble over to him in the locker room, my heart in my throat with nerves. I need to check if he wants to stretch; not an exercise that's easy when you're resisting attraction, but it's my job. And after the chat with John, I feel better about going to work. It's as if all the tension and anger I felt toward him has evaporated.

Turning the corner, I find Ben talking to another player. I pause, not wanting to interrupt. But from this angle, I can't help but run my gaze over his tight uniform. A swarm of butterflies hits my stomach.

I swallow hard, remembering what lies underneath the fabric. Wide shoulders, tight, muscled waist, and toned thighs making me warmer. As if sensing me staring, his head turns, eyes catching mine with a small lift of the lips. But just as quickly, he turns back around, and a wash of disappointment hits me. The other player walks off and my feet move closer to him. His gaze returns to mine, and I smile and pause in front of him.

"Are you ready to stretch before the game?"

He nods but doesn't utter a word. A twist in my gut forms as I watch him sit, laying a notebook next to him. Lowering to my knees in front of him, I ignore the rattle in my chest. I peer up to see his wide eyes watching me.

This is hard for me too.

He sits stiff and straight, his hands gripping the bench, his knuckles white, holding a breath. Waiting for me to check his knee.

"Do you want me to strap your knee, or just the ankle?" My voice comes out a little strained.

The touch of his warm skin sends a tingle down my spine and a twinge in my sex. It's begging for his attention.

He lets out a long breath. "No, just the ankles. Knee's good."

"What's the notebook for?" I ask curiously as I get to strapping his right ankle.

"It's my notes about every game."

That makes my lips quirk. I knew he loved football, but seeing how mentally and physically strong and passionate he is, it's admirable. I move on to the left.

"How does that feel?"

He moves his ankles around. "This is good. Thanks."

"How about we run through the normal stretches next?"

It's just an excuse to stop touching him before I'm in a puddle right here on the floor. I need to get my professional brain and body back. He really has done a number on me.

"Sure." He stands abruptly, and it makes his cock meet my eye level.

My lips part in shock.

"What are you two doing?" Levi's chuckle comes from behind us and panic rushes through me.

"Stretches," Ben answers, unaffected.

I stand so fast I almost topple over, losing my footing, and Levi laughs again. "Are you sure about that? Tash looks flushed and jittery and was on her k—"

"Don't," I choke out and hold up my hand. My lips curve into a smile. "Good luck out there."

Ben pauses, giving me his signature smile before winking at me.

Taking a deep breath to control the flutters in my lower belly from that one jaw dropping smile. I need to work, so I walk over to Levi, who looks amused.

"Ben was stretching. My job, remember?"

He doesn't flinch at my tone, just smirks at us. It pisses me off further, and I shake my head, not bothering to entertain Levi's little dirty mind.

Looking out from the sidelines, I watch the players for injuries.

John and I meet the opposing team's physicians. John knows them but he introduces me as the other physician and then, as we walk back, he talks to the head referee. Now that all the pre-game stuff is handled, I get ready for the most intense work of my life.

The opposition win the coin toss and choose to kick off. After the sixty-minutes the game was over. It was an easy win for us. The winning touchdown was scored by our wide receiver, but I got to witness Ben scoring a rushing touchdown during the game. The way they all come together and support each other is incredible. I had to stop myself from jumping up and down and wooing him.

The post-game rush is manic. The team left the field buzzing after chatting to the other players. Bens beaming with pride at another win, another step closer to the possibility of winning the trophy of his dreams.

Inside the locker room, the players go straight into listening to the head coach talk about where they went right and wrong. And what the schedule is for next week.

Then Ben goes to do his press conference. I wander around, checking on players, seeing if I can help in any way.

Once I'm done, I make my way to the locker room and see a reporter approaching Ben. Her hand immediately touches his bicep. With the way she's looking at him, you'd think they've fucked. I have to swallow back a "get your hands off him" comment. *He isn't mine.*

He talks to her with his charming boyish grin. I can't help but wonder if he wants her touch.

His face doesn't look disgusted or uncomfortable, so he must be okay with it. It leaves me feeling...jealous.

Me, jealous?

What the hell is wrong with me?

She leans up and whispers in his ear, and I nearly pop a blood vessel in my eye with the blood pumping through me. My blood pressure must be through the roof.

Get away from him.

He smiles politely and answers question after question, and I just fucking watch.

This sucks.

I sit sulkily until the hot reporter leaves the room, and he stands to turn to his locker to remove his gear. I approach quietly.

"Are you ready now?" My tone is sharp. I'm pissed, and I can't rein it in. My emotions are getting the better of me.

Turning around, he frowns, but doesn't comment on my attitude. "Yeah, let's do it."

"Let's start with the basics first, and then I'll do the rest," I say, and he gets into position. "You played well today. Nice touchdown. Are you sore anywhere?"

He smiles at my compliment but doesn't linger on it. "It was one of my best games. No new sore spots. I felt really good out there."

I want to tell him he looked good out there too, but I keep it to myself.

He performs each stretch and exercise with ease, then I rub some medicated cream onto his knee for some preventative pain relief.

I'm drifting somewhere else as we go on in silence, and I can't bite my tongue any longer. "Did you know the reporter?" I stand up, feeling better when I'm not on my knees in front of him.

A deep crease forms between his brows. "No, of course not."

"You seemed close," I mutter.

I know I sound like a brat, but I can't help it. I'm jealous and horny, and it's worse when he's standing here like a sexy sweaty snack.

"You jealous?" He gives me a playful look.

I straighten up. "Well, n—" But I don't finish. He knows I'm lying anyway.

We stand there, staring at each other, neither of us saying anything. The blood pounds in my ears while I figure out what to say.

His chin drops, and a chill runs over me, sending goosebumps covering my skin. I'm inside, yet the way he's looking at me right now makes it seem dark and gloomy.

"Natasha." He clears his throat, but the way his sad tone says my name sends my heart dropping. "I have given you all of me." He lets out a strangled laugh. "I'm feeling like I've constantly been chasing you while you haven't let down your walls for me."

I blink rapidly, a burn behind my eyes making it hard to see. Then I remember I'm at work.

"That's fair. Can we talk later?" I ask in a low whisper. I don't want to cry at work. And I'm going to if we don't stop this right now.

His face tightens as if that was the wrong thing to say. "What?" Shaking his head, he mutters, "Nothing. If you can't figure it out, then I'm not spelling it out for you. But for the record, no, I'm not interested in her. I was just doing my job and answering questions like a normal quarterback does." His voice is rough with emotion.

My mouth is opening and closing, but no words leave me.

I've pushed Ben so much, he's withdrawing from me. He's giving up hope, thinking there's no way he can change my mind.

This is the time for me to dig deep and think about what I want.

Do I want him with someone else?

It would be crushing.

If I don't change, I'll be alone and worse...let the possibility of true love slip through my fingers. Because I'm stubborn, hurt, and scared.

Where is my life going?

What do I want and what makes me happy?

Or should I say, *who* makes me happy?

CHAPTER 30

BENJAMIN

"YOU FREE TO TALK?" Natasha's voice breaks through the silent room. I take a breath, and then turn to face her.

She's walking toward me, biting her bottom lip.

My hands slide deep into my sweats pockets, watching her as she stands in front of me, her eyes not as bright as usual.

"Yeah, I was just packing up."

"I see." She runs her hand through her hair. "Do you need to go soon?"

"I have time to talk." I smile.

She nods repeatedly, staying silent.

Hating the pain etched in her face, I step closer. "Natasha. What are you thinking about?"

"So much." She breaks into a wide-open smile.

A deep chuckle rumbles from my chest. "Let's start with one thing."

She peers away, contemplating, and then looks back up at me to hold my gaze. "How much I enjoy being around you."

The corner of my mouth tips up. "Yeah?"

"Yes, but...this isn't about inflating your ego."

A full smile hits my face now. "Dammit."

"No, but in all seriousness, I do like you. It's just, I'm not ready for a relationship."

"Why?" I ask, running both my hands through my hair frustratedly.

"Because I'm not used to depending on someone. Especially a man and I need to accept you completely, otherwise it's unfair to both of us. With that said, this awesome new offer needs serious consideration."

I blow air into my cheeks. "But I don't have to go. Nothing's set in stone."

Her eyes grow brighter from a sheen that's forming in them. "This is a crazy good opportunity. John told me more about it. But it doesn't change the 'me' problem."

I grit my teeth with annoyance.

Of course he did.

Asshole.

"Don't be mad at him. I'm glad I found out. This is a huge deal. Ben, this is your future."

"I was hoping if I took this you might consider... us."

When her lips pinch together, my stomach bottoms out.

The look in her eyes stabs me to the core.

She steps closer, closing the distance between us. "I'm not saying no, so let me get that out of the way. But can you just go and see how things are between us when you're there?"

My heart jackhammers in my chest. I try not to touch her, but my hand can't help but reach out one last time and caress her cheek.

Staring into those ocean eyes, it makes it hard to say what I'm about to say, but I don't want to drag this out. She needs to be ready and willing to be with me. I don't want half of her. Fuck, I don't deserve only half.

I want her completely. All her mind, body, and soul.

And as much as it kills me to say this...I have to.

"I don't think that's a good idea," I say, pulling my hand away, watching her exhale a shaky breath.

When she opens her eyes, tears sit on her eyelashes.

"You should've seen Abby the other day when her brother was here." James pisses himself laughing, taking a sip of his beer before continuing. "He's like all serious and shit and she's looped her arms through his and practically skips down the fucking streets. Poor bastard looked in pain. Luckily, he loves her as much as me and would do anything to keep her happy."

"How long is he in town for?" Thomas asks.

"Just a couple of days, I think," James says.

"You don't know? What a shit brother-in-law you are." Joshua tips his head back, letting out a laugh. "This is fucking gold."

I chuckle.

A sting hits my arm, and I look at James pulling his hand away. My brows knit together as I ask, "What the fuck was that for?"

"Waking you up. You seem somewhere else." He squints his eyes at me, probably trying to read my mind.

Too much shit in there to untangle.

I can't deny and say I'm listening when I've barely muttered a couple of words in the last hour.

I ease back in my chair and drop my gaze to the table, then meet his gaze with a shrug. "Just a lot going on."

"You've been through a lot already. You were made quarterback and then you got injured. Now you're back and close to being in the Super Bowl, and that would scare anyone. But you've got this. You're well prepared, and you work hard. Hard work pays off."

I know that's true because looking at how he went from nothing to becoming a billionaire, I believe him.

He isn't just blowing smoke up my ass.

No. He means what he says. But I wish that was the real problem.

It's her...it's always fucking her.

"I know. I think we have a good team, even though I would love to have my man, Levi. I feel like this is it. Post football is for new opportunities."

"What do you mean?" he asks, rubbing his clean jaw.

I peer over at Thomas and Joshua. Thankfully, they're too busy talking, and munching on fries in their own world.

"Don't say anything, because I wanna tell them."

"Scout's honor." James salutes.

I shake my head at his idiocy before speaking quietly. "You're such a dick. Anyway, I was offered a coaching position in Seattle. I'm looking at a contract, but I don't want to leave Chicago."

James takes a sip of his beer, then lowers it back to the table. "Why?"

I really wish this water was alcohol, but it doesn't change the fact I'm about to share how stupid I am.

"Because I don't want to leave Natasha," I whisper.

He slaps my shoulder and wears a shit-eating grin. "Holy shit. A woman is making you not want to leave the fucking state." He drags his body closer to me and says, "Now I need to know all the fucking details."

I snort. "Then you'll know how pussy-whipped I am."

"So, this is more than a hook-up?"

I wince, hating how he thinks of her like that. Natasha is not a hook-up; she's never been one.

No, a hook-up is someone who you never think about again...a soulmate leaves an imprint in your heart that can never be filled. Natasha is my soulmate, and leaving her will be hard. Even if she doesn't want me, I can't stay away, even if it makes me a schmuck. Or in this case, a laughingstock to my friends.

"She's definitely not a hook-up, she's..."

Everything.

I run my now sweaty hands down my pants and turn to look at James, who's staring at me with an odd expression I can't read. "What? Stupid, aren't I?" I mutter and look away.

"Not at all, but I didn't know you felt that strongly about her. I would quit chasing her and follow your career, but that's just me."

This is my internal battle. I don't know what to do. I'm stuck between a rock and a hard place.

"My head keeps telling me to walk away, but my heart can't stop beating for her. I wish my heart would listen to my head."

"Wouldn't life be easy if we had no feelings?" James snorts.

"A walk in the fucking park," I mumble, rubbing my forehead with my hand.

"Tell me what happened the last time you spoke. When was that?"

The flash of her hits me, and I speak. "Game day. She checked on me before and after the game. And fuck, I wanted her right then and there."

James frowns with confusion. "Okay, you wanna fuck her, I get that, but what happened?"

I exhale heavily. "She said she doesn't usually depend on guys. And that it's unfair to me. Yet after the game, this reporter was flirting with me—" I hold my hands up. "I didn't flirt back, just answered the questions like the good quarterback I am. But when Natasha came to go through stretches, she was jealous, and I kind of..."

"What?" James pushes when I don't immediately answer.

I take a deep breath, feeling like I've been talking so fast and for so long, I'm struggling to breathe. Or is this how it is whenever I talk about her?

"I told her it's unfair how she doesn't want me but won't let anyone else have me. I was harsher than I usually am…it's just, I'm so fucking confused. The mixed messages are just fucking with my head."

"She sounds confused. If there's something there, you have to wait."

'Mm-hmm," I say back as I think about what he said.

"Is she worth waiting for?" he deadpans.

And I don't even need to think. "Honestly…I'd wait forever."

He squeezes my shoulder again and gives me a smirk. "Well, do that, Benny boy."

———

Training days are usually my favorite, but after the talk with Natasha, I'm not looking forward to seeing her. A part of me wants to, but I hate not being able to have her the way I want to.

I'm also dreading the awkward tension. I know it's going to be there, even if it's just from my end. I wonder how she'll be with me, guarded or sorry?

I guess I'll find out soon.

I have my head down, focused on my agility training, droplets of sweat running down my face as I push myself to my breaking point. I lift a knee and the other follows over each hurdle and plate on the floor. I'm pumped when I don't miss a one. It feels as if I'm training in a sauna.

"Smooth, Benny. Keep it up," I hear my coach call out in the distance.

I nod my acknowledgment, unable to speak.

After I complete my sets, I walk over, my lungs burning for air. I grab my water bottle and drink, spraying my face with it to cool down.

As I wipe my eyes, I sense someone watching me from the sideline.

It's her.

Before tossing my bottle, I lock eyes with Natasha, soaking in her beauty before I begin running back. It's just the re-energizer I need.

"Now, engage. Release. Good," Coach tells me as I approach the stand-up pads, and then he continues, "Now, turn, ball, good work."

I toss the ball back, stoked I nailed that. We repeat before moving to the pads. I swat the pads, swat left, swat right, repeating the movement with the coach. I keep my focus on being precise because that's what it takes to be at the top. The competition is high, so I need to be the best.

I get totally lost in every drill, then as I take another water break, I hear my dad say, "That's it, son. Good work."

Those words cause my chest to warm and a smile forms on my lips. I stare up into his proud eyes, and he smiles back.

I got this, Dad. I'm gonna do this for us.

I turn and walk back for the final time, my hands on my hips, my chest rising and falling as I hear my offensive line and defensive coach say, "Great foot work today. Let's do some catching drills."

I spend the rest of the session working on the speed and calculated movements to control my body.

"Nice work today. Totally controlled. Go cool down."

"Thanks, Coach," I say with a grin, knowing I'm playing well, and my knee isn't hurting at all. I haven't got much left of the season before my knee can rest completely, knowing it won't be this hard ever again.

I walk off the field, struggling now, but I need to do a little bit of conditioning before I can call it a day.

As I walk and take a seat, the skin on my arms rises as I hear her voice say, "Hi."

I look at her, and the feelings of desire creep in under the layers of my skin as she stands near me. She's pulling me back into her aura. And all I can do is stare back at her and offer a lopsided grin.

CHAPTER 31

NATASHA

I STEP CLOSER. MY nose is flaring with every intake of breath, his masculine scent strong and intoxicating. He worked hard at training today, and it was hard to not stare. His body moving effortlessly around the field, doing different drills, is something I always enjoy watching.

He lifts a brow at me.

You said hi first, duh.

"Um. So, your, uh, hips were flexible, and your movements were so fluid. You were fantastic out there," I say, ignoring my temperature rising from being so close to him. The air seems thicker, and I can't help but need to suck in an audible breath.

Get your shit together, woman.

This is work.

He's work.

He gives me a boyish, charming smile, and it causes my pulse to kick up. I can't but help offer a big giddy one back.

"Thanks. I felt good out there. Best I have in a while, must be thanks to all our sessions." He winks.

I scoff. "Don't be silly. You did all the work. It was a choice, and you rose to the challenge."

"I wouldn't say it was a challenge."

I tilt my head, not understanding. "What do you mean?"

He lets out an audible breath. "I'm a competitive guy, and my goal is to win the Super Bowl, so I had to get better. No other choice. Plus, my dad would whoop my ass." He chuckles.

"You still didn't have to. You could have let it defeat you."

When he stops laughing, his face turns serious. "I think your sessions have strengthened me, though."

I feel heat hit my cheeks. "It was my pleasure."

The air between us suddenly feels awkward. Or is that just me?

"Did you want help conditioning, or will you stretch and go home?"

I don't know why, but I hold my breath and wait for him to answer. Part of me wants him to need help, just to spend more time with him, but the other part wants him to go home to give me space to breathe easier. He still causes my thoughts to be foggy.

"Help, please. You know I want as much time as you'll give me." He stands to move closer and gently strokes my cheek.

I bite the side of my lip...this could be trouble.

So much trouble.

"Greedy, aren't you?"

"You have no idea," he growls, and the sound sends a tingle down my spine.

I turn and walk to the gym, needing to move and get this session started. My mind has been taken over by images of him showing me just how greedy he is on the nearest piece of equipment in the gym. Yep, I'm officially screwed. I need to hurry this session and get home for a very cold shower.

"Let's start with some crab walks."

He squats and his shorts tighten, riding higher on his thigh and showing me his thick quads with the blond dusting of hair.

I cross my hands over my chest tightly to keep them from twitching.

"How's your mom?" he asks, surprising me.

I smile and answer. "She's the same, but good."

"That's good. Did I win her over?"

I giggle at that.

Such a shit.

He knows exactly how well my mom loves him.

I roll my eyes playfully. "As if you don't know. You're her new favorite person. I've been replaced."

His smile widens. "Never. You're the apple of her eye. Anyone can see that. And definitely no one will take over the bond you two share...it's special."

I like that he can see the love my mom and I share.

"Thanks, I think so too. She's my best friend."

"Am I going to crab walk for the whole session? Because I'm starting to not feel my legs," he teases with a raised brow.

"Oh, shit, sorry." I drop my arms and grab some dumbbells for him. I hand them out and he takes them from my grip. The simple brush of our hands sends a current through me.

"You owe me now."

"Depends on what you're talking about."

"What? I'm innocent. I don't know what you're talking about."

I squint at him, knowing he's playing by the tone of his voice. "Hmm."

He pauses. "How many?" He holds the dumbbells up, so I know he's asking about the exercise.

"Do fifteen on each side and three rounds."

He lifts the weights and looks into my eyes. "What is something you wish you did more often?"

I think about the answer. That isn't the horny side of me that says *you*.

But I think about something I do dream about too. "I'd say travel."

He makes an approval sound from his throat. "If you could go anywhere, where would you go?"

He pauses his raises, resting in between sets.

I look at him and answer. "Somewhere with history, like Italy or Paris."

It's fun talking about exciting places in the world, but it's not like I can go. Mom can't travel with her back and frequent doctor's appointments.

"What about you?" I ask.

"Hey! This is me asking you questions." He smirks and begins his second set of raises.

"Nope, I like this." I cross my arms over my chest with a small grin.

A little too much.

"Me too." He smirks and continues, "I would say to relax and switch off more."

I frown. "You don't relax?"

"Not really. I train every day, wake early, and I never really take time off. I think our date was the last time."

My stomach drops. He sounds sad, and it breaks me. Their schedule is brutal, and to do it for years is taxing on both mind and body.

We finish that exercise and move onto dumbbell flies. I'm watching his back muscles contracting in a rep with my lip between my teeth. I remember the magical date and how it felt to have his body covering mine in one of the safest hugs and the heated kisses could have made me fall. But there is something bothering me.

I release my lip and whisper, "Will you take the offer?"

He pauses the exercise and straightens, and I lift my head up to look at him, waiting for him to answer.

"Yeah, but—" He sighs.

"What's holding you back?"

I don't know why I want to ask, but I feel like I *need* to know.

"Honestly...you."

I drop my chin and squeeze my eyes shut.

My heartbeat is in my throat and the wash of guilt rolling through me is making me nauseous. When I glance back up, he's staring at me with pleading blue eyes and I'm breaking.

"I wish I was what you needed," he says before bending down and pumping out the next set, and I feel my heart break, my blood pumping in my ears.

You are.

I want to be what you need too, but I'm scared.

But the words don't leave my throat.

I watch him and hate myself in this moment for hurting his feelings.

"The final exercise is bicep curls, and then, please stretch," I say, needing space.

"Cutting my session short?"

I open my mouth but close it again. No point in denying, since he knows I can't change my mind. I wish. We finish the exercise in silence and pack up.

I turn to leave, but he steps in front of me. A lump is in my throat as his gaze pulls me in.

"I won't go if you tell me not to," he says, leaning in and causing me to suck in a sharp breath from the unexpected move. His lips touch the corner of mine, and the kiss feels as if it's a goodbye. I feel a crushing sensation in the center of my chest and the backs of my eyes sting.

What am I going to do?

Am I going to let him walk away and out of my life forever?

I'm still thinking of his last words and what I'll do as I step foot in the door.

"Mom, I'm home," I call out as I wander in and see her sitting on the couch, so I kick off my shoes and join her. The feeling of the plush material under me feels so good. I sag in relief and lie back. "How was your day?"

"It was the same, really."

Her voice hesitates, and I shuffle to face her, worried something's happened. "Are you sore today? Did you need me to get your stronger pain relief?" I'm about to get up when she shakes her head and sighs.

"No, love, it's not that it's—"

I frown. What's going on? The feeling of nausea rolls in my stomach. I wonder if she had a phone call from her doctor and she received bad news. "Did the doctor call?"

She looks at me and offers a small smile. "No, love."

"Then what is it?" I ask in a rush.

"I've made a decision."

"Yeah...about?" I ask, holding my breath.

"After what happened with Ben—"

I sit up and face her properly. "I thought we spoke about this."

"No, it's just given me time to think about my life and what I want."

"And what's that?"

Her eyes have a new determination that worries me.

"You need to move out."

I widen my eyes. Surely, she's joking.

"What...but why?"

"I want a different relationship for you. I want you to be my daughter, not my twenty-four-hour caretaker."

"I go to work," I argue.

I'm growing tense and my answer was a little short, but I'm hurt. She's kicking me out and doesn't want my help. This is too much right now.

"I want to hire my own full-time caretaker, so now you can hang out with me like a normal daughter."

I feel like the walls are closing in. "What about cooking and cleaning? You can't do that."

"It's all been organized; you don't have to do anything. Just visit me." She smiles. But I can't return the smile. I'm confused and lost at this moment. I run my hands through my ponytail and tug out the band, holding my hair up. It's not helping with the headache that's beginning to form.

"I love doing it, Mom. I just don't understand."

I'm choking, but it's not from tears. I'm too spent to cry. I'm just shocked and struggling to form sentences.

"I know you do, but you're thirty-one and spending your free time with me. You need to move out and find out who you are. Get a hobby. Do something for you."

"But I don't have a hobby," I argue.

This makes her smile bigger. "Exactly. Go out and try stuff and find out what you like to do."

This reminds me of Ben asking me what I wished I did more of and I said to travel. But I could still do that and help Mom. ..only she doesn't want me to do it anymore.

I'm gutted and at a loss.

"I don't even want to do anything," I whisper to myself.

"Did you have fun with Ben on your date?"

"Yes, but—."

She laughs. "Love, please see what we all see in Ben. People like him don't come around often, and if you miss out, someone else will snatch him up."

"I don't know. I'm so confused," I say honestly, needing to tell her how I really feel.

"That's why people date. To get to know each other. Spend time doing things with each other. Fun things. You'll have plenty of time now...so you can't use me as an excuse."

Ignoring her talk about Ben, reality hits me. "Where will I move to?"

She shrugs. "That's not something I can answer. You need to start looking, though."

"It's a lot to think about."

"Yeah, but it's exciting."

I narrow my eyes at her. Isn't she supposed to be sad? I'll be leaving the nest? She seems way too thrilled for my liking. "Why are you so happy? You don't like living with me that much?"

She laughs and reaches out to grab my hand, squeezing it. "No, I'm excited to see you finally live your life. And where you decide to go on your own feet without needing me."

"I'll always need you."

"But I won't be here forever."

Tears well in my eyes at that.

"I didn't say I was going anywhere yet, but it is a harsh reality."

"A reality I don't want to think about."

"But it's a reality you need to come to terms with, because one day, it'll happen. It's better you don't dig your head in the sand. Go find yourself, so when the time comes, you'll still have a life you love, and you can continue on and hopefully have babies to run around after."

I feel like a bucket of ice was poured over me. "Oh God, Mom. Death, and now kids, you really know how to layer it on thick today. I already had a bad day."

She frowns. "Why? What happened?"

I sigh and lean back onto the couch. "Ben said he has an offer to go to another state."

She smirks. "He wants you to go with him?"

I scoff. "No."

"You can now." She wiggles her brows.

"No." I shake my head vehemently and continue. "Not happening. It's one thing to move out and not care for you, but I'm not moving states."

She rests her head back on the couch, watching me. "Fair enough. I can't force you to do anything. You know, I think you should give him a go, but this has to be your decision. Remember, this is it. Now your life is free of responsibilities revolving around me, so you'll have time for him…"

I can't help but laugh at her not-so-subtle hints. I just have to decide if I'm willing to change or remain the same.

CHAPTER 32

BENJAMIN

IT'S BEEN A COUPLE of days, and I haven't heard from her. I thought by now I would've heard something, with the way she reacted when I was close to her. Her body hums in sync with mine. She wants me as much as I want her, but she just needs to give herself completely to me. I can't keep doing this. So I'm taking the job. I felt like I had no other choice. She needed to make a decision, and so did I.

"I'd prefer to stay where I am and coach when there's an opportunity here. But I can't," I say to Joshua on the phone.

"That's fair, and fuck, I want you here. I couldn't imagine not seeing your ugly face on boys' nights."

We tease like brothers, and I wouldn't want to be too far away from them either.

"Who are you calling ugly?"

"You want me to call you pretty boy?"

"Fuck no," I say on a laugh. "What are you doing calling me? Don't you have a business to run?" I tease him.

"Pfft. Perks of being a boss. I can call my friends when I want to. Have you ever thought about running your own business?"

"Truthfully, no. It's never crossed my mind." I couldn't imagine myself owning a business. What would I do? No, James and Joshua were born business owners. Thomas and I are hard workers but not owner material. We aren't into control.

"You do have a trophy to win this year."

I smile at the thought of holding the trophy in my hands. "Trust me, we'll win it."

"All right, I'm coming," Joshua calls out to someone before saying to me in a whisper, "Ava is breaking my balls. I gotta go."

I chuckle. "All right, bud, you go, and I'll talk to you later."

"Thanks. I'll speak to you soon."

I hang up and shove the phone in my pocket.

I can't wait to play in a Super Bowl, but the thought of winning isn't helping me sleep at night. I haven't slept in what feels like weeks. To fill that missing piece that's in my heart, I need her.

She's what my heart needs to feel alive...and I only have a short window for her to stop me. And right now, I'm feeling like there's no fucking hope.

As I open the glass door into the coffee shop, I blink repeatedly, thinking there must be something in my eye because I'm seeing her.

I amble farther in and confirm it's Natasha with her back to me, standing in line. I run my gaze slowly over her outline, taking every curve in with a smile. She's wearing a green sweater and black slim jeans that show off her perky ass I love so much. It has my cock twitching.

Like me, he's reminded of how beautiful her skin looks from behind, flushed from arousal, and what her perfume smells like from desire. I'm salivating. When she moves forward, I instinctively take a step, wanting to be close to her again. But I won't go to her. I have to act as if I have my shit together...even when I just want to beg her to let me in.

After she pays and turns around, our eyes lock, hers widening.

"Hi, coffee stop?"

"Yeah, pre-gym pick-me-up."

Her gaze drops, running over my body. God, I love when she looks at me like she's drinking me in. When her gaze meets mine again, my smile broadens.

She runs her tongue over her lips. "I see. What are you training?"

"Full-body workout. What are you doing?" I question.

On a Saturday morning, I'm shocked to find her out and not at home with her mom.

Is she meeting a guy?

No. Don't be fucking stupid.

The line moves up, and she follows, waiting for her order. I don't remove my eyes from her.

"So, my...this is...God, this is embarrassing." A cute pink flush appears on the tip of her nose, which is causing my curiosity to pique.

The lady calls out her name.

Fuck!

"I'll be back."

I take a step forward and feel her beside me.

"Let me order. I'll be one sec."

She nods and moves to sip her drink, and I place my order, moving to the side.

"You were saying," I ask eagerly.

She tugs on the neck of the green sweater with one hand and sips her coffee with the other. "My mom kicked me out."

Well, fuck.

"Wow. That was not what I was expecting you to say."

She giggles at that, and it's like music in my ears. Adorable, just like her. And I miss the sound of her laugh.

"I was not expecting it. It was a complete surprise to me."

"So then, why did she do it?"

"She doesn't want me to be her caretaker anymore. She wants me to start living a life without her. And just visit her as a daughter."

Her eyes fill with tears, and it hurts so much to see her cry. Natasha is strong, resilient, and definitely not a crier, so this is worrying to me.

She drops her head, and I grab her chin, stroking my thumb over her soft cheek. I gently tilt her head back so I can see her eyes. "Please, come for a walk and tell me all about it."

She blinks, and a tear slides down her face. I have to resist not kissing it away. "Okay, but I don't have long. I have a condo to check out."

My order is called, so I grab my cup, and we leave the shop together. The breeze picks up, and she huddles next to me to avoid the wind. I ignore the attraction flying between us and focus on being a friend right now.

"Do you want me to come to the viewings with you?" I offer, not wanting her to do this alone if she doesn't want to.

"No, I'm fine, but thanks for asking. It's something I want to do for me."

I smile at that, knowing I'd be the same way. "Fair enough. But if you change your mind—"

"I'll let you know." She finishes my sentence with a small smile.

She drinks her coffee.

"Tell me what happened," I say gently, watching her lower her cup again.

She blows out a deep breath. "She told me to move out and look for my own place and that she'd hired different caretakers for all her needs."

I want to ask her how she feels about it, but I can see she needs to say more, so I wait.

"It feels like I wasn't good enough. I'm a physician. How can I suck this much that she hires people? It makes me feel incompetent."

I slip my free arm around her shoulders and squeeze her, offering her the comfort she desperately needs. "You are more than capable. Your mom wouldn't be doing this for that reason at all. Your bond is strong. She loves you and you love her."

She rolls her lips. I can tell this has been clearly weighing heavily on her. "I know, it just hurts. I love having her around, and I don't know what to do without helping her."

I haven't let my arm leave her and she hasn't asked me to move it. Instead, she leans in a little, and my heart pounds in my chest.

"My car is just up there." She points to the same car we met at months ago. "I don't want to be late for the first appointment."

"How many do you have to see?"

"Two today."

I nod. "I'm sure you'll adjust to living on your own. I won't lie. It's hard at first, but it gets easier—not completely."

"What do you mean?" she asks as we approach her car. Her face tilts to look up at me.

I turn to face her completely, her brows pinched tight.

I rub my neck with my hand. "I feel lonely sometimes. It would be nice to share my house with someone."

"That's what I'm afraid of. I don't want to be lonely."

I drop my hand, holding my coffee in both hands to prevent myself from touching her again. "Just take it one step at a time. Go see some places and see if any makes you happy when you walk in. I'm sure with the right house, you won't feel lonely. Or maybe ask a friend to live with you."

I see her eyes widen, and a deep chuckle leaves my chest at where her thoughts have gone. "I'm not offering, calm down. You do remember I'm supposed to be going interstate soon. Unless someone changes her mind and begs me to stay."

Her face drops, pain etched in every feature. I hate that I put that there. I should have kept my mouth shut.

Why the fuck did I have to say that?

"I'm not begging," she whispers.

Dammit. Here I was, hoping she would start the whole "please stay" speech, but again, that's wishful thinking on my behalf.

"Figured."

Her face scrunches up before she softens and asks, "What will you do with your house when you go?"

The words I don't want to hear from her.

"I don't know. I'm not going to sell it, but I don't want to rent it out either."

Horror splashes over her face. "Speaking of houses, I need to get going. I don't want to be late."

A twist in my gut pulls at me to say something, but I can't say anything other than, "You don't need it. I'm sure you'll find the right place for this new start."

"Well, um—" she says with a face that looks torn, and I'm a little lost as to why. "I guess I'll see you at the game."

Ah, it's the awkward goodbye.

I smile, trying to appease her guilt. "Yes, the playoffs, and then my new adventure starts. Look at us in our thirties and thriving." I wink.

"Thriving thirties." She giggles, playfully smacking my arm, and I lean in and give her a hug.

"Oh," she breathes.

I'm not leaving this goodbye without one last embrace. I nuzzle into her neck and take a deep inhale of her delicious coconut scent. Holding her, I enjoy her soft, plush body against mine, hating how much this hurts.

We pull apart, and I internally groan, not wanting to separate but needing to let her go to the viewing.

I kiss her on the corner of her mouth and cheek. Pulling back slowly, I watch as her lashes flutter and then open, showing me her pretty bright blue eyes.

I grin. "Good luck."

"Thanks," she says and steps around to climb into her car. I stand on the sidewalk and watch her car drive off, knowing it's the end.

The next day, I'm sprawled out on the couch, watching television. My phone vibrates with Natasha calling.

"Hi," I answer.

"Are you free for coffee?"

I sit up on the couch.

"Yeah. Where?"

"Bean? Say, in half an hour."

"Yep. See you soon."

Already grabbing my keys and shoes, I'm out the door in five minutes.

As I enter the coffee shop, I don't see her, so I take a seat at a table at the back to give us some privacy. I watch the moment she enters the door, and all the air leaves my lungs. She wears a blue top and a pair of blue jeans that hug her luscious figure. Her hips sway as she moves toward me, and when she arrives with a wide smile, I can't help but grin back. Standing to greet her, I pull out her chair and she sits, thanking me as she shuffles in.

Sitting across from her, I don't miss the cute pink staining on her cheeks. And the adorable twinkle in her eye.

"By the way you're smiling, I guess that the viewings went well?"

Her hands touch her cheeks. I chuckle.

She drops her hands. "Yeah, they did. One is a tad pricier than I want to spend, but it's bigger than the other."

"Are you telling me you have expensive taste?" I smirk, knowing I'm being a smartass.

She goes to answer, but then we're interrupted by the waitress, who takes our orders and leaves.

"No. I'm easily pleased, but I'm trying to decide if the extra space is worth the money."

I nod. "If money wasn't a problem, which one would you choose?"

She sucks in an audible breath and sits back. Her fingers touch her lips and it's transfixing. Those pillowy pink soft lips are taunting me.

She drops her hand away and leans forward. "Easy. The more expensive."

I look back up into her eyes and my smirk widens. "You have your answer. But if it's too much of a stretch, I have a friend James who'd be able to help you out if you need?"

"Thanks for the offer, but it's not a stretch. I think I'm just scared to commit." She laughs.

I freeze, staring at her, and I can't help but say. "Seems like in every area of your life."

"Ouch," she winces with a tease. "Commitment phobia." She raises her hand.

I can't help but chuckle at that.

"However, I'm committed to my job."

"Does that job make the hole that's left for love go? Does it really fulfill you? Because I thought I wanted to win the Super Bowl, but now I know that's not all my life is. There's more to me than just football."

She sips her coffee before lowering the cup. "Do you think the coaching job will fill that hole for you?"

I shake my head, knowing the answer right away. "No. That's me giving back, and I think teaching is something that'll bring me joy, but that hole will remain empty. I'm not going to lie; you've known for so long I've wanted you. And I don't want to keep repeating myself. You're what I want and need, but I can't..." And I sit on the last words, thinking of the best way to say it. Then I add, "You need to follow your heart, and I need to follow my head to protect my heart this time."

Her lip wobbles before she whispers, "I'm sorry."

"Me too."

There are no more words now, just actions.

CHAPTER 33

NATASHA

IT'S SUPER BOWL SUNDAY. Even though I'm not a player, the nerves are pumping through me as if I were.

The locker rooms are still, and I offer help to all the players. Talking to each individually, helping where I can. Having work to do helps the butterflies in my stomach. I haven't gone to Ben yet. But with only a couple of players left, I can't delay it much longer. Coach will want to talk to them all.

I make my way over to him. He's sitting alone with his head dropped. When I sit down next to him, he tilts his head to see it's me, smiling.

"Natasha."

"How are you feeling?" I ask quietly.

"Truthfully..." He glances around before whispering into my ear, "Scared shitless."

I laugh, but I hate when he pulls away.

"I would be too. Hell, I'm nervous, and I'm not playing." I elbow him.

"Won't be long, and all the nerves turn to adrenaline, and I'll be giving this body a massive beating."

I wince, not liking the sound of him in pain. "Please don't do that."

"I'm not going to give myself another injury, but I'm sure I'll have some nice bruises. And then I leave next Sunday."

"Sunday? You took the job."

He shrugs. "No point in hanging around."

My stomach hardens, but I can't blame him when I haven't changed my mind. "Is there anything you want help with?"

There's a slight smirk, and I know what he's thinking, but I don't comment on it.

"No, thanks. I'm good."

"Okay, I better go. I need to do a few more check-ins before you all go out."

He nods.

"Good luck out there," I say with a full smile.

"Thanks," he says with a wink.

As I'm about to leave, I peer over my shoulder and our eyes hold. He was watching me, and it's exactly what I suspected. I bite my lip and turn to leave. We both need to focus on the game ahead.

The referee calls the two-minute warning. It's a nail-biter game and watching the people you've trained and cared for win is emotionally taxing. But the person I'm most excited for is Ben. It's his last game and he's worked so hard to get here. I want him to win. I want to win. I want to prove to myself and to John, that I'm not just a female doctor the guys drool over. I've earnt this win just as much as the team. We are a team. Women and Men. Everyone working together on and off the field.

We're so close to winning. John stands next to me fidgeting, the stress rolling off him in waves. He's making me more nervous.

I look over at Ben standing proudly on the field, I smile. He's jaw is set; his eyes are pinned in front of him and his athletic frame showing off how much he's worked to get his health and fitness back. I'm proud of him. He's an unstoppable force. My gaze treks over his body. Determination written all over his stance. I shouldn't be drooling over him. I should be the doctor who's proud that his knee isn't giving him any issues. When he looks my way and his head dips, my stomach flips. I know underneath his helmet he's wearing a cocky grin.

He's got this.

I stand up straighter in my uniform feeling alive with the roar of crowd surrounding me. I soak up the next two minutes until there's no more time on the official clock.

The biggest game of my career has finished.

We won the Super Bowl by three.

Afterward, I stand waiting, hoping I can speak to Ben. Congratulate him and soak in his post-win glow. I want to see his handsome flushed face, talking to me in his breathless voice that I love.

"Let's go," John orders, breaking my fantasy.

I want to argue but I'm here to work. All I can do is settle for a heavy sigh and keep my eyes fixed on the man I'm lusting after.

Inside the locker room the players begin hitting the showers. It's loud in here.

Reporters haven't stopped asking Ben questions since he announced his retirement.

The question of if he's okay is still gnawing at me, so before he leaves to go home, I catch him.

"Ben, hey!" I walk over to him, chewing on my lip.

"Hi."

"Congratulations. It was a close one. Are you okay?" I ask, studying his face.

"Better now," he says, a mix of excitement and exhaustion swirling in his eyes.

I smile stupidly at that comment.

"I'm glad I can help. How's your body feeling?"

"Achy and badly bruised, but nothing I didn't expect," he states simply.

"Did you have a Gatorade?"

He looks at me baffled. "Yes, Doctor Blackwood."

I cross my arms over my chest and hide my embarrassment that's building inside me.

"You're always working," he teases.

"I can't help it."

"It's okay, I'm teasing, and it's definitely needed...winning is kind of fun."

"Kind of? I would have thought you would be buzzing," I say, amused.

"Oh, don't get me wrong, I am." A beaming smile sweeps across his face.

"Were the reporters harsh?" I ask with wonder.

He widens his stance and hesitates. "Surprisingly, not as bad as they could've been. I guess being my last game, they asked the questions I was prepared for."

Someone clears their throat behind us. I turn to see another reporter—the same flirty one gawking at us. This time, I'm not jealous. Instead, I'm annoyed she had to choose this moment to interrupt us. I flash him a well-done look.

"I just wanted to check in on you. I better get back to my office." I offer him a polite nod.

"Talk to you later." He surprises me by inching closer to take my chin in his hand, and leaning in. I can feel his hot breath on my face, and I stop breathing momentarily, wondering what he's going to do. My pulse is in my throat with anticipation.

The sound of the reporter's shoe tapping irks me. Damn her. I step back, causing his hand to drop from my face. Then I spin on my heels and straighten, walking out toward my office. Before turning the corner, I catch his eyes on me, and my heart swells.

I've been shopping with Sara, trying to keep myself busy. He leaves today, and I need to stop myself from thinking about him. We haven't spoken much, just a text here and there, but nothing of importance. I want to say goodbye, but I don't know if I can do it. I know I want to, and the more the day goes on, the more I think I should.

"Did you hear me?"

I shake my head to clear it. "Sorry, what did you say?"

"The red or back?" Sara asks, holding out a dress in two colors.

"The red, it's different for you."

She continues to stare at it before nodding. I follow her around the store, pretending to be paying attention to the clothes she's picking.

She tucks the dress under her arm and pauses to stare at me with a concerned squint. "What's going on? You're distracted today."

I sigh. "I know, I'm sorry. Ben's leaving to go to Seattle today."

She reaches out and rubs my arm, her face conflicted. "Ah, and you're second guessing whether you want to be with him?"

We're at the counter so she can pay for the dress. I don't want them to hear my conversation. Ben's name is still a hot topic for the news.

When we leave the store, I take a breath and explain. "Yeah. But I'm not ready to depend on him. That's not fair to keep him at arm's length when he's been nothing but caring and patient. While I'm such a mess."

A "hmm" leaves her mouth before saying, "I'll support you, but don't push him away because you're scared. Be brave and let those fears go."

I cross my arms and hug myself, trying to calm my stomach that's full of knots. "I know." I sigh. "I want to say goodbye, but I don't know if that's a good idea."

"It might make it harder on both of you. But if you want to, then you should."

"I don't know. This is why I don't need a guy. They interfere with my head. I had work and mom until he pursued me. Now he's in here consuming my every thought." I tap my temple.

She giggles. "That happens when you like someone."

CHAPTER 34

BENJAMIN

"WHAT TIME DO YOU need to leave?" Thomas asks as we all sit around our favorite bar and have a few rounds of drinks.

I glance down at my watch. "In an hour. I gotta leave to get home in time to grab my bag."

"It's going to suck without you," Joshua says, and I grin at my friends. It won't be easy leaving them either, but I need to do this for me. It's the best decision.

"I know, I'll miss these catchups, but there'll be times I'll come back, and here's a thought...you could visit me in Seattle?"

James snorts. "I'd rather not. Do you really have to go?"

I nod. "Yes. I need a change, to clear my mind. What better way to do that than a fresh start?"

"It sounds like you're running away," Joshua argues as he sips his drink.

"I'm not," I say, but it's a lie, isn't it?

I am running away.

I don't want to be around the stadium or the gym, remembering all the good times I shared with her. No, I want to move on and just be friends. Distance will surely make it easier because I won't see her.

"Why won't you visit?" I ask James.

"Because that would require leaving Abby," Joshua says.

He narrows his eyes and gives Joshua a dirty look. "Untrue. I travel for work all the time. But yes, I don't like leaving her, and I do enough of it for work."

"Where did my friend go?" Joshua asks with a smirk.

"What do you mean? Just because I don't hide my feelings and need to be macho all the time, you think I've changed. Well, I have for the better."

"Woah, calm down," Joshua says, raising his hands. "I was just saying what I'm seeing."

"And I'm saying, don't be a dick. I'm happy, and would like it if you could support me a bit more."

"Who wants another drink?" I stand, needing to get away from this. I'm happy they're all in love and shit. But today is hard enough; I don't need to sit here, listening to them talk more about it.

"Yeah, I'll come." Thomas rises from his chair.

As we approach the bar together, weaving through the mountains of people, I get recognized by a few fans. I stop to take photos with them, have a chat, and sign a few shirts. Eventually, we come to stand at the wooden bar and wave down the bartender.

He comes and takes our order, and I lean on the bar to face Thomas. "How's work?"

"It's really good. I'm still working on a couple of larger pro-jects, so it's costing me time with the girls, but it won't be forever."

I smile, thinking of his kids. "And how are the girls?"

He smiles broadly, and I can't help but match it. He's the quieter one in the group. His life turned upside down when he became a widow, so to see him and his girls, Rose and Lily, find their happiness again, it's good to witness.

"They're great, seriously; they love school, and Jennifer is managing at work, so life is great."

I nod and swallow the gravel that's lodged in my throat, knowing I want that, but don't have it. Maybe moving states will allow me to find my own Jennifer.

"And how are you going? You played such a good game. Fuck, it was a close, though."

I chuckle as the bartender delivers our drinks. Thomas picks his up to cheers with me. "To the future."

"To the future." I take a big sip before answering his question. "The game was brutal, both mentally and physically."

He leans on the bar and shakes his head. "I don't know how you do it."

"Did it," I correct him with a smirk.

"Yeah, that's a hard adjustment too. You being retired."

"It was time. I'm not young, and my body is getting torn up every game. I'd have to be careful on my right side. So before I have an accident that turns into a lifelong issue, I'll quit and move to coaching."

"Yeah, and what's the coaching gig about?"

"I'm trialing out at a college team as Head Coach and renting a place for three months. I didn't want to be committed to a job for, say, a year, when I don't know if I'll enjoy it. I want to find another job that fulfills me like football did."

"Good plan, because if you hate Seattle or the job, you can move back. What are you doing with your house?"

"It's being leased for a month at a time. I don't want to feel stuck in Seattle."

"Good idea. I'll visit with the girls, for sure. I have vacation time coming up, so expect us."

I love that idea, to have people I know visit will give me a lift. It's definitely something to look forward to.

"We better get these back to the guys. They seem agitated today." I look over to our table, and then back to Thomas.

Thomas chuckles. "They are extra touchy these days."

We carry the drinks to the booth.

"Did you guys get lost?" Joshua teases.

I peer at Thomas, thinking, "good luck with these buffoons." He just shakes his head and takes a seat. I don't say anything, but then I change my mind. "Next time, get it yourself."

———

Leaving the bar, I walk home, faltering when I see *her* waiting on my doorstep. I blink and glance around before I look back, and she's still there. Smiling, I offer her a wave and she does the same. I can't help the way my stomach twists with hope.

Is she going to change her mind?

Beg me to stay?

God, how much I wish she would, but the way she's standing there hugging herself, any hope vanishes of this being the "wait, don't go" speech. And immediately, my shoulders drop.

When I'm closer to her, I mutter, "Hey."

"Hi. I didn't know what time your flight was," she says, fidgeting with her hands.

I chuckle. "So, you were planning to wait here?"

"I hadn't thought that far."

"How long have you been waiting for me?"

She checks her phone. "About twenty minutes."

"Come inside while I grab my things and call the taxi."

"Thanks."

I turn and open the door for us. Inside, I can't help but struggle, having a flashback of her lips on mine and the sex against the stair railing I'm currently staring at. I squeeze the back of my neck; I should've had another drink back at the bar. At least being tipsy, I wouldn't be so affected by her or imagine a repeat of me on my knees.

I need to get out of this room and into a safer space. I clear my throat and ask, "Did you want a drink?"

"Do you have time?"

"I'll make time for you. Five minutes isn't going to make me late."

She nods. "Water, please."

I grab us both a bottle and I have to ask, "What are you doing here? You could have called."

She glances down, before lifting her head and saying, "I actually didn't think of that. I wanted to say goodbye in person."

I grin. "You want to give me a goodbye kiss?"

Her mouth parts, and it's not in horror. She looks more stunned. "No, that's not a good idea."

"I know, I'm just teasing."

She bites the corner of her lip nervously. "I did want to apologize for how I reacted about my mom. I over reacted."

My jaw goes slack and all I can do is nod. Because I never expected her to apologize.

"I'm..." She starts before removing the bottle lid and drinking some water. "I'm scared I'll lose her like I did my dad."

I can feel her pain as she said every word. My mouth opens to argue, but I close it again, because I've never been let down by my parents. Never felt the hurt of losing someone I love.

"Your dad is why you won't let me in," I say, still trying to wrap my head around her confession.

She slowly blinks, but her pain and confliction still swirl heavily in her eyes. I grab her hand, needing to comfort her.

She deserves the time and space to think about us. Whether it takes a day, a week, a month, or a whole fucking year, I'll be ready. A phone call away.

It's silent between us. I reluctantly remove my hand from hers. I check the time again. "I might have to go."

"You might?" she asks with a lop-sided grin.

"I have to go."

She dips her head, and I order a lift. She has a couple of minutes to change my mind.

"When will you be back?"

I lean on the counter that separates us, and our eyes hold.

"I don't know. I don't have plans to come back."

She swallows roughly, and I think the reality of me actually leaving is finally sinking in. I don't have a date to visit. I'm going for work, so I can't schedule time off yet.

"Oh," she mumbles, all animation having left her face.

She doesn't say anything else, and it doesn't look like she will.

"You can text or call me."

A car horn beeps and my phone chimes at the same time.

"I gotta go," I say, ignoring the odd twinge of disappointment.

She drops her lashes quickly to hide the hurt. "Okay," she says, slipping slowly off the stool, still clutching the bottled water, and I grab my bag.

We stand outside by my door, and I say in a strained voice, "I'll let you know when I land."

She nods, and it's strange; she's never this quiet, but I can't wait, I'll miss the plane.

I drop my bag and wrap her in my arms, and she sags against me. After a short hug, I pull back, "Bye."

"Bye," she says, lifting her eyes briefly, the pain still flickered there.

Opening the door for her, I watch her take the steps, taking me with her is my heart. I wish she'd choose me and happiness.

Not the darkness of her past.

I don't talk to the driver; I just ease back and stare out at the clouds in the sky, reliving the last ten minutes. My hands resting in my lap feel empty; they want to be wrapped around her again. Winning the Super Bowl didn't fill the void in me. True victory is only great if I could've shared it with her—someone I love.

CHAPTER 35

NATASHA

> *Benjamin: Just arrived. The rental isn't as nice as the pictures made it out to be. Look at this... (Picture of a twin bed, with a gray stitched headboard.)*

BEFORE I HAVE A chance to respond, a new text comes through.

> *Benjamin: How will I fit in that? My legs are going to hang off the bed, for sure. Now I have to buy a new one. Not a good start.*

I giggle to myself.

"What's funny?" Mom asks beside me on the couch.

Oh. Now, what do I say to that?

"Um," I mumble, avoiding her gaze.

"It's Ben, isn't it?"

I look at her and smile, unable to lie. "Yes."

"What's going on there? You haven't mentioned him in a while."

"He moved to Seattle."

She smiles warmly at that. "Good for him. Did you two have a fight?"

"No, obviously not." I held up my phone to remind her he texted me.

"Then why did he really leave? I thought you two were dating."

A wash of guilt hits me like a tidal wave. Tucking my legs up onto the couch beside me, I look over to TV before meeting her eyes to explain. "He said he didn't want to be here if he couldn't be with me."

She merely stared at me, tongue-tied, causing me to choke out a laugh. "What's with the face?"

"He actually left because of you?"

Pinching my lips together before they pop open. "Yep."

"And there was no chance?"

I stay silent for a moment, thinking of the right words.

"I couldn't commit to him."

Her eyebrows shot up in surprise. "You don't like him? I thought you did."

I smile tentatively. "I do. But if I was to date him, I want to completely trust and depend on him, give him all of me, not be unsure, it's not fair to him."

She makes the sound of approval in the back of her throat. "That's true."

Her cheeks are flushed. "Mom, are you warm?"

"Yes, actually, I'm wondering if I could have some Tylenol and water."

I get off the couch and retrieve the items immediately.

"Do you need anything else?" I ask with worry.

"No, let's finish our conversation. I'm fine."

I nod and settle back into the couch.

"It's a shame you didn't work out. He was lovely."

"He is, Mom, he is."

Our conversation ends, and I watch the TV, and when I look over, she's fast asleep, having her nap. I return to my phone and text him back.

> *Natasha: Ouch, I hope they can order you a new one quickly. What about the couch? Can you sleep on that until the new bed arrives?*

> *Benjamin: (pic of a small couch)*

> *Natasha: laughing emoji*

> *Benjamin: Glad you find this funny. Why is it that everything looks nice but isn't practical?*

Natasha: Most guys aren't like you.

Benjamin: Is this a good thing? Are you actually complimenting me? I need to screenshot it as evidence you can be nice.

Natasha: Yes, and hey! I can be nice.

Benjamin: You're more than nice...

It's been two whole weeks since he left. Work isn't the same anymore. Seeing the team, including Levi, and not having Ben is strange. I miss the company he provided and the laughs. I don't miss the sexual tension bouncing between us during our sessions, but thankfully, with all the other players, there hasn't even been a small patter in my heart. No, there're definitely no feelings for anyone else. Nothing even sparks my attention, not even a conversation. I turn up to work and do my job and go home.

"There you are." Mia's voice comes from behind me.

I turn and smile. "Some of us have to work."

"I work...sometimes."

We laugh together, knowing it's a lie.

"The perks of being a coach's daughter." She shrugs, and I can't argue with her there.

"Levi and I broke up," she says out of the blue, tilting her head to study her hands.

No way.

My jaw slacks. I had wondered why I haven't seen them together much. "What? Why?"

She sits down on the workout bench, and I take the one opposite her. Her brown eyes stare back at me with a glossy sheen, and her mouth is as pale as her cheeks. I hate seeing how she's struggling. I wish she had told me when it happened.

"He saw a text from my ex-boyfriend. He d-d-dumped me," she stammers.

"Oh, I'm so sorry, Mia. You should've called me as soon as it happened."

"Sorry...I didn't believe it myself, so I found it hard to reach out. He didn't believe me when I said I don't have feelings for my ex."

I reach out and hug her. She hugs me back. I whisper in her ear. "Maybe try to talk to him in a couple of days. He's probably too hot-headed right now to listen to anything. Give him some time."

She pulls back and a single tear slides down her cheek, but she swats it away. "Yeah. You're right. I don't even know why I'm crying."

"Because you love him, and you can't switch it off straight away."

"Well, it would be nice if the feelings would fuck off."

I can't disagree with her there. I know exactly what she means but I also know there's no such thing and unfortunately you have to feel every bit of the heartbreak.

"Did you want to go for some lunch and talk more?" I offer.

She gives me a weak smile. "Yeah, I need a margarita."

"Okay. Let me grab my bag."

We leave, and I can't help but text Ben.

> *Natasha: Hey! I hope I'm not disturbing you, but just FYI Levi and Mia broke up.*

We take our seats and my phone chimes.

> *Benjamin: Hey yourself. And thanks for letting me know, I had no idea I'll call him. What happened?*

> *Natasha: He broke up with her. Mia said something to do with him seeing a text from her ex-boyfriend.*

Benjamin: Okay, and how's Mia?

Natasha: She's understandably sad, but she'll be all right...

I think? I don't have experience in break-ups, but time heals all wounds, right?

"Who are you texting?" Mia asks curiously.

I don't know what to say, and I don't want to lie, but at that moment, my phone rings with Mom's name.

As soon as I answer, I'm hit with my own worst nightmare and my own bigger heart break.

———

I sit by Mom's bed, my head down, full of worry, thinking about tomorrow.

Come on, you can do this...just wake up and tell me you'll be all right.

"Let me tell you one thing, Mom, thank you for always being there for me. You were always my rock, and even if I don't know what my future holds now, I know you'll be there watching over me. You were always my constant companion, someone who I could talk to about anything."

The warm tears keep falling over my cheeks and onto the hospital blankets.

As my phone vibrates in my pocket, I sit up and disconnect one hand from hers, but refuse to let the other go. I want her to know I'm here. Dusting the tears away, I look down at the message.

Sara: Are you home tonight?

In the rush of calling for an ambulance, I didn't even think about telling anyone what was happening. Looking at the time on my phone, I realize it's almost been a whole twenty-four hours later.

Natasha: No, my mom is in the hospital

Sara: Shit, do you need anything? Is she okay? Are you okay?

Am I okay?

No. My world is sick and lying in a hospital bed, and I don't know how to help her.

What will I do without her?

Natasha: Thanks for the offer, but I'm okay. I don't need anything.

I hit send, but then I type out.

Natasha: Actually, could you please let Mia know.

I left Mia at the restaurant with the words. "I've gotta go." Then I ran out of there.

I remember mom's friend Patty; I hadn't even thought to call.

I don't want to talk to anyone right now, so I send her a text message too.

Sara: Yes of course, I'll do it right now. But please let me know if you need anything else.

Natasha: Will do.

I tuck my phone away and grab Mom's hands in mine again. This time, resting my head on top of our hands. My eyelids drop closed, and as heaviness hits me, I fall asleep from exhaustion.

A few hours later, my stomach is grumbling from lack of food. I haven't eaten since yesterday. I had only felt nausea rolling in my stomach, but now I'm hungry.

As I check the time, I notice a couple of texts had come through. One from Sara, one from Patty, one from Mia, and last, Ben.

I check the other messages first and respond to them, and then open his message.

> *Benjamin: Found another issue with the house.*
> *(Pic)*

He sends a picture of him attempting to stand in the shower, but the shower head is too short, and he has to lean to the side.

A smile forms on my face at how disastrous this house is. But I'm also grateful for his distraction; he makes me smile even when I'm in difficult situations and he has no idea. I don't want to tell him what's going on, so I just answer his message.

> *Natasha: That house is a disaster! It's one thing after another.*

> *Benjamin: Soon I'm going to think it's a sign I shouldn't stay here.*

I stare at the words, and I'm tempted to say, *"Yes! Please come back. Mom's sick, and I need you,"* but I can't be selfish. I still can't give him all of me, so I can't use him when I want to. That's unfair.

Natasha: Maybe, but all houses have teething issues.

Benjamin: It's like you're talking about a child and that's fucking weird.

I laugh at that, and I grip the phone in both hands to text back.

Natasha: You're weird.

Benjamin: Only with you.

I stare at the words and with nothing else to say, I put my phone in my pocket. Having a look at Mom, she still lies in the hospital bed, unchanged. I feel lighter than before and ready to call Patty, and I have Ben to thank for that. He has a way of making me feel as if everything will be okay.

I wake the next morning on the side of Mom's bed. The machines pumping fluid into her, and the nurses kept coming in overnight to do her observations and take blood. The way my eyes sting, I feel so exhausted; it's beyond anything I've ever felt. I need my bed and to be able to sleep for days. But until she wakes, I'll be staying right here.

A knock on the door sounds, and I turn my head, expecting the nurses, but what I didn't expect was—Ben.

I blink rapidly and rub my eyes, but he's still there.

"Hi," he whispers, holding two bouquets of flowers.

Swallowing hard, I bite back tears.

"Hey. What are you doing here?" I say in a choked voice. I rise, suddenly feeling awkward about how I must appear. I need a shower and to brush my teeth. Oh God, my teeth. I have furry teeth at this point, and this hot man is standing in my mom's hospital room, looking sexy. His blond hair tousled on top of his head. He's definitely been running his hands through it. His sharp jawline is freshly shaved, but his dazzling smile makes my breath hitch. I run my gaze over his navy top and blue jeans and bite my lip. It's as if I stepped out of a dream, but the noises around me remind me that I'm still, in fact, here waiting for Mom to wake up.

I run a hand over my messy hair and try not to be too self-conscious about the way I look.

"Mia called me," he says as he lowers the bouquets to the table.

My brows rise, totally taken off guard that she was the one to tell him.

"Thank you." I lift my chin in the direction of the flowers.

"One for you and one for your mom."

Tears fill my eyes, but I don't let them fall. Goddamn him and his kindness.

I need to focus on something else and not get lost in the little things he does for me.

"But don't you have work?" I ask.

"It's fine, don't worry about me. How's she doing?"

I turn and glance at my mother's lifeless body in the bed.

"They're still treating the infection, but it's scary."

"I can only imagine."

"Did you want to sit?" I ask, offering a chair.

He shakes his head and gives me a crooked smile. "No, thanks. How about I get you some coffee or tea?"

I smile back. It's like he read my mind, and I don't have the energy to decline. "That would be amazing, thanks."

"Did you want to shower or something?"

I frown and look over my clothes, embarrassed. "Are you telling me I smell?"

He chuckles. "No, it's a mere suggestion, because I'm going to have one guess and say you've been here all night with no food or drink."

"I've had water."

"You need to eat," he growls, not happy with my answer. "I'll get you something."

"I might take a shower before you leave, if you don't mind. I don't want Mom to wake up alone."

His eyes hold mine and neither of us moves. I wish I knew what he was thinking. I run my hand over my messy hair again and try to smooth it out, feeling uncomfortable under his stare.

"You are something else," he whispers before taking the seat I was asleep in before he entered.

I want to hug him, but I also want a shower first. "I'll be quick, and call me if she wakes."

He nods. "Alright."

I'm about to turn, but my heart is in my throat when he leans forward and grabs my mom's hand in his. His large one wrapping over hers completely. At this moment, my butterflies are back in full force.

He's the one who's something else.

How can a man just know how to take care of my mother the way I do?

A fresh, warm set of tears trickles down my face as I watch the exchange. My heart is so full right now.

He turns, obviously sensing me, and his face falls, but I shake my head with a smile and mime, "I'm good."

His gaze roams my face to read me, but I'm being honest. He holds her hand, but stays holding my gaze. Sucking in a deep breath, I turn, wiping away my tears.

For the next few minutes, I soak in the steam and hot water, feeling the freshest I have in the last twenty-four hours. Unfortunately, I have to wear the same clothes and maybe I should have taken Patty up on her offer to bring in some. When I'm finished, I step out of the bathroom, and he's in the exact same position with his hand on hers. The calmness running through me from his presence is surreal.

He turns when I touch his shoulder, standing to allow me to sit down. "I'll grab you some coffee and food. Anything in particular?"

"No, thanks. But a latte sounds wonderful."

"Coming right up. I'll be back soon. Call or text me if you think of anything else."

Sinking down in the chair, I hold on to Mom and wait for him to return.

"How long are you here for?" I ask him when he returns with our coffees and plenty of food for the next couple of days.

"I don't know. I told them I'll update them daily," he says as he leans back with easy grace in the hospital chair beside me. His large frame fills the whole space, making the noise of the monitors on Mom more tolerable. For the first time since being here, I'm not solely focused on every beep. And hitting the bell so the nurses can come in and check on her.

He has a sense of calm about him.

I bite into my blueberry muffin, not really having anything else to say. It's clear he won't leave until Mom is better.

"How do you feel about retiring? Has it been hard to adjust to?"

His gaze shifts to the ground as he shuffles in the chair. "I can't lie. It's been a struggle to wrap my head around it all." Meeting my eyes, the sadness staring back at me unsettles me.

"Do you regret it?" I whisper.

He shakes his head. "No, but it'll take a bit of getting used to." He takes a sip of his warm latte.

"Are you still training?"

"Not as much as before." He wiggles his brows, amused. "Is Doctor Blackwood coming out now?"

I bite my lip to hold back a giggle.

"No. I'm just curious. What you do in Seattle, and what it's like there?" I ask.

"You mean, other than the shitty house?"

I giggle again, remembering all the disaster pictures he's sent me. "Yes, tell me what it's like?"

"It's quieter, and the people are very friendly. The kids I met seem eager to learn."

Reaching out, I touch his hand and give it a gentle squeeze. "I bet they're thrilled you're there."

He nods. Movement stirs in the bed, and our eyes fly to Mom.

I practically dive for the bed, and he says, "I'll get the nurses."

I can't answer him with my heart in my throat as I grip her hand. "Mom, I'm here. Oh my God, I'm right here. You scared me." The last few words come out in a sob.

"Sorry," she speaks, but it's hoarse. I turn to look at the water, but I don't know if she's allowed to have a drink.

"Mom, don't speak, it's okay. I just want to double check with the nurse to see if I can give you some water."

I hug her, and when her door opens, I reluctantly pull back to let the nurse see her.

I wrap my arms around myself. My gaze fixed on Mom.

I didn't hear him approach, but his hand touches my back. I feel his powerful body behind me. He's supporting me. A new sting hits the back of my eyes.

"Ms. Blackwood, we're glad you're awake. How are you feeling?"

"Like I've been hit by a bus, my head is throbbing. And my back hurts."

"I'll get some medication for you. Let me check your vitals and call the doctor and let him know you're awake."

"Can I give her some water?" I ask, in a voice that doesn't sound like my own.

"Yes, of course." The nurse gives me a kind, sympathetic smile before she takes Mom's observations and then leaves the room.

"I'll let you have some time alone," Ben says, removing his hand from my back.

"No, stay, please," I beg, not ready for him to leave yet. Missing his comfort of his hand already.

"Hi, Ben," Mom says croakily.

His eyes flick to her with a full smile. "Hi, Ms. Teresa. Glad to see you're better."

"I can't wait to feel better. What happened to me?" She rubs her head.

"Meningitis was what the doctor initially told me, but I'm sure they'll talk to us soon," I say, giving Mom a cup of water to drink.

"I have to make a call, but I'll be back," Ben says.

When he leaves, Mom's face has a funny expression. "What?" I ask.

"Why's he here?"

I sit down in the chair next to her bed and peek at the door before looking at her again.

"Mia told him you were in the hospital."

"So, he came and brought flowers?" she asks, raising a brow at the biggest arrangements of lilies, roses, and carnations we've ever seen.

I need to take them home and put them in water.

"Yeah."

"He's way too sweet."

"I kind of have to agree."

"What are we agreeing to?" His voice booms through the door.

Mom smirks, and I bite my lip as a flush runs up my neck, hoping he didn't hear us call him sweet.

"Just that she'll be happy to go to dinner with you tonight," Mom says, twisting her lips into a wicked grin.

My lips part and my eyes narrow at her in horror.

"Ah." His face lights up, and his gaze flicks from Mom, then over to me. A devilish look enters his eyes. "That would be great. I actually know of a good spot, and I happen to know the chef."

"Of course, you do," I mumble, still shocked Mom threw me under the bus like that.

"Don't be smart, Natasha," Mom scorns, shooting me a cold look.

"I can't leave you," I argue.

"Patty will come and be here. I'm fine. Get out of here and have dinner."

I feel like I'm backed into a corner.

"I'll call Patty and check first," I say, standing to grab my phone.

She purses her lips. "If you must. It's like I'm the child and you're the mother."

I sigh, understanding her frustration, but she scared me. And if I'm going to go out for dinner with Ben, I don't want to be worried about her the whole time. "Mom, you scared me. Give me a break."

She waves her hand in a shoo action. "Fine, go call Patty. And, Ben, please book dinner. Patty won't say no."

I peer over at Ben, who's staring at me with compelling blue eyes, firm features, and a confident set of shoulders. His mouth melts into a buttery smile.

It looks like I'll be going out for dinner. Alone with Ben.

CHAPTER 36

BENJAMIN

I'M NOT SURE IF Natasha agreed to this date, or if her mom dropped this on her, but I'm not mad about it. In fact, I'm fucking elated to spend more time with her.

I return home, grateful James managed to push back on the settlement date so I can stay at my place tonight. There's something about sleeping in your own bed that just can't be replaced.

I have to fly back to Seattle tomorrow, and the thought alone breaks my fucking heart. After seeing her eyes brimmed with tears, it makes me feel sick, but I can't afford to take any more time off. I've already started off on the wrong foot.

Once I'm showered and dressed in a blue shirt and jeans, I make my way to pick her up.

The way my heart is beating in my chest for her is surreal. She has a way of getting under my skin and into my whole being. The closer I drive to her place, the more my nerves pick up to an uncomfortable rhythm. This is how I know she's the one. I just need her to get to the same point and submit to her feelings for me, and fuck...accept us.

Arriving at her place, I take the stairs, then ring the doorbell and wait for her to answer. Which feels like an eternity.

Finally, she opens the door, and my chest tightens. She's a vision in blue. It really makes her eyes pop, and I stand completely at a loss for words.

"Do you want to come in for a minute? I have to get my shoes and a jacket," she says as she opens the door wider, not noticing my frozen state.

I force myself to nod and step into the house. When I enter, I'm hit with a scent so strong it's like being on a tropical holiday. The scent is *her*.

I peer around at her new place, taking in all her furniture. Warm neutral tones and wooden accents give it a cozy-cabin vibe. Picturing myself reclined on her large cream couch with her snuggled up beside me, watching TV. I wouldn't even care what was playing as long as I was with her.

"Did you want a drink?" she asks, pulling my gaze down to her baby blues, where she's smiling shyly.

Even though I'm hot and thirsty, it's for a different reason.

"No, thanks."

"Okay, I'll be right back. Make yourself comfortable." She walks off to what I assume is her bedroom.

And it takes a lot of willpower not to follow. Because I can't help but wonder, what does her bed look like?

I sigh. Taking a seat on her couch, it definitely is as comfy as it looks.

I sit in silence and wait for her, scrolling through socials. The sound of her heels on the wooden floors has me tucking my phone away and rising.

The silver strappy heels compliment her outfit, and I let out a soft whistle. She's the sexiest date, and she is all mine. Well, for at least a couple of hours.

I run my eyes from her shoes to her beautiful face. Stopping at her newly applied red lipstick, I can't help the breathy compliment that falls from my lips. "I love the red on you."

She bites her lip, looking effortlessly sultry, and the pink stain to her cheeks makes me want to tell her every other nice thought I have flicking through my thoughts, but I don't want to suffocate her.

"Thanks," she whispers.

"Are you ready to go?" I peer at my watch and then back to her. "I made a booking for six."

I love the twinkle in her eye; it makes me want to do this again.

My chest heaves. That's right, I'm leaving tomorrow.

"Oh. You did. Where?" Her question pulls me back to the here and now.

"A surprise," I say, suppressing a grin.

She rolls her eyes cheekily and fixes her bag up on her shoulder. "We better get going then."

"We better." I walk behind her and try to keep my thoughts off her round, full ass. It's only when she spins at the doorway, I have to clench my teeth to stop myself from kissing her as I pass her. Thankfully, the cool night air hits me in the face as the perfect wake up call.

Turning around, I watch as she closes the door and goes to take the step, but she almost tumbles on her fuckable heels.

She laughs and I do too.

"Have you been walking long?" I say, poking her side, and she hunches over, laughing harder.

"Clearly, I've not been in heels in, well...forever."

"That's a damn shame, because they look fucking sexy on you."

I hold her hand all the way to the car. She doesn't fight me on it.

We arrive at my favorite Thai restaurant after a car ride filled with pleasant, albeit tension-filled, small talk. All I wanted was to have my hand on her thigh, to pull over and kiss her breathless, but I stayed strong.

We're escorted across the dark wooden floors to the back of the restaurant that's painted black but has hints of gray and gold trimmings. It's the perfect place for our dinner, away from other customers and possible fans. I don't want us to be interrupted tonight.

We reach a room that I know will be just ours, and our waiter takes our drink orders, then leaves us alone. My eyes are set on Natasha the whole time, who looks around in awe.

"This place is incredible," she stammers. I remember when I first came here, I felt the exact same way.

"Isn't it? It's my favorite restaurant. I come here with my family at least once a month."

That makes her tilt her face toward me. Her eyes shimmer under the warm lights. "I love how close you are to your family."

I shuffle forward in my seat. "Yeah, I miss them now that I'm away."

"Have you seen them yet?"

I grimace. "No, I'm going to see them tomorrow morning before I head to the airport."

She nibbles her lip before speaking again. "Oh, are you doing something special with them?"

Her teeth have some of her red lipstick smeared on them, making me forget all about her question. "Come here." I bend my finger to incline her toward me.

A cute line forms between her brows.

"You have lipstick on your teeth." I explain.

Her hand comes up to her mouth to cover it, and she mumbles into her palm. "I can wipe it off. You don't need to help me."

"I don't mind," I offer softly, not wanting to embarrass her further.

"Sure," she drops her hand and edges toward me. "Why not? I can't possibly embarrass myself any further tonight."

I reach over with a hint of a smile on my lips. Touching her face, I rub my thumb over her tooth gently. Watching the smudge disappear, I sit back when I'm finished and answer her question. "No, I'll just stop by the house and have some lunch."

"Is it better?" she asks, sweeping her tongue over her teeth.

She opens her mouth, showing me her brilliant smile.

"Yes." I grin adoringly at her. "Much."

"What time is your flight?" she asks.

My heart pounds strangely, but I swallow any dumb ideas down. "Five."

She nods, and the waiter arrives with our drinks, and we order food before he takes off.

Not wanting to discuss me leaving again, because it leaves a storm cloud over us whenever it's brought up, I change the subject. "So, tell me what happened to your mom."

She puts her hands under her chin to answer. "The other night, she had a temperature, so she took some Tylenol and went to bed. But the next day, she went downhill fast. I was on a lunch break with Mia when she called to say she didn't feel right. I raced home, and her temperature had climbed to dangerous levels, and she was so irritable...it was scary."

"I bet."

"Then they gave her meds to calm her down because she was confused and frustrated, to the point they couldn't treat her properly. When we got to the hospital, they gave her antibiotics before doing a lumbar puncture, scans, and bloodwork. She was out of it for most of what they did, then she just slept. It wasn't until you came in that she woke up."

Her voice is shaky by the end of the story. I hate seeing her anything but strong, but I'm just glad her mom is okay now.

"How long will she be in there for?"

She sips her wine and then answers. "I don't know. I imagine John will give me hell for missing work next week."

Trying to calm her nerves and let her focus on just her mom and not work, I say softly, "I'm sure he'll understand."

She raises her brow, unconvinced. "We don't have the best relationship, so I don't know about that."

"It's unfair if he doesn't give you a bit of time off. Season is over, so it shouldn't be as big of a deal now."

She sits back, dropping her hands to her lap, and nods. "That's true, and if he isn't nice in this situation, I'll have to reconsider working there."

That makes me feel a mix of emotions. I don't want her to leave the team that I know is full of wonderful people I've known for years. She's so valuable there. But it's not up to me; this is her career that she worked so hard for.

"Mmm. Would you go to another team?"

"Yeah, for sure. I love the job. I just want a good team around me. I spoke to John about how he treats me. He apologized, and he's been better since, but still, any hiccup could send us backward."

"I think talking it out was a wise choice. You gained his respect, and it'll help him to get to know you better. Under that wall is a sweet woman who loves her job." I say, knowing compliments are a way into her softer side.

She smiles bashfully at me.

"You're so cute when you blush."

Now she's crimson.

Fuck, she's adorable.

"Thank God, I've got this drink." She picks up her wine, bringing it to her lips to take a large sip, causing me to chuckle.

After dinner, we're quiet, getting inside my car. I'm surprised when she speaks.

"How long will you be staying in Seattle?"

A loaded question.

My lips are pressed together as I suck in a steadying breath. "It won't be for a while. This wasn't...planned."

I keep my eyes on the road, not wanting to read her face.

"No, I mean, like, when will you come back for good?"

I grip the steering wheel tighter. I thought she knew. "There's no return date."

The car grows silent.

I steal a quick glance at her and take in her slackened jaw before my eyes swing back to the road ahead. "Oh, I thought it might've been a twelve-month contract."

"It is, but I can't come back."

I can't come back with her here. Even now, with the tension swirling in this car, it's so fucking hard. But it's not like I couldn't not come. I wanted to be here for her in case something happened to her mom. I know how important she is to her and how devastated she would've been. This was the right decision; I don't regret it.

Pulling up to her house, I park outside of her house. I twist to face her, keeping my hands firmly in my lap to prevent reaching out and touching her.

She unbuckles her seatbelt and turns her head, leaning on the headrest, holding my gaze. "So, this is it?" she breathes.

"This is it," I repeat, leaning my profile on the headrest to mirror her.

I take in every inch of her face, appreciating her fully. The lines near her eyes when she smiles, or the way her lips have the perfect shade of pink now with the lipstick worn off. But the most beautiful thing about her is her heart; she is caring, giving, and tender. It's evident in how she treats her mom every day. Showing me the person she really is.

With the air around us charged and growing thick, I push open my door and suck in a deep breath of the crisp night air. The way my lungs burn for her is so unnatural; I just need to get away from a confined space because I want to respect her wishes.

She doesn't want a relationship with me, so I'm going to walk her to the door and drive home.

And we move to do just that without another word. She unlocks her door, and I stand still on her doorstep, trying to regulate my abnormal heart rate.

"Thanks for tonight. I had a great time," she says with a genuine smile.

I give her a wide smile back, feeling the same. "Me too. Good-night, and I'll text you when I'm back in Seattle."

Her face falls, as if she just remembered tomorrow and the fact that I leave. I haven't forgotten, not one fucking bit.

I turn to walk back to my car, chin down to lick my wounds.

"Wai—" She stands, holding the door with sad eyes. Adrenaline rushes through my veins like tidal waves. I can't hold back the flicker of hope that hits me as I turn back around. But then it's crushed when she whispers, "Okay."

I stalk toward my car. Once I jump in, I take one last glance at her sexy figure and stunning face before I beep the horn and wave. She offers a small wave, then spins on her heel to head inside.

A renewed wash of disappointment rolls through me, knowing she still hasn't changed her mind. And there's nothing I can do about it anymore.

CHAPTER 37

BENJAMIN

"YEAH, I JUST GOT here," I say down the line to James. I'm standing at my gate, in the back of the airport departure lounge, leaning against the wall and waiting for the announcement to board.

"We didn't even get a chance to catch up."

"I know. It was an unexpected visit."

He chokes out a laugh as I hear him type away on his keyboard. "You're in deep—"

At the sight before me, everything goes silent, heart thumping erratically at the familiar figure running in my direction, looking around frantically.

"I'll have to call you back." I pull the phone away from my ear and hang up on James.

In the next second, I'm pushing away from the wall, watching as Natasha comes toward me. Her flushed face stands out in the sea of people, her shiny blonde hair cascading over her shoulders, and then her blue hues find mine. Nothing else around me exists; it's just me and her.

She pauses in front of me, her heavy breaths matching mine, only I wasn't the one running. I can't believe she's here, within my reach. I fucking hoped she'd show up, but never in a million years did I think she'd change her mind. My mind rewinds the last few days, but nothing stands out. I try to control my breathing so I can speak. She's stunned me into silence.

Her blush spreads across her nose and onto her cheeks, and I have to stuff my hands in my pockets to stop myself from touching her. I need to find out what she's here for. I have hope that it's for me, but until she says the words loud and clear, I won't believe she's here for the reason I need her to be.

And right now, I really need her to fucking be here for me.

We stare at each other in silence for a few seconds.

"What are you doing here?" I ask in disbelief.

Her lips tremble as she chokes out, "Stopping you."

My body tingles as I take in her words I've longed to hear, but I keep my composure.

"Stopping me?" I repeat.

My palms are sweating as I wait for her to elaborate. I just want her to hurry up and spit it out so I can kiss the shit out of her.

"Don't get on the plane. Please..." She blinks up at me with the brightest, most hopeful, tear-stained eyes.

"I thought you said you wouldn't beg," I say, playing it cool.

She laughs and stares boldly at me for a moment. "Neither did I, but I can't do this anymore. Pushing the feelings I have for you aside and burying them so deep, just so I don't risk having my heart broken...but having you here for Mom..."

"For you," I correct, cutting her off.

"For me," she whispers, as if still not believing someone, or should I say, a man could be there for her when she needs them the most.

"The first time you left was hard, but our texts were things I looked forward to every day."

I smile, knowing I felt that same.

"The friendship and connection to you hasn't changed, even though you moved. I know you're starting over, and I hate how long it's taken me to wake up. You keep coming back to me, and I've got no reason to doubt you. Just because my past hurt, doesn't mean I should keep running away from certain feelings. Like love. And shit, Ben, you're my one."

I can't hold back now. Staring into her glossy eyes, I step forward to close the distance between us. I grab her face with my hand and lift her chin, bringing our faces inches apart. "I love you so fucking much it hurts."

Her eyes go wide, but I don't wait for her to speak. I crush my lips to hers in a heated kiss. She kisses me back with equal passion. This kiss is bruising, with all our emotions professed through our lips. Pain, hurt, happiness, but mostly love.

Disconnecting our kiss, I rest my forehead on hers and speak through harsh breaths. "Thank you for letting me in. I promise not to hurt you, leave you, or ever let you down. I'll always be there for you."

"I feel so understood with you, so loved by you, and that has never happened," she says, as if she can't quite believe it exists. I don't get a chance to respond because she brings her lips back to mine. When I taste her salty tears on my lips, it breaks me. I hate her in pain.

I pull back, grabbing her head in my hands, scared she might crumble beneath my palms. "Not having you in my life was so fucking hard, baby. But I needed to let you go so that you'd give me everything, including your heart."

"I am," she cries.

"Now what?" I gaze down at her, raising my brow, trying to get her to lead the way to our future.

"You come home with me, and you don't get on that flight to Seattle."

The air in my lung catches at hearing everything I've wanted to hear for so long. "You want me to leave my job?" I ask, holding back a shit-eating grin. Knowing if she asks me, I'll drop everything for her in a heartbeat.

"I want you here with me, but I can't ask you to quit if you don't want to." She glances away for a moment before bringing her gaze back to mine. She looks a little sheepish.

I know she wouldn't want me to quit my job, but I need her to know she's more important to me than that job. She's my future, and I'll give it all up right now.

"I want to be here with you too. The job isn't as important as you. You'll always be my priority. I can find another job here."

She gazes up at me with sad eyes. "I don't want you to do anything you don't want to do."

I'm still holding her face tenderly. "I know, but I want you. And what I really want is to go home with you and wrap you in my arms and not leave for the rest of the night."

Her expression flicks to a new determination. "I think we should get out of here and do exactly that."

I don't waste another second. I grab her hand and walk out of the airport with her, and she directs me to her car.

"Where're your keys? I'll drive." I ask, holding out my other hand.

She shakes her head. "No, I need to keep my hands busy."

I do a double take, thinking I've heard wrong. "What?"

She tips her head back and laughs. "I've never been so attracted to someone, and I badly want to do nothing but kiss you."

I stop walking on the sidewalk. She turns at the sudden movement, and I bring my face to hers. "I want to kiss you too."

I capture her lips, and she parts hers immediately, eagerly meeting my tongue. Her hands diving into my hair and bringing me down. She's super handsy, and it's making my blood hot and my cock so hard. It wants her right here, right now.

"We need to go home," I groan into her mouth.

She pulls away and turns, dragging me by the hand to her car.

The drive is fast, quiet, and I make a call to the coach of the team I was working with. He was a little disgruntled that I'm leaving before the whole trial is over, but having her near me, it makes me give no fucks. I'd rather be in trouble than leave her.

I'll deal with the consequences next week, and I'll organize for my stuff to be shipped back here. But my house contract may be harder to break. I'll have to talk to James. If not, I'll be renting somewhere else for a month.

Arriving at her house, we exit the car and walk to the door with hurried steps. As soon as she unlocks the door, I scoop her up into my arms. She squeals, and I kick the door closed behind us, striding directly to the room I assume is hers.

I lower her down onto the white blankets, leaning forward with my hands beside her head. Leaning over her, I kiss her collarbone, making my way up her neck to her ear. "Am I dreaming?"

Her skin erupts in goosebumps, and she giggles lightly. "No."

"Thank God, because I'm only just beginning." A rumble leaves my chest.

"You better. I've missed you."

My chest expands, and I almost think I'm hearing things, but the way she's looking at me, I know she speaks the truth. I love her with every part of me.

I kiss her lips and just take a moment to soak this in.

That this is real.

Our tongues tangle, and it causes my cock to become rock hard.

Moving my mouth down along her neck, I take my time to go slow, and have her writhing under me by the time I finish. She makes this sexy purr that has me struggling to hold back.

I lift her top up and kiss her exposed stomach. Pushing the fabric higher, I trail kisses over every square inch of her. Reaching her bra, I pull back and help her remove her top completely.

Squeezing her breasts through her bra, she moans, and I hiss at the sound. As I sit up and remove her bra with urgency, her moan sets me off. I try to regain control and take my time, but it's just been too long, and I'm about to burst.

I pause a moment to appreciate her breasts, but I don't wait too long. I take a pebbled nipple into my mouth and roll my tongue around it, causing sounds to vibrate from her chest that spur me to keep going.

I reach for her jeans next and pop the button and zipper, then make quick work of getting them off. Which leaves her quivering in blue panties. She moves her hands to my top and pulls it off me, skimming my back, shoulders, and arms when I'm bare to her.

"Your body is incredible. I've fantasized about it more than once."

I growl. "While you touched yourself?"

She nods.

"Fuck. You could've had me. The real me, not some stupid fantasy."

"I was stuck in my own head."

I snort. "You mean, you were stubborn."

She giggles. "That."

Her hands don't stop exploring my body, and the rhythm is adding more and more friction and heat.

"Well, you can touch me whenever you want, baby. I'm yours to have in any way."

She gives me a full smile. "Sounds like heaven."

I slide her panties off effortlessly, the wet patch showing me evidence of her arousal. She lies wet and ready, and my cock is aching to take her.

"I need you. I need to be inside you."

"Right now," she encourages shakily.

Leaning down, I kiss all over her neck and up to her cheek, breathing into her ear. "Right fucking now."

The connection is so raw and real, and I need her to consume me already. She has her legs parted wide, and she's panting.

Fuck me.

I hold my cock and rub the tip through her opening, and she trembles at the sensation.

Leaning on one hand above her, I inch myself inside. Her wonderful heat tightly wraps around me, and I'm thankful she's so wet, because there will be no taking our time now.

My thrusts are deep and powerful right from the start, hitting her all the way every time. She whimpers and moans, saying my name on repeat, and it's sending animalistic grunts from my chest. Our eyes are locked, her back arching, creating a new glorious angle.

I gasp her name, and she tightens down on my cock, pleading, "I want to come."

"Not yet, baby. Almost. Just keep milking my cock. It's so fucking perfect."

She does exactly that, and I tingle with the need to fill her. "That's it...just like that."

I thrust a few more times, and her eyes close, her head tipping back. Exposing her bare neck, and I lean over and kiss it.

I trail kisses up her neck, and when I get to her lips, I say, "Come with me now."

A cry I've never heard leaves her. It's loud, feral, but so fucking hot. I'm unable to hold back my orgasm, so I climax hard inside her. When I finish jerking, I try to catch my breath, both of us holding on to each other. I look at her and, in this post, orgasmic state...and in this moment, she owns me.

CHAPTER 38

BENJAMIN

As I LIE HERE holding Tash in my arms with her sexy body curled into me, I can't help but wear a crooked smile. I can't stop thinking about how happy I am. It's been easy to slip into a relationship. Once she lowered her walls and let herself be happy, it's been as simple as breathing. The last month has been a comfortable state of bliss. Full of hot sex, laughter and, dare I say it, normal domestic activities. Like who would've thought folding laundry with her would be so fun.

She practically lives at my house, sleeping over every night, but we've yet to discuss long-term living arrangements. I don't want to push her. As long as I get to have her in bed next to me every night, I don't care who's house I'm in. Gone are the days of just casual sex and dreams of winning a Super Bowl. Now my life is full here in Chicago, with a girlfriend, who I love. It's nice having someone to talk to and plan a life with.

She's still working with John and my old team. Levi's back training hard. I don't know how much longer he has left in him, but with Natasha, I know he's in good hands. She continues to prove to John she was the best choice for the position. Funnily enough, John has been more welcoming of her. Even giving her more opportunities than usual. The way she speaks of work with that starry-eyed look makes me endlessly happy for her.

For me, I'm also loving life. Since I left the job I was offered in Seattle. I found a local college team to work with as their defensive coordinator. It's been the best decision and I'm grateful for where my life has led me.

Her fingers are distracting me as she draws lazy circles over my abs, up and down, in the most delectable way, moving lower with every minute that passes.

"Mmm," I groan.

Her head twists, her chin now resting gently on my chest. She stares at me intently. "I was thinking..."

"Yeah. About what?"

Our gazes stay fixed on watching her movement.

"Would you be open to living together?"

My body turns rigid, and my eyes widen in shock.

"Ah, yes. Move in here. Like, today." I chuckle, but I'm not joking.

She smacks my stomach playfully. I pull her up over me, ignoring the erection she's given me, because it seems I'm always hard whenever she's around.

Her eyes bore into mine as her soft body lies over me. Those gorgeous blues have a shine that wasn't there before.

I lick my lips and search her face. "You really want this?" I don't want her moving faster than what's comfortable for her.

But fuck, if she gives me the green light, I'll be calling in favors and getting all her stuff moved this week.

Her hands trail up to my hair, pushing it back off my face. As it flops back on my forehead, I bite back a smile.

"Yeah, I don't see why I don't. I'm practically living here anyway. Also, I don't like the thought of waking up alone ever again."

"I like the sound of this a lot."

She scrunches up her nose, and her eyes squint at me. "I'm surprised you haven't asked me."

I poke her nose, and she sticks out her tongue.

My eyes flare with heat at the idea of kissing her mouth and tasting her tongue. But we're still talking, so the dirty thoughts need to hold off for a little bit longer.

"Don't think for a second I didn't want to. Because I did. But I've been the pushy one, and I needed to slow down and go at your pace."

Her gaze drops to my chest and my expression pinches. "So, you would've asked if I hadn't?" she asks in a quiet voice.

Sensing her uneasiness, I grab her chin and tilt her face up, bringing her eyes to meet mine.

"Baby. You know I would've. I've been biting my tongue to stop myself from begging you."

Her face wears an amused expression, struggling to stop the laugh from bubbling out of her lips. But she fails epically.

I frown, pretending to be serious. "Are you laughing at me?"

"No. Never." I tickle her ribs, causing her to erupt into laughter.

"Good. Just checking."

I'm expecting a comeback, but instead, she leans in and captures my lips in a soft, breathy kiss, and she whispers, "I love you, Ben."

Fuck. I rub my face. I'm dreaming. Surely, this isn't my real life. She's more than I deserve, but everything I need.

"I love you too. So fuckin' much."

EPILOGUE

NATASHA

WHAT THE HELL DO I pack to take to Italy? I toss everything
onto the bed and hold up each item, but I'm not excited by any
of them. When I check the time, I curse. I've wasted an hour
already, and Ben will be home in less than thirty minutes.

With no more time to waste, I pack the maybe items into the
case, and it isn't long before the door opens. He takes the stairs,
and when they stop, I peer up to find him sinking his body on
our bedroom doorway, watching me. I pause and give him a
wistful smile. He gives me one of his lopsided grins and steps
over to me. My gaze falls over his fitted white top that's a little
tight and should be illegal for him to wear. And my God, the
jeans flatter his thick, muscled thighs that I love so much. My
mouth is suddenly dry from my inspection, and I wonder when
I'll get my fill of him. Because I'm struggling to get enough of
him lately.

When I return my gaze to his, I have to ignore the way my
body responds to him in a hum. "Of course, you look hot, and
I'm standing here a sweaty mess, trying to figure out what to
pack."

"You're hot, and I can make you even more sweaty if you want?" he insinuates, as he wanders even closer to me.

"Of course, your mind drifts to sex. You're a sex maniac."

"But you love me." He winks, coming to stand in front of me.

I peck his lips. "Yes. I do. So much."

"So, you don't want sex, but do you want some help?" he offers, kissing my lips again.

"How?" I ask.

"You could model your outfits and I can say yes or no?" He wiggles his brows at me. I know exactly where we would end up. Having sex, and I'd still have an empty suitcase.

I laugh. "Any excuse to get me naked, huh?"

His smile widens, and I can't help but smile back. It's infectious.

"What? I can't help but want you in every form. But no, I actually came to help you fold or go to the shops for any last-minute items."

I know he isn't all about sex, but I love to tease him. It's a part of our relationship that I enjoy, and I don't ever want it to change.

The fact he wants to help me with mundane activities is one of the reasons I love him. He's so thoughtful and selfless.

"Thanks. I might get you to help me with the clothes because our room is a disaster and I want to tidy it. I don't want to come home to a mess."

I start picking up items of clothing and folding them.

"Before I do that, I want to ask you something." His hands drop from around my waist, and he steps back, causing my hands to fall to my sides. His hand goes to his pocket, and he drops to one knee.

And my heart feels like it's beating outside of my chest. He hasn't said a word, but warm tears already stream down my face, as I know what he's about to ask me.

"Natasha, ever since I met you when your car broke down, I knew I liked you. You're driven, kind, and loyal. Those beautiful blue eyes are a bonus, but the beauty in your heart made me chase you. I knew we'd be a perfect match if you'd just let me in. Finally, here we are, in love and traveling the world. And I don't want this to stop. I want to keep doing life with you. The house, kids, and future. So, let's start by taking the next step. Natasha Blackwood, will you do me the honor and become my wife?"

"Yes." I choke on a sob and watch him slide the ring onto my finger.

I stare at the cushion-cut white-gold diamond on my finger before leaning down and kissing him. He stands and I cuddle him, trying to calm my erratic heart.

We kiss again before I say. "I need to call Mom."

He gives me a large knowing smile. "She knows."

I pull away, confused. "She knew?"

"I had to ask for her hand in marriage."

Oh. My. God.

"You did?"

And if I didn't already feel so deeply and utterly in love with him, I just fell all over again.

He nods. "I did."

"Thank you." I hug him with everything that I have. He's always a step ahead of me, and I need that. It soothes me. Being able to rely on another person to take the weight off you makes you breathe a little easier.

"But I'm sure she'd love to hear it from you," he suggests.

"Did she see the ring?" I ask.

He dips his chin. "Yes. I wanted her part of the process; I knew she'd have good ideas."

More tears spill over my cheeks. He's perfect. Hell, this moment is perfect.

"Thank you," I say between sniffles.

He lays a gentle kiss on my lips. "Go call her."

I bite my lip and pull out my phone and video call her.

Her face comes into view. "Natasha," she drawls.

"Mom. Hi," I choke out.

"Hi. What's wrong? Did you need help packing?" Mom asks, clearly looking for something in her kitchen.

"No, I wanted to call and say I'm engaged!" I scream.

I hold up my ring to the video, moving my hand around, so she can get a good view as warm, happy tears are still falling again, but I ignore them.

"Oh, honey. I'm so happy for you. Tell me how he did it, tell me all the details," she says as she finds her keys, and she stops pacing her house to focus on me.

"You don't know?" I ask with shock.

"No, I wanted that to be a surprise."

This makes me happy because I want to tell her. I always would've wanted to tell her first before all my friends.

"I was packing for Italy when he got down on one knee and proposed."

"I love it, darling. It's so simple, but so you. I'm glad he listened and didn't do anything crazy like a hot-air balloon or a public proposal I think you would've hated it."

I giggle and nod vehemently, knowing that's way too much for me. "Definitely, this was the perfect proposal. Intimate and so...me."

Sensing him, I glance up from the phone and smile at my now fiancé.

Getting off the plane, I'm yawning. I'm still tired, even though we flew first class. There were too many good movies to watch and the thrill of going on a holiday with Ben prevented me from sleeping. From never wanting to do this because of my mom and John. To finally accept a well-earned break. If I'm honest, Ben needs it too. He's been working hard with his new job, and it'll be nice to spend two weeks in Italy, exploring with no work distractions. It's just him and I.

Arriving at the house we're staying at, I step through the doors and drop my bag and gasp.

"Surprise!" a crowd scream out.

All my friends and family cheer, including my mom. She steps forward, and I wrap my arms around her before pulling away and looking over at my fiancé in awe.

How did he do this?

"What is this?" I ask no one in particular.

"I wanted the proposal to be just us. Simple and real like we are. But I wanted a fun engagement party, so I organized everyone to meet us here and celebrate."

"Everyone is here for us?" I stammer in shock.

"Yes."

Mom rubs my back in circles. I'm completely overwhelmed. So much love and support for me and I don't know what to do with it.

Mia comes over, grabbing me by the shoulders. "Come on, let's go get ready to party. I've got some alcohol to help with the nerves."

I smile and whisper. "Thanks."

"Anytime, I got you." She winks, whisking me up the stairs. I take the house in as I walk. Loving the red wooden floors and the red internal bricks. The homes here are so different; there is more character and less modern.

We find the bathroom and it's smaller than I'm used to. I turn to Mia and Sara.

"I—"

"I've got you a dress," Sara says with a big smile.

I let out a deep breath, knowing it'll be stunning because she would have pulled some strings at work to get me it.

She exits the bathroom, and Mia hands over a shot of alcohol.

"A shot?" I raise a brow.

"Yeah, what's wrong with that? Are you nervous or not?" she asks, amused.

"Terrified," I answer her honestly. I've never had a party before. And I've definitely never been the center of attention. So right now, this is a lot for me.

She giggles and so do I. I take the shot and let the burn flow down my throat before Sara comes back and hands me the prettiest sage green dress.

"Oh, Sara. This is incredible." I touch the fabric between my fingers, admiring the soft silk touch and color.

"I know. Put it on, and we can help you put a little makeup on," Sara encourages.

"Yes, I'm way too shaky to apply anything right now. But first I need a shower, so you two please meet me in the room and I'll be a couple of minutes."

They leave me alone and I grab the sink, sucking in a few cleansing breaths. I need to reign in the shakes that have taken over my trembling body. This night couldn't get any better. I have a shower and then join the girls.

"Oh, Tash, it's perfect for you," Sara gushes, clapping her hands excitedly.

"This was made for you," Mia says.

I peer down at the way the dress sits delicately over my body; I rub my hand over my hips. "Technically, it wasn't, but I get you," I say with a smile. "Thanks."

I sit down on the edge of the bath and close my eyes as Sara adds a little makeup while Mia curls my hair.

Then I'm ready. I re-join everyone and find my fiancé.

"Baby, you look so beautiful." He kisses my cheek.

"And you look devilishly handsome." I look over at him seductively, admiring his outfit change. A white linen shirt and cream dress shorts. Of course, they complement me, and I have to laugh to myself at how coordinated they've all been to make this perfect for us.

My mind wants to pull me down the spiral of I don't deserve this, but I push it away. Not allowing myself to delve into them.

This moment is beyond my wildest dreams and better than anything I could've organized myself. We hold hands as we spend time walking around, thanking people for joining us. So many are asking when the wedding is, of course.

I smile and say the truth, "I have no idea when it'll be yet." But I have had a little thought about eloping. I love the idea that I can keep our day just between him and me. I feel like we've spent enough time separately because of my stubborn ass, and I would love it to be just us. But he would have to agree because, looking at him right now, I'd give him anything he wanted just to keep those blue eyes fixed on mine. He gazes at me like I'm the most important thing in his world.

If only he knew he was now the most important one in mine.

The End.

If you enjoyed this story could you please leave a rating or review? Link here

Have you read Doctor Mike Taylor's love story? If not, read it here.

Did you want more of Benjamin and Natasha? I have a small bonus and deleted scene. Read it here.

Also by Sharon Woods

AFTERWORD

To keep up to date with my new books releases, including ti-
tle's, blurb's, release date's and giveaways. Please subscribe to my
newsletter here or www.sharonwoodsauthor.com

Want to stay up to date with me? Come join my Facebook reader
group: Sharon's Sweethearts This is a PRIVATE group and only
people in the group can see posts and comments!

Acknowledgments

Firstly, I'd like to thank my husband and two kids. You're my world and I love you all so much!

Thanks to all my friends and family. I seriously have the best cheerleaders in the world.

This story was shaped by the help of my beautiful betas: Amy, Kirstie, Ashley, Kerissa, Nadelle, and Dee. You have no idea how grateful I am for all your comments.

Thanks to my wonderful team Word Emporium, Naughty-GirlNiceEdits, Lilypadlit, Enchanting Romance Designs and Wild Love Designs.

To you my readers, I want to shout out a massive thank you for reading my words. Your support has been amazing.

If you enjoyed Benjamin and Natasha's story please leave a review on Amazon. It helps authors so much.

About Author

Sharon Woods is an author of Contemporary Romance. She loves writing steamy love stories with a happy ever after.

Born and living in Melbourne, Australia. With her beautiful husband and two children.

http://www.instagram.com/sharonwoodsauthor

http://www.facebook.com/sharonwoodsauthor

https://www.tiktok.com/@sharonwoodsauthor

http://www.sharonwoodsauthor.com

Printed in Great Britain
by Amazon